P9-DTE-978

Rode Hard, Put Away Wet

★ ★ ★ Lesbian Cowboy Erotica ★ ★ ★

RODE HARD, PUT AWAY WET

★ ★ ★ Lesbian Cowboy Erotica ★ ★ ★

suspect thoughts press
www.suspectthoughtspress.com

This book is a work of fiction. Names, characters, places, and incidents are either products of the author's imagination or are used fictitiously. Any resemblance to actual events, locales, or persons, either living or dead, is entirely coincidental.

Cover design by Shane Luitjens/Torquere Creative
Cover photographs by Rhonda Oxley
Book design by Greg Wharton/Suspect Thoughts Press
Print management by Jackie Cuneo/Little Jackie Paper

First Edition: June 2005
10 9 8 7 6 5 4 3 2 1

Library of Congress Cataloging-in-Publication Data

Rode hard, put away wet : lesbian cowboy erotica.
p. cm.
ISBN 0-9763411-0-7 (pbk.)
1. Lesbians--Fiction. 2. Erotic stories, American. 3. Western stories. I. Green, Sacchi. II. Valencia, Rakelle, 1967-

PS648.L47R63 2005
813'.0874083538'086643--dc22

2005003757

Suspect Thoughts Press
2215-R Market Street, #544
San Francisco, CA 94114-1612
www.suspectthoughtspress.com

Suspect Thoughts Press is a terrible infant hell-bent to burn the envelope by publishing dangerous books by contemporary authors and poets exploring provocative social, political, queer, spiritual, and sexual themes.

PUBLICATION CREDITS

Grateful acknowledgment is made to the following publications in which these stories originally appeared:

"Last Tango in Paris, Texas" by M. Christian first appeared in *Faster Pussycats*, Trixie, ed. (Alyson Books, 2001).

"Bull Rider" by Sacchi Green first appeared in *Body Check*, Nicole Foster, ed. (Alyson Books, 2002), and in *Best Lesbian Erotica 2003*, Tristan Taormino, ed. (Cleis Press, 2003).

"The Flight of the Prairie Lily" by Sacchi Green first appeared in *Best Women's Erotica 2005*, Marcy Sheiner, ed. (Cleis Press, 2005).

"Dry Hearts, Dreaming" by Jay Lake first appeared in *Clean Sheets*, Susannah Indigo, ed. (www.cleansheets.com, 2002).

"To Fuck a Cowboy" by Rakelle Valencia first appeared in *On Our Backs*, Diana Cage, ed. (November, 2003), and in *On Our Backs: The Best Erotic Fiction, Volume 2*, Diana Cage, ed. (Alyson Books, 2004).

Contents

INTRODUCTION

Cowboyin' is a way of life. It's a job today as it was in yesteryear, hard, gritty, and as much down-to-earth as it is high in the saddle. The cowboy is a legend that can inspire romantic as well as lustful desire. This living tradition, this state of mind, can shake a body from the crown of their Stetson, past the gleaming rodeo prize buckle and well-worn leather chaps, all the way to the jinglebobs on the spurs of their boots. Imagine what it could do for a woman who dreams from within posh polo shirts and khakis or capris.

Some of the best cowboys aren't boys. There are plenty of women at the job. As Rakelle Valencia points out in "To Fuck a Cowboy," plenty of girls get hot at the thought of a Marlboro *Woman*. The stories we've been lucky to gather for this book portray cowboys riding a horse by day and a woman by night in a wide range of gender flavors, from Julia Talbot's tangy "Sweethearts of the Rodeo," through Bryn Haniver's voluptuous Park Ranger in "Off Her High Horse," to Jake Rich's Daddy/boy pair "Franky and Johnny," and to Connie Wilkins' ex-Union soldier still passing as a man in the Sierra gold country in "Snowfound."

There's a wide range of flavors in the leather and lust of it too. Fair warning: Many of these stories have a decidedly kinky kick to their gallop. All that rope! In Nipper Godwin's "Three Loops and a Hooey" and Stephen D. Rogers' "Tether is the Night," roping becomes a fine art with almost as much humor as heat, while Val Murphy adds an iron to the mix in "Rope 'Em and Brand 'Em."

In Crystal Barela's "Ridden," the riding is rough by choice. Then there are the barns full of tools and implements, and handy mounds of hay. Chuck Fellows makes steamy use of horse tack in "No More Secrets." C.B. Calsing's rodeo bull rider takes a newspaper reporter for a fling on a tire swing before tumbling her in the hay in "Ranch Hands...and Tongues." And C.A. Matthews' pair of ranchers play a dark game of dominance and submission triggered by their find beneath an ancient stable in "Spanish Silver."

Our cowboy theme wouldn't have as much depth without stories set when the Old West was young, and we were fortunate to acquire a bonanza of these. In "Wagons Ho," Fargo Wellington puts a new spin on the oxen-drawn prairie schooner. Caralee Levy's "Independence" takes an ex-slave and her former owner on a post–Civil War voyage of discovery and adventure. A captured Indian woman finds harsh joy in a reunion in "Squaw, 1863." Rakelle Valencia's excerpt from her novel "Mail Order Bride" involves homesteaders on the primitive frontier. Then in Sacchi Green's "The Flight of the Prairie Lily," a rebellious girl takes an erotic ride, not on a horse, but in a hot-air balloon. Much closer to the present day, though still far enough in the past for nostalgia, "Bull Rider" chronicles the adventures of a Montana cowboy in the fleshpots of 1980s Amsterdam.

Every story has sex at its core, but some of them have scenes of tenderness as intense as their erotic passion. In Cheyenne Blue's "The Other Side of the Rockies" and Jay Lake's "Dry Hearts, Dreaming," women in pain are saved and healed by loving sex. Skian McGuire's "Pleasure Ride" is a scorchingly sweet story of long-time partners, while Amie M. Evans' "The Coal Miner's Other Daughter" explores young love and discovery. Shanna Germain's "Western Pleasure" and Toby Rider's "Petroglyphs" tell of the strong bonds between old friends, even though they seldom meet. And in "Last Tango in Paris, Texas," M. Christian shows that heat can flare even when the fire of love has gone out.

So here we offer you the plethora of cowboy visions our wonderful writers have shared with us, and hope that you'll feel their erotic intensity as much as we do.

Sacchi Green and Rakelle Valencia

To Fuck a Cowboy

Rakelle Valencia

She was still there at the end of that long, dusty day as I picked up my discarded rope halter from the dirt and lashed a coiled lariat to the empty saddle of my big quarter horse gelding. She was still there. And that's how we ended up in her bed.

Everyone wants to fuck a cowboy. It's the American way, Mom's apple pie, hot dogs, and all that. Cowboys are rooted in our heritage. They're a rare breed nowadays, girl "cowboys" being even more rare. Cowboys are a daydream of the old Western heroes. They're a fantasy. Who hasn't gotten hot over the Marlboro Man and wished there was a Marlboro Woman? Who hasn't wanted a rugged, rangy body of sinuous muscles wrapped in cotton and denim, accentuated by long, worn, tight, leather chaps? Who hasn't wanted to be ensnared in a cowboy's rope?

No sooner did the gate on the round corral close than did the door of her rented double-wide trailer. She kissed me as the lock clicked. I noticed that her small, soft hands rested lightly at my lean hips, not wandering from the thick, harness leather of my belt, not committing themselves like her insistent lips had promised.

I dropped my gear bag, using the thud to drive home the point that I was there, and staying, at least for one night. The contained weight of my horse-breaking equipment and a fresh change of clothes resounded on the hollow floor. In reply, her hands tugged the embroidered Wrangler logo shirt from my leather-belted waist. I knew that in the morning the two-toned, embroidered, trophy shirt would be gone, a memento, a token to remind her of the time she fucked a cowboy, a real, working cowboy, a filthy rendition of legends.

I took her mouth then, sucking on her lower lip with the hunger and the thirst of a ten-hour day in the sun, in the saddle, chasing down eager colts anxious to throw a leg here and there, much as I was anxious to do now. She returned my fervor by forcing her tongue into my mouth. The pleasantries were over.

She was short, petite and cute, and I knew what to do, even if I hadn't caught her name. Shit, it's what I do, rope 'em and break 'em. But that sounds harsh. It's not. I gentle 'em until they're in my hip pocket. Then I like to get my legs around them, feeling the power that surges in my groin.

They say the cowboys like it rough, but that don't matter. We like the ride, any ride, and we like to ride all day, all night too if we can, and all the better if each ride is different. It don't matter, so long as it's not boring and you're not on the hell bitch.

I don't mind being bucked if she's got a little of that in her. But when I settle into the rhythm I'm there to stay, all the way to the buzzer. They call me "Stick," not referring to my physique, although it could. They say I can ride anything, and I haven't been thrown. So when I finally get a leg over, I mean business, but that's not to say it won't be fun.

I tore my mouth away to watch my finger trickle down the line of pearly white snaps along her plaid, Western-yoked, pink and purple, femme dress shirt. Mesmerizing pearly white snaps, good for only one thing. I grasped each side, under the collar, just above her breasts and ripped the snaps apart. I love that sound.

Her little white, conservative, cotton bra plopped out with a heavy load. My tanned, weathered hand trailed dust over the pure whiteness, an alluring contrast, and I had to have my mouth on her. Suckling greedily, I released her tin buckle and peeled her faded jeans open, thrusting fingers deep into a cleanly shaven crevice. Smooth flesh was hot in my hand, and I could feel in my palm the hardened nodule.

Her ready wetness gave me pause. I wanted her. I wanted this ride more than the last ride, more than any ride, because it was here and now, and I knew just how I wanted to saddle and mount her.

"I'm going to ride you every which way before dawn calls me back to the round corral." I grasped her hair, entangling my fingers through the cheap, bottled dye-job, and dragged her downward until she was kneeling. My slickened fingers left a snail's trail of wetness from her crotch to the hollow of her pale throat.

"Open the gear bag and wait."

Unbuckling my rugged leather waistbelt, conservatively

highlighted with silver conchos, one directly center, I wrapped her slight, feminine wrists with the looped buckle end, inverting the leather length through her legs, following the seam of her untarnished buttocks until that center concho rested against her clit.

The tail of the western working leather firmly in my grip, I liberated from my bag a worn piggin' string, the short length of which is used for tying off the legs of a roped calf. Soon I had this waxed, thin rope knotted to the belt's tail, thrown around her pasty throat and back to hold that studded strap in place. Oh, she could release the pressure to her wrists, clit and neck by dropping her hands, but I didn't think she would. In my experience, none of them did. In fact, they all learned to pull on it, rub on it, gyrate their cunts over that silver protrusion, oiling that leather strap until it slipped into their cracks and teased their eager, camp follower's puckered asshole, too.

But, while I could give, I was here to get. I was eager for the promise, the ride of that waiting filly I found standing at the gate all day long. I gathered and tugged the tendrils at the nape of her neck, to set her head. I wanted her to look up at me. I wanted her to search my eyes as my cunt would be searching her open, red, pouty lips.

My long thin fingers deftly plucked the brass button of my Wrangler jeans and pulled at the gritty zipper to expose the trimmed, runway strip of my shaved pussy. A musky odor escaped, born of the hot day's work and the even hotter imagination that plagued me. Denim dropped toward the unswept floor. I wanted to thrust her nose into my smell, bury her face in the erotic crease between my legs, but I would be more gentle than that. I didn't want to break her too soon. I wanted her to come to me willingly, with every aching inch of her being offered for service, there for me to ride.

I showed her what she should do by tracing small circles over my stiffened clit shaft, plunging my fingers into my own wetness. She licked her lips in response, telling me that she understood, that she was thinking on it, like an eager filly during round-penning work. She wanted it too, and my will would become hers. I stepped up for that first ride.

Mounting her mouth, there at the doorway, jeans trapped on my boot tops, gear bag open at my ankles, I could find no other bliss outside of the pen. I was born to ride, compelled to ride something all of the time, anywhere. I moved my pelvis from a walking pace into that of a brisk, two-beat jog, wrapping my fingers in this filly's mane to stay with her in case she bucked or tossed around. I pulled on her hard, sinking into my seat, thrusting along with her movements until we were one.

I felt a quivering beneath me, her whole body joining into the rhythm with a creak of leather and a straining of taut rope. I had to have more. Not faster, just more of what I had now.

As if she read my thoughts, her tongue pushed its way into my hole. The pointy tip of her petite nose bumped my rigid clitoris fiercely as her long, pink muscle explored my cavern. Her face was sopping wet from the ride, the vision nearly ungluing me from my human saddle. I drove harder, lengthening the rhythm, the stride, into an uneven three-beat.

She began to bounce beneath me, her mewling turning into throaty moans, then gasps and snorts like that of a rogue stallion challenging in the night.

Splashing, a tumultuous waterfall slit the air, the sound lunging at my ears, and I broke then. I was the one to buck, twisting and writhing from atop the saddle, forcing my mount to stay with me as I pitched and slammed through this first ride. It was nearly impossible.

Not one to ride 'em hard and put 'em away wet, I reached to release the cinch on my downed filly. She rolled to all fours. I smacked her rounded rump and drove her into the disheveled bedroom.

LAST TANGO IN PARIS, TEXAS

M. Christian

You know the El Rio? Down on Cortez? Well, I'm not surprised; I'd be surprised if you did. It's not exactly what you'd call a memorable "establishment." Nothing, really, but a cinder-block bunker in the middle of a red-dust parking lot. Hell, you wouldn't even know it was a bar except for the pieces of neon in the black, narrow strip of window. It didn't even say "El Rio" anymore—so maybe you know the "E io"? Down on Cortez?

Whatever. It was the dive of dives, the black hole of Paris, Texas, frequented, as far as I know, by alcoholic kangaroo rats and inebriated rattlers, or at least the two-legged equivalents.

I do know that once a year, for two or three days, they hung a very tired rainbow flag in the doorway. I liked that a lot. I mean, as far as I know he wasn't a fag (and don't tell me a gal ran the place), but for a couple of days a year he looked up from the red dust, the flickering Budweiser sign, and looked us right in the eyes.

It wasn't really "our" place. We didn't have that kind of relationship; we just hadn't picked up those kinds of things—no song, no holiday, no place. It was just Shelly and I, the thin blonde and the big butch. Just in case you haven't figured it out yet, I'm the butch and she's the blonde. We didn't have a certain place, but we'd been to the El Rio before, and that little queer oasis just seemed to me to be the right kind of place to end it.

It wasn't like I didn't care for her. God knows we'd been up and down the ride enough times together. It was just...well, it was just over. I had this girlfriend back in the '70s who used to get real stoned and then real perceptive. One of my favorites of hers is that dykes just have so much juice in them, like gasoline. They run hot and fast, and then, well, there's just nothing left. We just run out of gas. Rattle, rattle, gasp, sputter—nothin'. Who wants to push a relationship along? Not me, that's for sure.

I think Shelly knew this was it. I'm not great at hiding my feelings; good enough, though, because that one girl back in the

'70s didn't see the breakup coming. Not before she looked me straight in the eyes and said, "Ruthy, you always make the wrong decisions."

Fuck you, bitch. I've made my share, but I've also scored a few times. My truck started out just a rusty pile of shit, but it became a thing of beauty after I got through with it. I've got a pretty good job. Working for a Western apparel store isn't exactly brain surgery, but I've done a lot worse.

With Shelly and me...it was just over. Didn't need to see a lot more to know it just wasn't working. It had been fun, but the gauge was tapping E and the engine was seriously sputtering.

That morning we'd rolled out of bed like every other morning and crawled into our stuff. The usual denim work shirt and jeans for me, with boots of course; pink turtleneck and cotton dress for her. We didn't say a lot, but that wasn't anything new. We'd been slipping down that quiet road for months. Still, it wasn't like we hated each other. Just run out of gas.

I still loved her, but I'd taken the capital letter off that months ago. She still made me laugh, and I still looked at her with that fluttering thing in my stomach, but just not as much. I knew I'd miss seeing her when I came home from work, sitting there at the kitchen table reading Carlos Castaneda, Aleister Crowley, Margot Adler, or some such shit, something classical booming on the stereo (we'd gotten four complaints the first month she'd been living with me). Clove cigarettes. Haunting the flea markets for weird stuff. Little trips across the border. Sudden volleyball games with crunched-up typewriter paper. The poster for *The Burning Times* that was one of her favorite things. At first we had talked a lot; but then we started being just roommates, and recently, almost strangers.

I'd driven by the El Rio the night before, seen the rainbow flag, and suggested we go out for beers. I had my whole speech prepared, a little combo of what had worked for me before, spiced with a few words I thought she might like: "destined," "allowing us to follow our paths," and so forth.

It was night by the time we showered and shaved (or at least she shaved), the bright sodium lights making the city look like one of those weird pieces of jewelry she picked up. I smiled at that as I drove the truck down Cortez.

The place was deserted. Dirty linoleum floor, red plastic

stools, a bar that was almost black, the usual crazy glassware behind, BUD in buzzing neon, an ancient jukebox, a handful of tiny tables. Just us and the bartender. "Anything for ya?" he said as we walked in from the harsh, yellow night, blinking at the darkness of the place.

He didn't look like a fag, but I usually can't spot the boys. He was young, which surprised me, with bright red hair, like rust or something. I asked for my usual Bud and Shelly chipped in for a Daniel's on ice. We didn't make a lot of bucks, me working for the Western-wear chain and Shelly down in the courthouse, and we couldn't afford much. I remember I got this little stab of pissed-offness—like she either didn't care we were almost broke or was determined to have me pick up the tab for her parting shot.

We sat at one of the little tables for a few minutes and talked the usual bullshit: me about Wrangler's new 20x jeans and Ariat's line of lace-ups like they were God's gift to mankind, and she bitching about the drones in the courthouse.

Like I said, I'm not the best kind of person to pick up on stuff, so I didn't know what to say when she said, "I'm going to the can—come with?" I probably just sat there like an idiot as she smiled at me, then turned and walked toward an ugly door marked CAN.

It wasn't really about the sex. I mean, if there was one thing I'd bitch about it was how she really didn't give a flip about money, always buying things when we didn't have a dime. I'd have to pay the rent and find out we had jack in the account because she'd gone off and bought some CDs or something.

Sex was not the problem, at least not until recently when it all started to slide. But that look she flashed at me, that brought me way back; back to when she first moved in, back when we never seemed to have our clothes on.

But, thickheaded me, it took a couple of seconds for me to remember that look, and hear exactly what she'd said. After it finally sunk in, I got up, almost knocking my chair over onto the floor and with that red-haired kid watching followed Shelly into CAN.

For a sec I thought she was attacking me or something. I had one foot in the door and wham! She's right there, arms wrapped around me, kissing me like mad. I freaked a little, trying to push back against the door, but she kept right on at me, pushing her little self against me, squishing her little tits against mine. Her tongue pushed past my teeth, pushing against my own. Like I said, I didn't get it at first, but when her hot breath filled my mouth and her tongue really started to work I figured it out.

So there we were, a couple of dykes tongue-dancing in the bar of the El Rio. It was hot. Did I just say hot? I was fucking melting, man. Shelly had always been a damned good kisser. For a little slip of a thing, with those sly little lips, she knew how to do it right: tongue—oh, yeah—but also with these little playful "bites"; and she'd rub her tiny nose on my big honker, which always made me giggle like a damned little girl. Good? She was the best.

Then she was at my tits. You could park a bus on my ass, but I really liked my tits. What was great is that Shelly liked them too. Kinda bothered me sometimes, when she'd just sit down in front of me and touch them and touch them and touch them, then lick, then kiss my nipples—like the world had shrunk down to just this little girl and my big boobs. But sometimes, like that time in the CAN of the El Rio, God was in Her Heaven, because Shelly's hands went to my shirt, frantically unbuttoned it and pushed it aside like a curtain to a damned hot show.

I like sports bras, and so does Shelly. She smiled wickedly up at me, eyes shining like polished dimes, as she stroked me through the stretchy stuff. Damned right my nipples were hard, and my cunt was getting wet. No duh. I remember I leaned forward, like I was begging for another of those kisses—which I was—but she just kept up that cat-and-cream smile and flipped up my bra, flopping out my tits.

Right then I realized that I was in the CAN of the El Rio. I mean, I knew that, but with Shelly's tongue down my throat I was lucky I could remember my last name, let alone where the fuck I was. It wasn't like we were just necking in my truck or sneaking in a wild quickie on a hillside. This was a sleazy dive that once a year just happened to hang up a queer flag, and we were necking like horny teenagers in the fucking bathroom.

But tell that to Shelly. I don't know what the barkeep put in that Daniel's, but I should buy stock in the company; at least, that's what I thought at the time. I wanted to haul her out of there and off to a quiet, dark street in my truck, but all she did was playfully bat my hands away from where I was trying to pull my bra back down and then she latched her sweet lips onto my right nipple.

Damn, that did it. I knew some girls who look on their tits like they belong to someone else, but not me. I've got one of those nipple-to-cunt hookups: get someone who really knows how to put lips to tit and I'm all off in a fuzzy place just letting the comes wash over me.

She knew how to kiss, and she sure as hell knew how to suck tit. Lips, tongue, the whole damned thing right there on my nipple. My legs went all limp and my eyes just plain faded out. Back against the door, I felt myself lose motor control. Shelly smiled around my fat nipple, gave me an evil look and kept right on sucking. I'm not what you'd call a fast come, but BAM, right then and there I came the fastest I'd ever. I remember it because this little part of my mind thought for a second that I might be having a stroke or something. Then I realized that it was a damned religious experience, and I found myself saying so without realizing it, "Oh, God!"

She quickly shushed me, putting her little hand over my mouth. "Unless you want to have someone else in here," she added in a low, husky voice.

I definitely didn't want that, and shook my head at least once or twice. We kissed, but this time her hands were on my nipple tugging at me and twisting, just enough, back and forth. Her hot breath mixed with mine, bringing me up to a boiling point. While she worked my tit, her other hand was working my crotch, kneading my cunt through the thick denim of my pants. I started to pant down her throat; it was that good. I knew it was that good because I wasn't doing anything by myself. My body was on its own.

Somehow I realized that her hand had left my nipple. God knows how long it was until I figured that out, but there you go. I opened my eyes, feeling them pop against the sweat that was almost gluing them shut.

What did I see? Oh, man, it was so tasty. I think about it a lot, even today.

The first thing I thought was that the damned CAN in the El Rio was really a pit: piss-yellow sink (I tried really hard not to think about that), bizarre Jackson Pollock floor (something else not to think about), stalls covered with billions of years of filthy graffiti.

The second was that Shelly had never looked so pretty. There she was, standing close, eyes half-shut, one hand on my right tit, one hand up between her legs. That wild gypsy skirt was bunched all up around her waist, and her little hand was working at her hot little quim.

For a long time I just stared down at her. Her mouth was also half open, her hot breath warming my face. Distantly, I could hear the little slick, slick, slick sounds of her fingers flickering between her legs, over her clit.

I've regretted a lot of crap over the years: all those times when I fucked up, made the bad call. That day I did one that I've kicked myself over ever since, but at least I did one thing right: I kissed her.

Shelly and her kisses. They were always good, but that time in the CAN of the El Rio in Paris, Texas they were the best they'd ever been. Her hand on my tit, her hand in her cunt, it was the best it could ever be.

We didn't really come together, but we were damned close. Her panting breaths in my mouth pushed me right over the edge, and as I shook and felt my legs get all tense—then loose—I could feel her do the same in my arms.

Holding each other up, we panted some more until the blood eased a little bit out of our cunts and a bit more into our brains. Sniffling and weak as all get-out, we put ourselves together. It felt like hours, but probably had been only a few minutes.

She kissed me then, leaned forward and planted one right on my cheek. I said I wasn't good at hiding things, and she proved it: "That's the best goodbye I can give."

Outside the red-haired guy just smiled at us as we limped and stumbled back to our rickety little table. We smiled, for a while, then I had to struggle off to the can (sex always makes me have to piss). Ever try to take a leak in a place you desperately try not to touch? Try it some time if you really want a challenge.

Like I said, that was the end of it. It might not have been the best call—especially not after that time in the bathroom of that pit—but that's the way it was.

The worst thing, though, is that after we broke up I didn't have sex for over two years.

And Shelly? Shelly married the bartender.

Three Loops and a Hooey

Nipper Godwin

I grabbed a handful of her hair and cranked her head to the side.

"See that?" I let her have a long look at what used to be the beautiful hardwood floor of my immaculate foyer. She winced, her eyes tearing up with pain, and gave me a sidelong pleading look, still too startled to speak.

"I asked, do you see that?" I gave her hair a tug. There wasn't a whole lot of it. Just enough for the pompadour she liked to affect, Saturday nights down at the Silver Spur.

She licked her lips, wincing again, and answered, "Yes, Ma'am." She wriggled her hands and shifted her butt against the strain of her position; being trussed up like a calf must be just plain uncomfortable, all by itself. Out of sympathy, I let go her hair and grabbed the tie instead. Her eyes were watering, but probably not from pain—it took a lot more than that to make my strong silent cowboy of a girlfriend cry. It was only her ego suffering.

"Do you remember what I said I'd make you do, next time you tracked horse manure all over my nice clean floor?"

"Make me..." She stopped midsentence while I drew her up and let her dangle with just her shoulder blades and one heel touching the boards. When I released my grip, she fell back to the floor with a grunt. She swallowed hard and went on, "...lick it up." I caught her ribs with the toe of my shoe. "Ma'am," she finished properly.

"So what's your excuse, pilgrim?" I towered over her, my hands on my hips. The hall mirror caught my eye, and I have to admit I cut a handsome figure. I'm what they call Junoesque; I have six inches of height and fifty pounds on her, and my skinny drink of a sweetie doesn't stand a chance. With my luxuriant chestnut hair pulled as severely back as a schoolmarm's, I looked positively frightening. I smiled. My makeup was perfect, too. I gave myself a come-hither look, just for the heck of it. From the corner of my eye I could see her watching me admire myself, and the expression on her face was priceless. "Is there any reason I shouldn't?"

"Please, Ma'am. Please." She squeezed her eyes shut against the tears. "Please don't make me, please, please, please..."

I love it when she begs. It just makes my heart melt. Well, other parts of me too.

"Please, oh, please, oh, please...," she murmured fervently. Did I detect a note of some other kind of urgency?

I rummaged in my purse on the side table and quickly came up with what I was looking for. I unfolded the hoof knife I'd confiscated from her jeans the last time she'd been careless enough to leave them in the laundry without emptying the pockets; she hardly ever made that mistake anymore. I'd boiled it clean before applying a little 3-in-1 oil, to keep it limber, and it opened real smooth.

"Well, you're gonna have to give Mama some sugar, then."

Her pleas stopped abruptly. I showed her the knife. A look of recognition crossed her face, then fear. I bet she thought she'd lost it in the barn. No such luck.

I fondled the knot lightly, just enough to make her relax her shoulders and heave a sigh of relief.

"Ah, ah, ahhh," I said, snatching a handful of denim where it was loose in the inner thigh. Her free leg flailed, and I had no choice but to kneel across it. She fell still when I poked the point of the knife through just shy of where the seams meet.

"Oh, no, honeybunch, please don't, not my favorite..." I gave her a look that made her go wide-eyed as a calf. "I mean, Ma'am, please Ma'am..." I started sawing through the denim.

"Aw, gee. Aw shucks, now." She jumped as I pricked her left buttcheek. I wasn't trying to be careful. "I'd be happy to give you any little thing you want, darlin', just let me..." I pulled up on her thigh to give the knife room and sawed through the layers of fabric. She gasped when the point touched flesh. "If you just let me up, sugarpie," she resumed in a slightly higher pitch, "I swear I..."

I dropped the knife to grab both sides of the opening and rip. The tearing sound filled the hall. "Oh my goodness," she said in a weak voice. I picked up the knife again and reached through the opening for a handful of cotton brief.

"Oh, now, I don't know about that, there, now, sweetness,

wouldn't you rather let me up and see about cleanin' up the mess I made then maybe afterwards you and me could..."

I pulled up the stretchy fabric and gave it two quick slices before you could say Jack Robinson. One quick yank—being none too careful about rope burn, I'm sad to say—and I had the scrap of cotton out through the slashed jeans and stuffed in her mouth in a jiffy.

My sweetie rolled her eyes back and closed them with a gag-muffled sigh. I tugged the gap a little wider to let the cool air hit her moist pussy—I didn't even have to touch to know how wet she was, and would she dare try to tell me she didn't love every minute of this?—and ran a polished fingernail ever so slowly up the outside of one swollen and happy lip. She wriggled and stuck her free leg out a little wider.

"Ah, ahh, ahhh," I said, and stood up. "I told you, you're gonna have to give Mama some sugar," I said, leaning down to yank the gag in one swift motion that left her mouth hanging open. I lifted my skirt and settled over my cowboy's surprised face. I wasn't wearing panties.

"Yeee-hah," I said softly, making fun of her just a little. I can't say my lover's equine fetish is a mystery to me—she grew up in a place where riding is as natural as breathing, and being in love with the beasts makes perfect sense—but I don't share it. I grew up in a nice Connecticut suburb with insurance executives for kin; and even now that I live with a barn full of them, I've never been on a horse. I've taken in the finer points of rodeo competition by osmosis. Friends say my Seven Sisters education is no longer apparent in my speech. These last few weeks, watching her out in the dusty ring on Daisy, throwing rope after rope over the sawhorse she rigged into a practice dummy, I had to admit that it looked like fun.

Not the riding part. And I surely wasn't going to admit it to *her*. But mornings, when she was gone to school her youngsters—last year's fillies and a very rambunctious colt—I thought I'd try my hand at it. There was something meditative about letting the smooth rope play out through my gloved palm as the circle flew like a crazy big halo toward its target. It didn't take long before I got good at it, standing still at least. I felt like I could finally understand my father's attitude toward golf.

"Mm, mmmm," I murmured encouragingly. My sweetie

does indeed have a silver tongue when she wants to, and not just to tip her hat and grin like a snake-oil salesman and spread flattery out like fine unguent to grease the path of something she wants. No, my sweetie knows how to lick pussy.

She nuzzled, she licked, she sucked, she nibbled. I came three times on shaking thighs before lifting myself away from her, her neck straining to reach me as I rose.

"Oh, don't go away, now, darlin', I only just got warmed..."

I stuffed the underwear back in her open mouth. Did I call her the strong silent type? Well, she can be. But it's nice to have a gag handy.

I stepped over the slack rope, still tied to the banister where I had snugged it. Without an intelligent and highly trained partner like Daisy to pull the rope taut, I'd done the best I could with the resources at hand. Caught by surprise just inside the cathedral-ceiling living room, she'd let the rope fall straight over her head and shoulders without a peep and hardly struggled when I drew it up tight just at her elbows. I secured the end around the banister's finial before she even started to back away, and a well-placed throw rug took her feet out from under her without me even having to break a sweat. Five seconds flat. I could imagine the crowd cheering.

Planning is everything. I reached into the drawer of the hall side table and extracted the rather large dildo and lube I'd secreted there earlier in the day. It's the one she likes to call a horse-cock. I thought it was appropriate. Her eyebrows shot up to her hairline when she saw what I was holding, but I have to hand it to her—she didn't spit out the underwear.

Oh, she was wet all right. I played with her clit through the ragged opening of her jeans until she was breathing hard, nostrils flaring like a winded thoroughbred. Then I dropped on a generous dollop of lube just cool enough to make her twitch. I smoothed it out with the head of the enormous toy.

"You want it, don't you, baby? You want to get fucked?"

I slid the cockhead up and down her slit, bouncing it on her clit in passing. I poised it at her opening, pressing ever so slightly in, then pulling it away to repeat the process. She made a sound like a whimper, muffled by the wad of cotton cloth in her mouth.

"You want me to fuck you?" I pushed the tip of the cock just barely inside her and left it there. She moaned. With my free hand, I pulled out the gag.

"Please fuck me, please, please fuck me, Ma'am, please," she breathed in a dry-mouth rasp. She hadn't even paused to lick her lips.

I pushed the head in a bit further then pulled it out. She whined in protest. I slathered the dick with more lube and put it back where it had been. She sighed.

"You want it?"

"Yes, please, yes, plea..."

I slid the head all the way in and slowly, deliberately, thoroughly, pushed the cock into her all the way to the hilt. She groaned. Her bound leg relaxed and her knees fell open. I pulled slowly out and began to fuck her.

"Oh," she said with every stroke. "Oh, oh, oh," picking up speed as my hand picked up speed, getting louder until she was nearly barking as I rammed her. Her hips rose to suck the enormous cock back in every time I pulled out. I rammed her like a steam engine, my hand slick with juice on the base of the big piston. I pounded her like hooves galloping across a prairie. "Oh, God, yes, don't stop, please," she yelled until she came like thunder and her cunt grabbed the rubber cock so hard I thought I'd never get it out again.

I lay down beside her and propped on one elbow to kiss her. "You're gonna have to relax," I told her. "Be hard to ride with that thing stuck in you as a permanent fixture."

She chuckled and let her muscles unclench. I pulled the dildo out with a pop and laid it on the floor beside the rucked-up throw rug. The toy could go into the dishwasher later, and the floor—well, it had to be cleaned, anyway.

She must have been reading my mind. "You're not really gonna make me lick that up, are you?"

I glanced down the hall. It was a mess; surprisingly so. She really does know better than that. I raised an eyebrow at her.

"Did you do that on purpose?"

Her look was a little too coy. "I'll never tell," she said.

"Hmmmph." I groped for the knife and reached to cut her bonds.

She frowned, watching the blade. I stopped short.

"You used my bathrobe tie for a piggin' string."

"I thought the real thing would hurt you, love. Your wrists

aren't covered in cowhide."

She sighed and nodded at the plaid wool sash wrapped in the requisite three loops around her wrists and ankle. "Probably right," she admitted, then grinned. "I swear, the sight of you with that bathrobe tie in your mouth and a rope whirlin' over your head damn near paralyzed me. It wasn't a fair catch."

I tried to loosen the knot, but it was no use. The bit of hardware I'd fastened it with wasn't a real hooey, just something I'd gotten from a mountaineering catalog. I sliced through the cloth. "I'll make you a new one."

She smiled fondly at me.

"I'll get the bucket," she said, stretching her cramped limbs. We stood up together.

"Don't think you're gonna get away scot-free, Mister."

She looked meditatively at the trail of horse manure down the front hall, then quirked an eyebrow at me.

"I'm going to have to pick out a cane and give you ten of my best, if you did that on purpose."

My cowboy's face lit up in a very broad grin. Luckily for me, horses aren't her only fetish.

The Other Side of the Rockies

Cheyenne Blue

The man in the suit, from the agency in Denver, looked me up and down doubtfully. I stood tall, as straight as my gammy leg allowed, raised my chin and stared him in the eye.

"There's a ranch out east," he said finally, while my black eye swelled under his assessing gaze. "They need a cook."

"I can cook."

I wanted that job, whatever it was. And "out east" wasn't Kremmling, wasn't the western slope where Colorado falls into the Green River and Utah. Wasn't the Lazy Haitch, where Jeb waited cracking his stockwhip among the sagebrush. Wasn't the home that wasn't home anymore.

"You cooked for ranch hands before?"

"Steaks and beans, meat and potatoes, stew, chili. I can make bread, can preserve if there's anything to preserve. Puddings too, sometimes."

The man in the suit nodded. "Well, there's no one else. Guess you'll do. For now." He pushed the forms over to me. "Fill these in. Name, address, social security number. You got one, I take it?"

I nodded, sat down and scuttled the forms over, started filling them in before he could change his mind.

The Red Door Ranch squatted out on the plains, hulked down against the wind. They had the spread of land here, yellow with the grass husks, but it was parched into submission. It was another drought year already. I thought wistfully of the gray-green of the Rockies, but then I thought of Jeb and his hamfists and thought again.

I was shown to a two-bed bunkroom, and the manager told me I'd have to share it with Matty, then left before I could ask if Matty were man or dog.

The hands seemed okay, the usual mix of loners, desperados, and dream chasers. Couple of old timers, some brash lads, skinny as peeled willow sticks. I saw a few rodeo buckles flickering a gleam from under their coating of dust, one man limping so bad that if he were a dog you would've shot him. I didn't find out who Matty was until that evening, when I dished up chops and mash.

Matty came in last. Course, I didn't know it was Matty then, I simply saw another rangy hand, more angular than the young ones, hipbones jutting like fence posts. It wasn't 'til she held her plate out that I saw she was a woman, taller than most, a long string of nothing and limber but with a man's flat figure.

"Matty," she said, by way of introduction. "Guess you're Darlene. We're bunkmates. Hope you don't talk in your sleep."

And that was it. I gave her three chops; she scooped spuds onto her plate with a few carrots and left, taking her dinner away from the others, out onto the verandah. She didn't seem to want to talk to no one, and the men left her alone.

As a bunkmate, she was self-contained, didn't bother me any. I had the bottom bunk as I rose before her, creeping out into the purple mornings to get the breakfast started. I grew to like that time of day, rising when the moon was setting, going out into air so chill and crisp that the world seemed reborn, and my mouth froze and dribbled as if I'd had a triple shot of bourbon. I'd step into my jeans, tread into my boots, and close the door quietly so as not to wake Matty.

I tried not to stare at her, give her some privacy, but of course I'd see her dressing and undressing—impossible not to in our little room. I'd normally be first in bed, but sometimes I'd watch her through slitted eyes, feigning sleep, as she shed her clothes with economical movements. A dusty, flannel shirt, dirty Wranglers stiff with horsehair and sweat and plain boots—no fancy tooling and wheeled spurs for Matty.

She didn't wear a bra. I guess she didn't need it as when she took her shirt off, her breasts barely swelled from her chest. Her nipples were large and dark, and there were faint silver lines running out from them. I wondered if she'd had a baby. She slept only in her underpants, and every night she'd move to the ladder at the end of the bunks. Her head and those small plum breasts would disappear from my line of sight and there'd be only her muscular legs, lean and strong, climbing the ladder. Her underpants were gray with age, simple, no frills, sturdy looking.

They suited her well. Sometimes, if the moon was high and its cold light bathed the room, I could see the fuzz around her bikini line, the unevenness of her hair underneath the close-fitting panties. She didn't shave, and her shins were covered with an overlay of long dark hairs, like the leg barring on a good dun pony. There was a line of fluff running down from her navel, under where the waistband stretched over her angular hipbones. I wondered if her pubic patch were diamond shaped.

'Course, we talked a little. Clipped sentences, a short laugh sometimes, but you couldn't really call us friends. There weren't the shared confidences, the frilly laughter of women. But then, Matty was an odd sort of woman.

Jeb's letter came one day in fall, when the plains scraped clean, the yellow grass withering away like day old bumfluff. The manager passed it to me with raised eyebrow. In the four months I'd been at the Red Door I'd never had a letter before. I recognized Jeb's writing, and my arms chilled into bumps like it were winter, not the low light of fall. Stuffing the letter into my back pocket, I thought I'd read it later, alone.

Alone came that afternoon. I'd taken the buckskin pony I favored out to my favorite spot on the creek, a nearly dried up trickle in the hard ground that still managed to support a stand of cottonwoods. There was a curve in the trunk of one that supported my back, and I could look out over the piddle of creek water and out to the Rockies, way out west on the horizon. Kremmling was on the far side of them, but I didn't think about that often.

I ground-tied the buckskin, and sank down against the tree, the letter in my hands. I was starting to pick at a corner of the envelope, when I heard a cough. I knew that sound: Matty's cough, a short, sharp little bark, not the phlegm-clearing hack of the men. Looking around, I caught a movement on the far side of the creek, her horse shifting from hoof to hoof, half-hidden by a thicket of willow.

She came from around the trees, zipping her jeans. I guessed she'd gone for a pee.

"Knew this was your spot," she said when she saw me. "I've seen you here before, looking west at them mountains. You miss 'em?"

I turned the letter over in my hands. "The mountains, yes.

Who's in 'em, no."

"Husband? Lover?"

"*Ex*-husband." The stress on the first word came out harsher than I intended.

"Was it him gave you that shiner you had when you first came here? And the limp?" Matty settled down next to me, her back against the same tree, half turned away so that she faced the plains and the distant blur of Pawnee Buttes.

I nodded, though she couldn't see me. "He messed me around a bit."

She turned at my words, flipping around to kneel in front of me. Her thighs spread wide, and her shirt hung loose out of her jeans. Surprisingly gentle fingers pushed my hair back, tucking the stray wisps behind my ears. Her fingers were rough and grazed my cheek. "No woman should put up with that shit," she said, and her voice was gritty, resolved. "That why you left?" Her hand fell down, rested on my thigh.

I pretended not to notice. "Yeah. He only hit me once."

"Once is enough." Her hand moved slightly, picked a grass seed from the inner seam of my jeans.

I trembled at the touch, stiffening. I'd heard the talk of course. Cowboys aren't very forgiving of women who don't like them, and Matty was so often alone.

"I have a letter from him. He wasn't supposed to know where I am. Guess that sonofabitch in the agency in Denver told him."

"What's it say?" Her fingers curled around my thigh, but it felt good, supportive.

In answer, I handed her the letter. "Don't know. You open it."

Brown eyes searched my face for a moment then Matty nodded. Taking the letter, she ripped the envelope across, pulled out the single sheet, torn from the ranch ledger. It didn't take her long to scan the contents.

"Fucking prick." She crumpled the sheet up tight, wadding it into a ball and threw it hard across the creek. It lodged in the thicket of willow, out of my reach. "You don't need a jerk like him."

"Gonna tell me what it said?" I looked down, at her brown paw and broken nails, rimed with the yellow dirt.

She shot me an inscrutable look. "Threats. Comment about you being a lousy lay. Something about him coming when you least expect it."

"He always came when I least expected it. Don't all men?" I tried to sound tough, worldly, but my voice shook. Jeb's threat coiled in the pit of my stomach, making me want to run far, far from the Red Door, out east, to a city maybe, where he'd never find me.

"Wouldn't know 'bout that." Matty's words were flat. "But then, I like women. Guess you've heard the talk."

I nodded and focused on those distant mountains. Kremmling was over there, but now it didn't seem so far.

"You don't mind?"

I switched my gaze to her. "Why should I?"

"Some women do. They think I might do this."

And suddenly, the hand on my thigh moved, slid higher, curled around and grasped my crotch hard through my jeans. I jerked instinctively, color flooding my face, but I didn't move away. In that second, I knew I wouldn't, that Matty could give me something I needed.

The flat planes of her face were unreadable in the low afternoon light. A leaf spun down from the cottonwood, the first leaf of fall, and caught in her short-cropped hair. I swallowed hard, aware that the next move was mine, but not sure how to go about it. Did she want romance, this tough cowboy? Would she accept tenderness from me? Or did she want to use me as Jeb did? She swallowed once, and there was a faint tremor in one finger where she gripped me.

I leaned forward and stroked a finger over her thin lips. "Will you protect me?" I asked.

"The price of your compliance? Don't want that." Her hand withdrew.

I wondered if calves felt this way when the branding iron lifted. "No."

"What then?"

"Jeb will come." I spoke steadily. "If you can't protect me, then it's best you stay away."

In answer, she leaned forward, her hands on my thighs, thumbs pointing toward my pussy, and pressed her lips to mine. Her lips were firm, skinny and hot, as if the heat of summer had been sucked into them. One hand raised and unbuttoned my shirt, tracing the lines of my collarbones over and over. Her hand palmed down over my stomach to the snap of my jeans.

"Lie down."

The ground was hard, littered with small seeds and animal tracks. Matty hovered above me then lowered her face to mine. The kiss lingered and clung. She was assured, parting my lips to slip between. She tasted of cinnamon, the gum she chewed I guessed, and she took my breath, stealing it so that my head spun, rustling like the cottonwoods. Her hand moved to my breast, squeezing it, pinching the nipple.

I flinched; Jeb used to do that, but Matty's touch wasn't harsh like his, she knew the line between pleasure and pain. My nipple peaked, bloomed into her hand, and I arched up toward her. She stroked my breasts for a minute, carefully circling over my bra.

"Take it off." Her eyes were dark, unreadable in the rosy sunlight.

I sat up, shrugged out of my shirt and bra, spread the shirt on the ground and lay back down. Waiting.

Matty returned, and her warm lips closed over my nipple, her rough tongue lapped at me like a kitten. I held her hair and let the sensation flow over me, small shafts of pleasure arrowing straight and true. Over her head the cottonwood branches moved slightly, and more leaves floated down, brushing her face before settling on my skin.

My confidence building, I reached for her, eager to feel those planes of muscle, smooth and flat under my hand. I wanted to explore the hollows of her hipbones, bury my face in the curve of neck and shoulder and inhale her scent. But she evaded my seeking hands, a small flinch, just enough to get the message across.

"Not yet." She raised her face from my breasts. "Not until I've fucked you." Pulling away from me, she sat back and tugged at my boots, briefly rubbing my feet in her strong hands. My jeans followed, then the black lace panties that Jeb had liked so much.

I couldn't read her face as she crumpled them in her hand and put them in her pocket, but I knew my own reaction as her fingers lowered, probed, then pushed inside. She rubbed with skill, sliding through the wetness, rubbing me just as I rub myself. I closed my eyes, so that there was only the sunlight dappling behind my closed lids and Matty's fingers, bringing me closer to the edge.

Then, just as my heels were digging into the dirt, arching my back up, pushing helplessly against her fingers, just as my orgasm hovered a breath away, she stopped, withdrew. I lay there panting, and I heard the scrape of her zipper, the sound of jeans being pushed down. In the next moment, she was on top of me, and a hard cock probed my folds, found its place, and with one sure thrust was inside.

My eyes widened in shock, and for a suspended moment, I was back in Kremmling with Jeb pounding away on top of me. Pushing at her shoulders, I twisted, but I couldn't move. Her hips rocked against mine and the cock pushed deeper.

"Matty!"

She must have seen the terror in my eyes, as she rose up on her hands, so that our bodies separated. I felt the loss of her weight.

"It's okay." She soothed me gently, unlike her normal brusque tone. "Feel."

I felt down over my belly, down to where her cock wedged open the lips of my cunt. Hard silicone jutted between my folds, and my questing fingers found the straps that held it to her pelvis. She moved gently, and the dildo slid easily to and fro. My fingers traced where it joined her body, feeling her pussy hairs curling around the edges of the harness. I pressed the cock back against her body and she made a small, abrupt sound of pleasure.

The balance was restored. I fumbled with the buttons of her dusty shirt, wanting to see her small breasts again. Her nipples were bitter chocolate drops, big dark pennies against her pale skin. I traced one of the silver lines, first with a finger, then with my tongue. My arousal, which had withered, surged again, fiercer than before, and I curled a leg around her thighs, feeling the embedded dust and grit abrade my calf.

Matty didn't need any more encouragement. She began to rock again, increasing the pace until she was fucking me fast and deep and hard. Yet her lips dropped down, caressing mine with a sweet and gentle tenderness.

I came fiercely, shivering around the pounding cock, pulling her into me so that my tongue could mate with hers. I couldn't reach her cunt to slip my fingers inside, but she didn't seem to mind, and her strokes built to a pounding crescendo.

We lay together afterwards without speaking, Matty and me, watching the way the branches swayed above our head. The sunlight dimmed and Matty raised her head.

"Storm coming."

Over toward the west, dark rain clouds boiled out from the mountains in a thick, charcoal mass. Our horses raised their heads and stood alert, ears pricked, glancing uneasily toward the storm.

I dressed hurriedly, trying not to see the amused look in Matty's eyes as she tucked away her cock, and zipped her jeans. I found I didn't know what to say to her. The natural thing would be to tuck myself under her wiry arm and curl a hand around her waist. Whisper words of pleasure and thanks into her ear; let her play the role of my protector.

Matty had no such doubts. She waited 'til I was dressed, then pressed her hips into me, hard enough that I could feel the outline of her cock, and kissed me possessively. "It'll be okay," she said when she'd finished.

She caught her horse and swung up, leaving me standing facing the mountains. The clouds were sweeping closer, bringing with them the smell of rain. The air was heavy, oppressive, the birds silent in the face of the storm.

"Come on," she said, impatiently. "We need to ride fast if we don't want to get wet."

I mounted the buckskin and we turned their heads for the ranch, urging them into a fast canter. Their hooves thudded on the hard ground, and they ran faster, the wind under their tails as they raced the tumbleweed east. I wanted to shout aloud to the wind, sing into it. Instead, I pressed my cunt hard against the saddle, feeling the new tenderness.

The rain caught us as we reached the yards; the first fat heavy drops hit the ground like tea stains. The manager was waiting for us as we led the horses into the barn. If he knew what we had been doing from the state of our clothing, or the bulge in Matty's jeans, he didn't say nothing.

"Visitor for you, Dar," he said, jerking a thumb over his shoulder. "Over at the big house."

Matty had vanished like a ghost. Her horse shifted from hoof to hoof in front of his stall. The manager looked around for her, shrugged, then put her horse away himself, dragging off the heavy saddle and throwing it over the partition.

"What's got into her?" he asked, seeming not to notice me frozen in place.

A visitor. There was only one person it could be. The joyful afternoon and the afterglow of loving vanished, leaving me small and scared, shrinking into my boots. Gingerly, I touched my eye, remembered the ache of his fist and the gentle touch of Matty's lips. Gone, both of them. I didn't have a truck so I couldn't leave, and there wasn't anywhere I could hide on the ranch. Someone would find me eventually, and chances were it would be Jeb with his heavy footfalls and his tracker's instincts.

Instead, I took my time settling the horse, checking the water trough, stirring his feed around and around in the bucket, then taking a brush and removing the sweat from under the cinch. The manager had gone, back to the big house, and I would have to follow. Time to cook for thirty hungry men.

The wide yard and stock pens were between the house and me. A step. Another. The space yawned wider than the gulf between me and my ex-husband. But it was Matty's fickle callousness that stung the most. Stand by me. Yeah, right.

I was three-quarters across the yard when I saw Jeb's figure loom in the doorway opposite, and start across toward me. The heavy raindrops darkened his hat in uneven blotches. I could see his expression, and it had the gloating look he got when something rightfully his was returned. I'd only seen it before when he got money, a calf, a stolen stock saddle, but I knew it well. I swallowed, and kept walking, concentrating on my stride, one, two, marching in even beat.

The blue pickup came hurtling around the side of the house. Lucky the gate was open, or I think it would've crashed straight through. It skidded to a stop and the passenger door flung open, rocking with the abruptness of the halt.

"Get in, Dar."

Matty leaned across the stick shift, her expression low and glowering. I hesitated, a look at Jeb, at the stretch of dirt between us.

"I said, get the fuck in!"

Across the yard Jeb broke into a run and reached for the knife that hung from his belt. I'd seen him use it before, on baling twine, willow sticks, steak, downed calves. I knew he liked the feel of it in his hand.

I leaped into the truck, slammed the door. Matty didn't look at me, simply set her face in hard lines and gunned the throttle heading fast for Jeb, fast for the gate. Jeb flung himself to the side nearly in time, but the pickup struck him a glancing blow on one shoulder, spinning him against the gatepost, then hard into the dirt.

I looked back, over the pickup's tray, over the jumble of Matty's and my mixed possessions—our clothes, everything we owned thrown in a hasty pile in the back—and saw him, his face black as he held his shoulder.

As we jounced off down the corrugated dirt driveway, the storm broke with a crash of thunder, a dark curtain of water, sweeping the road to mud. The fresh, sharp scent of rain was in the air and I thought I could smell the sagebrush.

ROPE 'EM AND BRAND 'EM

Val Murphy

The muscles across my back and shoulders burned as the lariat strained taut in my gloved hands. I lost my footing and face-planted in the scrub.

I'd gotten a loop over a good-sized heifer with her mind set on heading down into a wash and over the Mexican border. I'd lost my hat, my horse and now my dignity trying to keep her from renouncing her citizenship as a future all-American burger.

"You could just let go. Heck of a lot easier than that body-surfing through the brush."

Shit. All I needed was an audience, and it had to be JT. "You could get a rope on her and help get her back to the herd," I shot over my shoulder as I regained my feet.

"I suppose I could, though it seemed you had a plan there for a second or two, and I didn't want to interrupt. A woman and her rope work are a fascinating combo."

I managed to lock the rope half around a Joshua tree and looked to where I'd heard the voice, ready to let loose with a stream of descriptive phrases. JT already had a loop out and was swinging it lazily over her head. She took the shot. The rope floated, landing like a caress over the runaway's head. She snugged it up with a flip of her wrist. Taking a turn of the rope on her saddle horn, JT set her horse back to take up the slack. That settled, she shot me a wry grin.

"I like that you don't quit. You were taking quite a beating."

I let my lariat drop and slapped the grit from my Wranglers and shirt. "I've taken better," I replied, peering at her through sun-squinted eyes.

"Really? Didn't know you made a habit of rounding up your cattle for branding this way. Does save on the horses, I guess, but hell on your wardrobe, I'd say." JT reached into her saddlebag and pulled out my crushed straw Stetson. I stalked over to retrieve it, popped out the crown and reset the brim, as well as it could be, and settled it on my head.

"So. What was that about taking a better beating? If you don't mind my asking."

I wasn't paying attention, focused on getting the sand out of my leather gloves, picking kindling out of the cuts on my face and restacking jeans over my boots. I was silent while JT's question registered in my shaken brain. "Just what I said. I've taken better."

The leather split rein caught me twice across the shoulders. The slap with its tingle made me jump and turn to face JT.

"Then maybe you'd better learn to take the best." JT swung free of the saddle, pulling her work gloves off. She grabbed my shirtfront in one hand and started a rhythmic tattoo against my cheeks with the sweaty leather palms of the gloves clenched in her other hand. Each impact rocked me back and forth. Her steel-gray eyes locked with mine, neither of us giving way. She shifted her hand on my shirt and began to pluck and twist my nipples, the gloves never stopping. My pussy soaked the crotch of my jeans in the afternoon heat, and the scent rose between us.

"Are you getting off on this? Are you getting wet on this? Your wires are crossed, girl." The derision in her voice was punctuated by the thud of cowhide.

She knocked my hat off, the strokes getting harder. My cheeks stung from sweat and grit.

"Is that why you let those bitty calves drag you around the desert? You're whacking off? You haven't had better if that's what's getting you off. You think you've had it good do you?" The slaps stopped. "Well, do you?"

I'd hired JT a couple of months after buying the place at auction. I'd been a rich daddy's girl who rode primped, pampered show horses in the ring, with cowboy dreams and a couple of dude ranch vacations under my belt. It wasn't long till I'd figured out that life on a cattle operation wasn't *Bonanza*. That was just about the time my friends quit coming to spend imagined bucolic days, when instead they wound up getting put to work mending fence and hauling feed. I'd been getting ready to pull up stakes when JT had driven up in a battered red Ford with her horse in the back and her saddle on the passenger seat.

"Pay attention!" Whap. My head and body were both spinning. She had me over and down on one side, hands and a single foot wrapped in my own piggin' string before I could catch myself.

"Were you thinking about Wild Bessie over there in her rope?" JT jerked her thumb in the direction of her horse and the runaway. "You jealous?" JT stood and looked down as she stepped over me. "You like to play with little heifers. Well now, so do I."

I lay there doubled and watched as she built a fire, pulled down her saddlebags and started laying out the irons.

"I'd say it's about time all the cattle on this place get their brands. That way there'll be no disputing who owns them if they decide to wander." JT laid the patterned ends up close to the fire, not yet in the coals. She walked to me and crouched by my hip. "Now, we hadn't discussed where exactly you wanted brands placed on your cattle. But I know exactly where I want mine." JT flipped open my belt buckle and popped the button on my jeans. Grasping both front belt loops she pulled them apart, forcing down the zipper, then the denim to my knees.

"Nice big roasts here." JT slapped my ass. "You've been feeding up well by the looks of it. Though it does look to be tough. Maybe with a little tenderizing it'll soften a bit." JT rolled me up onto her lap and began spanking each cheek hard. She pummeled my ass bare-handed and then pulled on her glove and continued until tears and my pussy poured. I was on the edge. JT sensed it and stopped.

"Now that looks better, nice and red," sliding her hand into my sopping twat, "and juicy." She turned my face to her and offered her gloved hand to be cleaned. "Don't you agree?"

I met her eyes, looked at her hand, and then licked the leather clean, slinking my tongue between, around and up the seams, suckling her fingers like a newborn calf.

JT moved her free hand back to my cunt and slipped her fingers in, mimicking my suckling, picking up my rhythm. She danced around my G-spot, teased my asshole with her thumb. Never varying from what she felt on her leather-clad hand.

I sucked her fingers into my throat, up to the palm, and JT slid her cupped hand into me. I pulled my mouth free.

"God! Please JT. Now! Hard!" I broke. JT went with me.

She paced me now, driving me, tweaking my nipples with her gloved hand. "Go on, get up there. C'mon." She chided and kissed me, riding herd on my orgasm. "You're almost in there girl. That's it. Step it up. That's it. Now! Come now!"

I bucked and spurted, soaking JT's shirt to the elbow and her Wranglers beneath me.

JT slid her fingers free and gently put me back on the ground facing the fire. She stepped over me again and picked up her irons, placing the ends in the heated coals. She wasn't saying anything now.

I watched, still tripping, as she heated the ends and then pulled one free and came toward me. The cherry red shape was indecipherable in its mirror image. JT stepped over and behind me. I felt her grasp the waist of my jeans bunched at my thighs. She dropped a knee over to lock me down. "Don't move."

I wouldn't have thought to. I saw the iron swing down out of the corner of my eye and could feel the heat radiate as it neared my skin. I heard the searing sound and waited for the pain to come but it never did.

JT leaned over, released her hooey from my wrists and ankle and stepped back.

I reached to pull up my jeans, feeling heat come off of my leather belt. I turned to look at JT.

"Well the way I see it, the brand would be hidden anywhere else when we're out here. And if anyone decides to adopt your style of roundup, well, I'll know which one's mine."

Sweethearts of the Rodeo

Julia Talbot

"You really oughta watch that Charlene, you know." Jodi didn't know why she bothered. Chrissy Payne was a rodeo queen from the top of her pretty blue hat to the toes of her shiny ropers. She rode like a dream, had a smile like a hundred-watt bulb, and could be so cool butter wouldn't melt in her mouth. Chrissy was a shoo-in for this year's Miss Deltarado Days.

Maybe that was why it bothered Jodi to see the girl cozying up to last year's queen like it would help her get ahead. Charlene was bad news. Jodi knew that much.

"I don't know *what* you mean, Jodi Lancaster. Except that you're jealous because you know you've got no chance at it, for all you got Hiram Mayfield to sponsor you with his tractor sales."

Jodi sighed. She didn't really want to win. She was only running for the queen deal to throw mud right in Charlene's eye. She stuck her hand in the pockets of her Wranglers, bought in the boy's section at Tractor Feed and a heck of a lot less fancy than Chrissy's Rocky Mountain jeans, and rocked back on her heels.

"I just mean she's meaner than a rattlesnake and twice as sly. She'll only help you for one reason. Worse than any steer-dogger for that."

"What I do with Charlene is my business, Jodi." Chrissy tossed that head of jacked-to-Jesus blonde hair, sniffing disdainfully in Jodi's direction.

Jodi just shrugged, shaking her head. "Well, it's up to you. May the best woman win."

"She will."

Jodi watched Chrissy walk off, ass swinging, and hoped to heck Chrissy was right; hopefully Charlene wouldn't win this time. The price was mighty high.

The end of the week saw the choosing of the new Deltarado Days queen, and sure enough, it was Chrissy Payne. There was a big old party and a contra dance and Jodi found herself in the unlikely position of alternate and a member of the queen's court. Her, with her beat-up old boots and her big, dapple, gray gelding that couldn't run a barrel if his life depended on it. Jodi was a working girl, with a working horse. She might know her way around cattle but rodeo parades and flag carrying? Well, damn. They weren't her thing.

Now that didn't mean it wasn't worth it, Jodi figured. She slipped out of the dance before two-stepping and drinking turned to brawling, with a smile on her face. Charlene'd been furious at her, any fool could see that. While Jodi didn't think of herself as a vindictive girl, she was happy enough to put the rage in Charlene's sloe eyes.

She was on her way to her truck when who should she spot leaning on her fancy little Ford Ranger crying her eyes out but Chrissy Payne. Jodi wavered for a minute, knowing she should just up and leave, but headed that way against her better judgment.

"Hey. What are you crying about? You won."

Chrissy looked up, all hung-over raccoon with her mascara running that way. Her eyes were red as anything and she wasn't so darned perfect. It made Jodi like her better.

"That bitch Charlene. She wanted me to...she tried to get me."

"What? She wanted you to have sex with her?" Hell, she'd called it, hadn't she?

"No. With her boyfriend. Fucking bitch said she'd got me where I was and now I needed to blow him."

Jodi looked at Chrissy closely, noting no sign of swollen lips. "I'm thinking you didn't."

"No." Now Chrissy was looking at her, a weird expression chasing the last of the tears away. "No way was I touching him." Suddenly Chrissy moved in on her, hands coming up to cup Jodi's cheeks. Jodi was just about paralyzed with the shock, because out of all the things Chrissy could have done, that one was the last she had expected.

"Uh. Chrissy, honey, what are you doing?"

"I'll touch you, though."

Lord. Jodi jumped back a good foot. "Honey, if you think I'm gonna be your consolation fuck, you got another thing coming."

"I don't want consolation." Chrissy followed as Jodi retreated, finally backing her into the side of a big diesel dually. That girl just invaded Jodi's personal space, smelling of beer and Lady Stetson. "I want you. She said awful things about you, you know. About how you were a frigid bitch, about how you wouldn't give what you promised. I bet you just got wise to her a lot faster than I did."

Chrissy was close enough to kiss. Jodi kept her hands and her lips to herself by sheer dint of will. "Honey, I don't think..."

"Don't think. Or if you do, think what Charlene's face will look like when she hears we had each other."

Oh, God. When Chrissy leaned right in and kissed her, Jodi was a goner, mouth opening under those lipstick-smeared lips, letting Chrissy in. They were all over each other, just like that, Chrissy's hands sliding down Jodi's throat to her shoulders, holding her close. Jodi felt her way down Chrissy's back to that lush ass, so well defined by those pocketless jeans, cupping and squeezing.

Chrissy tasted good. Salt and lime and beer, maybe a few tears. The look on Charlene's face wasn't the only thing that would make it worth it to Jodi. Having Chrissy Payne would be an experience to remember.

A truck backfired close by. They both jumped, breathing hard as they pulled apart.

"Where?" Chrissy asked, holding Jodi's upper arms hard enough to leave marks.

"There's my truck."

"No. Need more room."

Room. Right. Jodi tried hard to think over the sound of her heart and the feel of Chrissy's thigh between her legs. Fuck.

"The, uh, exhibition house." It was only a stone's throw away, and dark and quiet.

They stumbled there together, Chrissy pulling Jodi along so she just couldn't catch her breath. Not much caught her off guard, but this heat, this need that had sprung up between them did. She never would have thought it.

The old twist lock on the door yielded easily to Chrissy's rattling and pushing. The place was cool and shadowed, the quilt racks and art boards for the fair next week already in place. With the same determination that made her a champion barrel racer and rodeo queen, Chrissy stripped Jodi right down, looking her over and touching her. Made Jodi feel weird, made her feel out of control.

It was as thrilling as it was frightening.

"God, you're pretty." Chrissy petted her, neck and collarbones and breast, one finger sliding over her nipple. Jodi gasped, blinked, her nipple drawing right up, legs shifting restlessly.

"Not pretty like you," she said, fingers flexing at the thought of sinking them into Chrissy's hair, of holding that hot mouth right to her crotch.

"You let me decide that." Backing off a step, Chrissy started to strip, heavy breasts falling free as she took off her bra and sent it flying. Jodi pretty much drooled.

Her own breasts were small, "pert" someone had called them once, but Chrissy's were lush, with dark nipples. Jodi reached for one, cupping it, weighing it. A sharp sound met her touch. Chrissy arched her back and looked happy as a cream-licking cat.

They moved then, coming back together and sinking right to the floor, landing on top of Jodi's clothes, thank God, because who knew what was on that floor. Chrissy pushed Jodi back, struggled out of her jeans and boots and straddled Jodi's hips, managing to look at once triumphant and horny as hell. Jodi got another taste of that mouth, Chrissy kissing her deep and hard, making her feel it. Her lips burned and so did her belly, way down in and needing.

Jodi touched Chrissy, her face, that hair. It was softer than she'd thought, not stiff with Aqua Net. Chrissy humped her, encouraging her with sounds and motions to touch more and there was no way Jodi could resist. The skin at the base of Chrissy's neck was softer than the skin on her face, less sunburned and wind-weathered. Chrissy's back was all smooth skin and bumpy spine and her naked ass was enough to give Jodi palpitations.

The floor was damned hard, even harder against her back as Chrissy finally got down to business, grabbing Jodi's hands and holding them down on either side of her head, bending to suck up a mark on Jodi's neck.

That stung. Hurt just right, made her try to wrap her legs around Chrissy and hump some herself but she couldn't. Not with Chrissy sliding down to sit between her thighs and biting at her little nipples, one then the other and back again. Jodi was gasping, heaving, trying to get to Chrissy any way she could and Chrissy just kept driving her crazy.

"I want to taste you."

Jodi blinked; tried to think. "Thought you did already."

"No. Not your mouth. Here."

One of Chrissy's rein-callused fingers slid between Jodi's thighs, right up between her wet lips, pressing against her clit. The fireworks might still be a week away but Jodi was getting a preview.

"Yeah. Hell, yeah. Please."

"Oh, damn. I knew you had it in you to beg."

Jodi wanted to deny it but it was true, wasn't it? She was spread like a staked-out goat, thighs wide open, wet and glistening. And she was begging. Just fucking pleading for it. She got two fingers as a reward, pushing right inside her before pulling out and spreading her own moisture over her clit. Jodi cried out, making Chrissy smile and slide down even more and put her mouth there, licking and sucking, even biting a little.

Made her crazy. Made her thrash and groan. Chrissy kept at her until Jodi was sure she was louder than the music over at the barn, until she was sure she would just downright explode. When she came, it was with Chrissy's tongue inside her, Chrissy's fingers pinching her clit and her own hand in her mouth to muffle the screams.

It didn't take Chrissy long after that. Not when the woman pulled up and rode one of Jodi's thighs like it was a bucking bronco, that wet pussy sliding against her, leaving trails of moisture. Jodi helped all she could with her brains melted, hands moving clumsily on Chrissy's breasts and belly. When Chrissy threw her head back and hollered it was fiercest thing Jodi had ever seen.

They stayed there together for a good while afterward, getting their breath back, until finally Chrissy sat up looking for her clothes. Jodi found her shirt and jeans but only one sock and no bra.

When Chrissy picked up her pretty blue hat, Jodi saw the glint of the little tiara the rodeo queen got to wear. Chrissy caught her looking, and laughed.

"Sorry I beat you."

"I'm not." Jodi climbed to her feet, feeling bruises popping up all over. It was a fine ache. "I only entered to piss Charlene off."

"Yeah? Well I reckon we sure will do that, when she finds out about this."

"Sure. I reckon so. There's just one thing."

"What's that?" Chrissy looked over at her, brushing dust off the butt of those jeans Jodi liked so.

Jodi grabbed Chrissy and kissed her. Hard. Knocked that pretty hat right off. "I think it will piss her off more if we keep on doing it."

Oh, now. That got her a blink and a blush and an almost shy smile. "Yeah," Chrissy answered. "I do believe you're right. I think you need to become a permanent fixture in the court, Miss Alternate."

Jodi laughed out loud, nodding and offering Chrissy her arm. "Whatever you say. You're the Queen."

Western Pleasure

Shanna Germain

I'd been looking, not looking, for Gina all morning. Thought I caught the shimmer of her blonde braid near the fence-line while I was trying to guide Sage up to the mailbox in the trail class. But Sage was tossing his head and snorting at the mailbox like he'd never seen one before. By the time I got his fat ass close enough that I could reach in and grab the paper out of the box, the plait of hair was gone.

By four thirty, when the fun classes were about to start and I still hadn't seen Gina, I was worried that maybe she hadn't come this year. Ten years straight we'd been meeting at this show. Never missed a one. I wondered if I should call her to make sure she was okay. Realized I didn't even have her home number.

Sage was rolling the bit in his mouth by that time, and I could tell from the way his hip jutted into my thigh that he had that back foot cocked up. Either my low energy was getting to him or he was tuckered out. I leaned over his sweaty neck. Ran my fingers under his short gray mane.

"That's all right, boy," I said. "We'll skip sit-a-buck and call it a night."

I felt the horse up next to me before I saw it; a shadow, a huff of air, Sage's neck cresting beneath my cheek. Gina's voice sang across to my closed eyelids.

"Why? You afraid Darlin' and I might kick your ass back to Montana?"

I slid up from Sage's neck. My heart thundered at the sight of Gina, blonde hair in double-braids, sky blue eyes, lips like a red apple split in two.

"Where in the hell have you been?" I asked.

I could barely keep from leaning over and taking her into my arms. Last time I'd seen her, she'd been naked, ass up, in my trailer, my hand making marks against that pale, pale skin, branding her until she'd cried just a little. Thinking about it made my stomach drop between my legs.

Gina put her big teeth over her bottom lip. She shook her head.

"Don't ask," she said. "We've had one of those summers."

She pointed down at Darlin's head, like the horse was a two-year-old who'd been throwing temper tantrums all day. Gina looked at the reins in her hand and fiddled with the leather. "I think this is my last time here," she said. "It's a long way to come for a small show."

I didn't know what to say to that. We'd been meeting at this show for nearly a decade, our bodies lying together after. It didn't matter what was happening at home, or who was dating who or what else was going on in our lives.

Gina bobbed her head toward the ring and broke those red lips into a smile. "So, we doing this, or what?" she said.

"Hell, yeah," I said. I didn't want to think about her not coming back next year.

Darlin' pranced a little beneath Gina, ready to move on. "Good," Gina said. "Then prepare to get your ass kicked, sister."

I wrinkled my nose at Gina and settled my butt a little lower into Sage's bare back. "I doubt that," I said.

For the sit-a-buck class, you ride bareback. Just a fiver tucked between your thigh and your horse. And this particular sit-a-buck class always drew a crowd—it was a jackpot class, meaning the one who could keep that bill under their leg the longest got to keep the pot. And with the five-dollar bills being a solid raise from the normal buck-a-pony, it was usually the fullest class of the show.

I had no worries, even with all that extra competition. Sage was steady as a tabletop, and about as wide—bills stuck to his back like a magnet. Darlin', on the other hand, was a dumb-as-they-come mare that had a reputation for being skittish around anything that shook, rattled, or wiggled faster than a fence post. Damn beautiful animal. Her coat was shiny red in the sun. She looked more Corvette than horse. She had that fine Arab head too, soft-as-satin muzzle, and those big black eyes with eyelashes most women'd kill for.

However beauty's nothing if you don't have the brains to go with it. Last year, Darlin' tried to take Gina's leg off on a cloverleaf barrel after one of the judges snapped her gum on the sidelines. Gina's knee got all bloodied up from the lip of the barrel. I could have killed that damn horse.

But Gina was loyal if nothing else, and she believed in the good in things, including skittish horses, growling dogs, and hard-assed women.

"You're the one going down," I said.

The truth is, we didn't care who won. We weren't really there for the show. We were there for each other. Not that we'd ever admit it.

Gina gave a grin, that wide smile I'd fallen in love with the first time I saw her.

Darlin' spooked at something and tried to crabwalk into the horse in front of her. Watching Gina's ass in jeans work against Darlin's bare back was killing me. I couldn't tell if it was Sage's wetness seeping into my jeans or the other way around.

I let Sage's reins drop. Showing off his temperament. The way he'd stand still for hours just because I asked him to. "What's a matter?" I asked. "Got spooked by her own leg again?"

Gina twisted her lips sideways. She gave Darlin' a little pat on her prancing shoulder. "Won't say she's the first woman who's gotten spooked by her own leg," she said, looking right at me.

I gave Sage a soft kick, to get him in position. I didn't have anything to say to that.

I leaned over and tucked a five under my thigh. When Gina and I started riding this class, it was only a buck. The winners, if they were lucky, might have brought home a whopping ten dollars. That first year, Gina won. She bought a bottle of Boone's and some crackers to celebrate. Then had me naked before we'd even opened the crackers.

When she took my nipple between her big teeth and twisted, I could feel the shock waves all through my body. Just that mouth on my nipple. She didn't touch me anywhere else. She made me beg and beg until, finally, I brought my own hand down when I couldn't stand not being touched anymore. She'd sat back and watched the whole thing. It was the first time I'd ever done that with someone else's eyes on me.

I've won the sit-a-buck pretty much every year since, and I still buy that bottle of Boone's. Although we never open it now. We always leave it in the barn for some grounds crew to help themselves to after we're gone.

This year, the stakes were higher. Five bucks a pop meant seventy-five bucks for ten minutes worth of riding. That was something worth working for. I could buy a girl dinner with that. Or a shitty hotel room.

"All right, boy, here we go," I whispered. Sage turned one ear backward, game for anything.

I watched as Gina slid a bill beneath her jean-clad thigh. I could practically feel the heat coming off her and Darlin'. I could, if I squinted a little, imagine that I was that piece of paper going under Gina's leg.

Gina saw me watching and winked. Then she dropped her hand into her crotch, and cupped it there, like it was just an innocent movement, like she was reaching to touch Darlin's back. No one would even think twice about that. No one but me. All I could think of was her in the back of my pickup a few years ago, back arched, fingers digging into her lips, legs wider and wider. The shine of her pale skin under the stars...me just watching...unable to move until she finally, finally said my name, pulled me to her, with her fingers sticky and wet on my skin.

Sage lurched under me, and I realized we'd started. I squeezed my legs against his sides and kept my eye on the back of Gina's braid.

"Trot!" yelled the judge, and the circle stepped up. Sage had more of a rock than a trot, and I focused on just moving my body with his, hips forward and back, forward and back. It could have been Gina below me, me on top, one hand inside her, taking her forward and back, rocking.

A few horses ahead of me, a bill fluttered through the air, and a man astride a dappled gelding moved to the inside. The rest of us kept going. Round and round. Canter. A hand gallop. Back to walk. Trot. Fivers fluttered down every couple of turns around the ring. The group of disqualified riders in the middle of the ring grew. Maybe thirty or forty bucks were on the ground now.

Ahead of me, Darlin's footsteps quickened. "Shit," Gina said as the bill fluttered from beneath her thigh. I watched the paper fall. Gina gave me a thin-lipped smile, no teeth, and ducked her head. The judge motioned for her to ride Darlin' into the middle. She headed that way, and then, quick, turned Darlin's head toward the gate instead. I watch as Gina talked to the man at the gate, her hands waving in the air. He shook his head. Leaving in the middle of a class wasn't allowed; I knew if she went through the gate, she could forfeit her right to compete.

Sage and I went around the ring again. I held my breath, tightened my legs around Sage so hard that he tried to speed up beneath me. Then Gina slid off Darlin's back and opened the gate herself. She led Darlin' through, not looking back.

In front of us, another bill fluttered. Another horse went to the inside, but I barely noticed. I was watching Gina's back, so tiny next to Darlin's hind end, walking away. I'd seen her walk away so many times—at the end of each show. I'd never stopped her knowing we'd meet again. But maybe not this time. Maybe she was going for good.

The judge had us slow to a walk. My heart kept moving at the faster beat. I could barely feel Sage beneath me for all the thumping up in my throat. I lifted my thigh just a little. The fiver under it stuck for a moment. Sweaty.

I gave it a shove with my finger until it fell onto the ground. The judge gave me a curt nod. I felt the others waiting for me in the middle. Instead, I followed Gina's vanished back as if by radar, through the still-open gate and down toward the place I had last seen her.

Gina was cooling off Darlin' behind the barn by the time I found her.

"You all right?" I asked.

"I will be," she said.

Gina gave me that damn smile again, those little dimples on each side, her teeth sticking out just a bit. I always got the insane urge to lick them.

"That was about the fastest win I've ever seen," she said.

I slid off Sage's back and started walking him out beside her, as close as I could get to her without Darlin' freaking. My nipples were tight beneath my shirt, moving toward her, already begging for her touch.

"There are still half-a-dozen idiots back there, duking it out over a fistful of paper," I said. "I couldn't wait. Didn't want to wait."

Suddenly, getting it out there, putting the words in the air for her to respond to or not, I felt better. My heart was still excited but no longer galloping in panic.

Gina reached over and took my hand without saying anything. We walked the horses silently for a while to cool them off, the horses' breathing slowed, they swished their tails against their thighs, hooves crunched through the grass.

Wherever I am, these sounds remind me of Gina. They remind me of the way her nipples bloom into soft, sweet buds when you touch them, the way she tosses her head back when she's about to come, the way she was so damn far from me that I couldn't remember her taste on my tongue.

We stalled the horses, then stood in the sunshine for a minute. I guess I was waiting for a sign, something to tell me what do next. Gina reached her callused palm out to my face, ran it downward, scratching my cheek just a little. "You got a piece of hay there," she said.

Those red, red lips came closer. I couldn't bear to close my eyes. I wanted to watch her there, lips against my lips, until I went old and blind.

"Don't stop coming," I said, when our lips parted.

Gina looped her finger through my belt and pulled me right against her, giving me that big toothy grin. "How could I?" she said.

NO MORE SECRETS

Chuck Fellows

My late dinner was peanut butter on white bread again, and, of course, my coffee. I was sitting on one bale, leaning back on another, and trying to ignore the prickly roughness of the hay pressing through my thin T-shirt. I hadn't felt the need to eat properly ever since Cassie left six months ago. I never bothered with grocery shopping either, since Cassie had taken care of that. I just didn't want to waste the time. She always came down to the stable with a proper meal, come lunchtime: soups, salads, fancy recipes she wanted to try out.

Cassie was bored here, never really wanting to live this far from the city. She wanted dancing and parties. She wanted to play at dressing up and going out, and, well, I had to be here, didn't I?

I had a lot of money invested in this place, and at that time, six months ago, I was boarding thirty-two horses. Sure, less than half were mine, but I was still responsible for all of them. Thirty-two horses isn't really too many with six hands working for me, but for some reason, around the first of the year, all but one worker moved on. And Cassie started to feel like I wanted to keep the stable running more than I wanted to keep our relationship moving along. She had been gone now longer than she'd shared my bed, but I still missed having another woman to share my life with.

I don't know. Maybe it wasn't Cassie I was missing after all. Maybe it was just the sex I wanted back. When I first met her she said she loved the smell of leather, but back then I misunderstood. I work with leather every day: bridles, reins, saddle soap and the like. Something always needs to be cleaned or repaired around here. And now every day when I work the leather, I think of Cassie.

Well, like I said, maybe I'm not specifically thinking about her. But I keep seeing a slender back flowing down to round womanly hips, straining against the ropes as I lovingly stripe pale skin with buttery soft reins.

As I sat, working the peanut butter from the roof of my mouth, I thought about the first time Cassie showed me a little something about kinky sex. I'd been working late in the tack room, trying to clean up the mess left by young boarders on Saturday night, in too much of a hurry to go out and party. I thought I heard a noise in the barn and when I looked up there was Cassie, walking toward me, naked as the day she was born. She was carrying a coil of my best rope and nothing else.

"What are you doing, Cassie?" My heart got stuck in my throat when I contemplated who might drop by the stable at nine thirty on a Saturday night. She ignored me completely and started threading the rope through eyebolts in the wall near the bridles. How the heck did those bolts get there? I wondered, briefly. I'd sure never noticed them before.

I didn't watch them for long, since Cassie's ass was my much more immediate concern. Each time she lifted her arms to thread the bolt her ass moved just a little from side to side. Watching her move, catching just an occasional glimpse of breast, I realized my breathing had changed. I didn't know what she was doing, but I was already enjoying the show.

The coil of rope was stretched evenly between two eyebolts, knotted at each, with a couple of feet hanging on either side. Cassie turned and smiled at me. "I want you to tie me up," she said as she handed me one of the ends.

"What?" I didn't have a clue as to what she was talking about. All I could do was look at her nakedness and wonder at the flush on her face and chest.

"Circle my wrists a couple of times and tie it off with a slip knot. I promise I won't pull it out. Come on, it'll be fun, you'll see."

I was starting to figure it out. Cassie wanted me to tie her up and...and do something to her. I'd heard about such things, but in all my forty years had never actually thought about doing it. Now here she was, and I could feel my clit getting harder by the moment.

She turned and faced the wall again, stretching her arms up and out to grasp the hanging ropes. Hesitantly, I bound her wrists as tightly as I dared, half hoping she would change her mind and pull her hands loose. But she didn't. And when I was done and she was secured to the wall, I tried to imagine what I could do to her now. We had never talked about this stuff before. I wasn't even sure I could ask her what came next.

But Cassie was a pro at whatever she did, and told me to start by running my hands all over her body. When she instructed me to pick up the reins I'd been cleaning and slap her backside with them, I felt myself get warm and even more excited. I gently tapped her ass with the last six inches or so of the inch-wide leather straps. She just laughed at me. I swung harder, connecting solidly with her skin, and watched in fascination and horror as two red welts appeared.

"More," she gasped. "Do it harder. And don't stop."

More redness and more welts came up on her ass. When I started worrying about ripping her soft, beautiful skin, I moved up onto her shoulders.

Cassie was panting and moaning now, and dancing about trying to move out of my range. But she had told me to keep going, and I couldn't stop until she had all she wanted.

Suddenly I just had to touch that reddened skin. Dropping the reins to the floor, I touched her back with both hands, marveling at how hot her skin was. I suspected the coolness of my hands was something of a comfort to her, but with each caress her moans grew louder, and my excitement grew with them. There was nothing I wanted more at that moment than to fuck her then and there.

Reaching between her thighs, I found her lips swollen, her sex wet and wide open. There was no thought on my part, only reaction. I plunged two fingers deep in her cunt and she staggered, struggling to remain upright. Regaining her footing, she arched her back, giving me better access to fuck her.

Half standing, half squatting, I pumped into her with my hand. She was so wet each time I pushed in or pulled out there was this glorious slurping sound. The slapping noise my knuckles made against the wetness dripping from her fueled my own desire. I fucked her pussy as hard as I could, almost lifting her with each thrust. Her fingers scrabbled against the solid wall, desperately seeking purchase, but not finding any.

Suddenly she was coming, loud, and hard, and strong on my hand. Her cunt pulsated, sending wave after wave of silky wetness over my hand, until finally she slumped, still partly suspended by the now uncoiled rope.

"Hey, come back." A sweet voice startled me out of even sweeter memories. Jo was looking down at me with concern etched on her face. I realized I was breathing heavier than I should have been and turned beet red with embarrassment. Jo didn't seem to notice; or maybe she was just being polite because I was her boss.

I never should have hired Jo. The job was physically challenging, and, when she'd signed on, Jo was definitely not in any shape to do it. She was on the short side, with little spindly legs and all barrel up above. Her arms were flabby and there seemed to be no way she would ever be able to keep up with the rest of us hauling bales of hay and buckets of water for the horses. But Jo had a nice smile and dark, dark eyes that reminded me of a mare I once loved. Well that part is true but, let me be honest here, she got to me because she looked enough like Cassie to be her sister. And Cassie had walked right out of my life less than a month before. And God, did I miss her.

The first few weeks it was painful to watch Jo struggle. Occasionally someone else would step in to help, but she refused all offers. She volunteered to come in early and always managed to hang around late, and we all stopped offering to help her. By late spring the whole stable got busy with new people always dropping by, new horses to be boarded, new kids wanting to learn to ride, and I stopped looking out for Jo. She was handling the job. She was getting stronger. I didn't need to worry about her anymore, so I hardly ever felt the need to check up on her.

Then one day, oh, maybe six months after she came to work for me, Jo showed up in a tank top and shorts. Suddenly she caught my eye. The round belly was gone. Her arms were toned. And good Lord! The girl had calf muscles! Tanned and fit, Jo was working much harder and much faster than any of the other stable hands. All I could do was lurk just out of her sight and watch those muscles ripple whenever she moved.

And now Jo was standing in front of me holding a brown paper bag.

"I brought you some dinner." She grinned as she handed me cold containers of potato salad and cheese.

"Thanks, but you didn't have to do that. How come you're still hanging around, anyway?" I asked, popping open the lids while reaching in the bag for the plastic fork I had seen there.

She looked at the floor. "I wanted to talk to you alone about a couple of things."

"Oh?" I raised my eyebrows.

"Yeah, that Zangri kid. She's gonna ruin Blaze's mouth the way she jerks that bit around. Somebody has to talk to her. She won't listen to me."

The Zangri kid was really no kid. Katie must have been in her late twenties, not much younger than Jo, but she did have a heavy hand with Blaze, and this was not the first time someone else had noticed it. "I'll catch her the next time she comes in and have a word with her. She does know better."

"Thanks," Jo murmured, kicking a bit of hay around with her toe.

"Something else?" I asked around a mouth full of wonderful potato salad. The silence stretched out.

"No, not really. Well. Maybe." Jo looked away again.

I swallowed, my fork hanging in midair for the next piece of business. It must be serious for Jo to hold back.

"Um. Well. Yeah, right."

"What is it, Jo?" The last bite of the salad disappeared.

"I've also noticed you watching me." She still wouldn't look in my direction, so I never saw it coming.

"Yes, I have, and you're doing a great job. I've gotten no complaints about your work."

Jo turned, her dark eyes staring down directly into my own. "No. That's not what I meant. You've been watching me."

I blushed. I couldn't deny that, and she knew it. I swallowed hard, not sure what to do or say next. Should I apologize? Or what?

Jo leaned down and kissed me full on the lips. What could I do? I kissed her back. I had wanted to do that for weeks now. Her tongue pushed between my teeth and from somewhere deep inside of me came a moan of want and need.

I tried to set the empty container down on the edge of the bale and missed, knocking my coffee over in the process. Her fingers, strong and rough, caressed my cheek and slid down to the back of my neck, holding me close against her. Jo's lips were cool and insistent as she kissed her way down my neck, leaving a trail of moist places along my skin and an even wetter place between my legs.

I gently pushed her away so I could stand up.

Jo took a step back and looked down again. "Sorry," she said, suddenly embarrassed.

"Don't be." I picked up her hand and kissed her palm, then walked toward the tack room pulling her along. Once inside, I locked the door behind us and turned to face her, feeling brave and wanting her more intensely than I had ever thought possible.

Turning her around to face the door, I pushed her up against it and held her there while my tongue followed the line of her jaw and down her neck. With teeth pressed into that tanned shoulder, I bit hard until she let out a cry of pain and surprise. I paused only long enough to lift her tank top over her head, using the material to bind her arms loosely behind her. My breath coming faster now, I leaned in and asked, "Is this okay?"

"Yes," Jo panted, "I want it hard."

I pressed my thumbs roughly into the flesh on her back, squeezing and pinching, then sliding around to pull on her nipples through her silky bra. "I want this off," I said, unclasping the hook in front, pulling the pink lacy thing down to further bind her arms.

My hands slid over her smooth sides, around to her belly and up to cup her breasts, rolling her nipples tightly between my thumbs and forefingers. Pinching and twisting Jo's large hard nipples made her squirm quietly. I pinched harder, and she cried out. "What shall I do with you?" I murmured in her ear just before my teeth clamped down on her earlobe.

"Anything, please, something. Whatever you want. Please!"

I stepped back, took hold of the waistband of her shorts, and pulled them down, panties and all. She stepped out of them. Her asscheeks, high and round, were white compared to her tanned legs.

I followed the crack of her ass with my fingers then slipped them between her legs. Jo wanted this as much as I did. Her lips were wet and swollen, and her clit was a hard pebble under my finger.

"Yes," Jo whispered, as I used my boot to slide her legs apart. She leaned her cheek on the door and pushed her ass out toward me.

I squatted on my haunches, running my hands down one leg to the top of her heavy boot and back up the other side. Her ass stuck out by my face, and I breathed deeply the scent of her excitement. With one hand on her thigh and the other holding her hip, I took a mouthful of cheek and bit down gently. But not too gently. Jo pulled her ass back in far enough to press her stomach to the door.

"Now Jo," I said sternly as I stood up again, "are you going to pull away every time it hurts a little?" Her ass moved backward again and I smiled.

My hands, rough with a lifetime of calluses, traced her arms up to her shoulders. I turned her to face me. Her hard nipples puckered when I took each in my mouth, my tongue flicking over and over.

Jo's eyes closed as she leaned awkwardly on the door, her arms still bound behind her. She whispered something too quiet for me to hear. I stopped my gentle sucking and stood to look in her eyes, now open and pleading.

"What did you say?"

Her eyes closed again, and in a tiny voice she said, "I want you to hurt me. I know you know how."

Well, there was no way she could possibly know, but that didn't stop me from walking her to a clear space on my workbench and bending her over it. I removed the tank and bra and she moved her arms, muscles rippling, to rest on the bench over her head.

Gathering up the bridle lying there, I draped the strips of leather over her lower back, holding the bit in my hand. My other hand rested on her shoulder. "Are you ready for me?"

Jo laughed. "I've been ready and waiting for weeks."

I set the bit down on the small of her back, the reins hanging to one side and puddling on the floor at her feet.

"Don't let that fall off," I whispered in the direction of her ear.

Scanning the bench, my eyes rested on nothing but possibilities. Lengths of leather, pliers, a hoof pick left out for no apparent reason, a rubber currycomb with the handle missing, and yes, there was exactly what I needed. An old cotton cinch, starting to fray, colored by years of horse sweat and rain and who knows what else. It gave my own pussy a jolt.

The whole piece was maybe thirty-six inches long, with a round metal ring on either end. I doubled the cinch up, threading my fingers through both rings, feeling the heft of it. Not heavy at all, but certainly capable of providing a little stinging sensation when slapped against the tender, exposed white ass before me.

Jo stood very still, her ass waiting for whatever I wanted. I gently tapped the folded cinch on her cheeks, moving from side to side, gradually striking a little harder, ending with a solid *whack*! She jumped and cried out, almost losing the bit balanced on her back. Changing my angle, I swung back and forth, hitting close to her pussy without quite mingling her juices with those of a multitude of horses.

I stopped long enough to slip my fingers between her thighs and pushed my knuckles up into her, feeling the heat and wetness of her desire, just to tease her. I wasn't ready for this to end quite yet.

Pulling my hand back out, I lay the cinch across her back. With my dry hand I squeezed her right cheek, pressing my fingernails deep, creating half moons in her flesh, while the hand moist with her juices slapped down hard on her left.

"More!" Jo gasped.

I left the cinch where it was and started spanking her in earnest, blow after blow. Her ass got hotter and redder with each slap.

The bit was dangerously close to falling off, the reins slithering across her back as she shifted her weight from foot to foot. The air seemed filled with the scent of her excitement, and my own cunt had soaked the crotch of my dusty jeans.

I didn't want to wait any longer. I wanted to hear her come and scream for me.

I pushed a finger deep inside her cunt, feeling the heat and wetness. Pulling it out, I plunged it deep in her ass. She moaned loudly, and pushed hard against my hand as the bridle slid the rest of the way to the floor.

My other hand found her unfilled hole, opened wide, hot, wet and ready for me. Jo's cunt absorbed two of my fingers without even trying, and I quickly added a third. Pumping hard into her, I alternated hands, almost coming out of her ass while pushing hard in her other hole. In and out. Slurp and smack. Slurp and smack. Slurp and smack. Moving faster, harder, pressing in, pulling out. The knuckle of my little finger hit her clit with each thrust.

"Come on, Jo, come for me. I want to hear it," I panted as I pounded both her ass and her cunt.

"Oh, yes, yes, yes," she chanted breathlessly, matching her rhythm to my own.

My hands moved faster, pressing in, sliding out, shoving Jo's body hard up against the workbench with each thrust. Her cries got louder and more insistent with each pounding into her sex and her beautiful ass. I pushed harder, moving her whole body with the force of my fingers. The feel of her clit growing larger and harder against my hand inflamed my own excitement.

I wanted to hear her now. I pulled my finger out of her ass and slapped down hard on her cheeks, moving from one to the other, still pumping in her cunt.

Suddenly her pussy clenched down hard, trapping my fingers inside. Jo let out a loud scream, and hot, wet juices flowed over my hand as she came. Wave after wave of spasms ground my fingers together until I was sure they would break in two.

Jo finally sank down, her knees giving out, unable to hold her up because they trembled so. I caught her as she went, and lowered her to a pile of big clean blankets. Wrapped safely in my arms, she rested and tried to pull herself together.

"Don't you want to know how I knew you could do that?" Jo asked at last, looking up at me from the crook of my arm.

I looked down at her, confused at first, and then remembered. She had asked me to hurt her, had said, "I know you know how," and yet, I couldn't imagine there was any way possible she would know of my recent past.

Jo looked away, unsure of how I would take this news. "I needed a job, and one night when I was driving by late, I saw a light. I figured no one but the boss would be working that late, so I pulled in and walked through the barn toward the back where the light was on. I figured if the boss was working late, he must need help, and that was when I heard two women's voices."

She glanced up at me, flushed, and looked away again. "And then I realized what I was hearing wasn't just conversation, but something hotter. I couldn't help myself. I sat down and listened until I thought you were almost through. Then I left in a hurry, not wanting to get caught."

Jo took a deep breath and turned to look directly into my eyes this time. "When I managed to come back during daylight hours to look for work, I had trouble not blurting out anything about what I'd heard. I recognized your voice right away, and I was so afraid you would know something was up, but I needed to hear that voice every day. And here I am."

I smiled at her, not believing my luck. "And here I am, too. Do you have other secrets I should know about?"

Without waiting for Jo's answer, I kissed her, my tongue slipping into her mouth, my fingers sliding down her body, reaching for more. Reaching for her.

FRANKY AND JOHNNY

Jake Rich

Even though it's been nigh on five years now, Franky is still known to shake his head when thinkin' on Johnny and him. Shakes his gray-haired head much like that ol' mare Bessy Come Too, that no one, especially not Franky, can bear to put down, even though she's older than old these days. She just pads around the "out back," behind the new red barn Franky and Johnny pretty much built by their own muscle and grit, otherwise known as determination and plain stubbornness.

You see, it just don't seem natural to Franky, no matter how many years have taken place between him and Johnny. Franky—well, Franky is what you call old school, as in Old School Butch. And Old School Butch just don't take up with another Butch—no matter what, no matter what for. Just ain't done. Not proper, ya know? And never mind that, like Bessy, Franky is getting' on in years too. Franky always knew he'd be "tied down" for sure by now at his age, but damn it, with another butch?

What would that ol' gang of his think of him betrayin' that most sacred of sacred, that dance of Butch and Femme? With the answer to that question sittin' hard on his mind, Franky shakes his head, and grumbles somethin' about somethin'. Then leave it to Johnny to ask the Elder, "Whatchya say there, Franky?" Not in that sing-songy way femmes have about them, but a direct no-nonsense kinda way. You know, the way butches talk, especially to each other. And addin' to that is the way butches shake hands, too. A firm and direct grip, eyes searchin' each other out for signs of that unspoken way of livin' the life that only another butch fully understands.

Now, don't be mistakin' here. Franky and Johnny are butch for sure. But when it comes down to it, let there be no doubt, they have an abiding love for one another. And not just the love of brother to brother, butch to butch either, mind you. There have been plenty of times in the last five years to show for somethin' more than just that. Like the christenin' of that new red barn of theirs. Well hell, you'd a thunk that barn would of burned down for all the sparks a flyin' in there. And Franky startin' it too, of course.

Franky had just finished up in the kitchen, cleanin' up after supper. He had made his special homegrown green fried tomatoes and a fresh snap-bean salad. Plus a just-out-of-the-oven strawberry-and-rhubarb pie topped with scoops of French vanilla ice cream, served with "cowboy coffee," that rounded out the evening's vittles.

By the time Franky was puttin' away the last of the dinner dishes, Johnny was already out back puttin' the finishin' touches on that new barn. A couple more dabs of paint here or there, along with boltin' on the last few black iron-tack hangers, and that barn was done. Finally, done. It had only taken the two of them a little over two summers to build, but it seemed like forever and a day before they would see the end of all the back-breakin' work that was to be put into that shiny cherry-pie-red barn.

Johnny the Younger stood at the back of the barn, fussin' with the last of the tack hangers. He knew the tack needed to be accessible for more than just animal care. This barn was built for a couple of reasons, and only one being the care and boardin' of Bessy and the other ranch horses.

Johnny wanted their new playground to be perfect, and was lost in thought as he worked that last screw into the solid oak beam. He visibly shook as he roused himself out of his Daddy-Fuck-Me daydream, only to look up and see Daddy himself leanin' on Bessy Come Too's stable door.

"Daddy! We're done—the barn is finished!" Johnny said with a toothful grin. His Daddy held back, resistin' his urge to give the boy a huge bear hug.

"It's not quite finished yet, boy."

Johnny's face couldn't hide his disappointment in hearin' this news. "No, really Daddy, it's done. I just put the last hangers up, and that's all that was left to do."

"You arguin' with me, boy?" Franky asked with no other movement than his right eyebrow movin' up toward his forehead.

"No, Sir!"

"Good. Then git over here and finish the job boy."

"Yes, Sir." Johnny slow-poked his way over to Franky.

Johnny knew somethin' was up, once he saw that gleam in Franky's eyes, that gleam Johnny knew so well. The one that says, "You're my boy and I am gonna give it to you good."

"Come on, boy, git a move on!"

Right quick Franky pushes Johnny down to his knees, where Johnny comes eye to eye with Daddy's Dick stickin' right out of Daddy's just-plain-wore-out blue jeans. Without a word, Johnny stuffs that Daddy Dick into his mouth, and sucks on it. Up and down, up and down Johnny goes, lookin' kinda like a kid bobbin' for apples. The more he takes into his mouth, the more he gags, and the more his privates feel like they're stuck to that electric fence guardin' the farthest edges of the horse ranch. Waves and shocks and pulses of electricity surge through his cunt ass. Up down pulse, suck suck shock it goes, 'til Johnny thinks he just might explode.

That's when Franky grabs both of Johnny's ears, and starts face-fuckin' him but good. Hard rammin' that Daddy Dick of his over and over, and chokin' Johnny somethin' awful, 'til he's got tears streamin' down his cheeks.

"You like Daddy Dick, don't ya boy?" Franky's lettin' out a low grunt that keeps perfect time with his thrustin' rod. "Don't...you...boy...?"

Johnny's tryin' to keep pace with Daddy's Dick and tryin' to answer Daddy at the same time. 'Tain't an easy thing for Johnny to do in his situation, ya know. He tries so hard to say "Yes, Daddy, please, Daddy, yes, Daddy." And Daddy's still ridin' that boy's mouth like there's no tomorrow. Then Daddy grabs a fist full of Johnny's curly black hair and gives a full-on yank, and comes hard.

Franky shudders, then pulls that boy off his knees, still holdin' on to that fist full of black hair. "Whataya say, boy?"

"Sir, thank you for lettin' me suck your Daddy Dick, Sir."

"Good boy," Franky says. Then with a sudden click, Franky's got his grandpappy's ol' straightedge shavin' razor pressin' real hard up against Johnny's throat. "Don't move boy, this razor just might slip, and cut ya up but real good."

"Yes, Sir!" Johnny ain't movin' a muscle, and he's tryin' real hard to breathe slow and shallow like, but he just can't seem to do anythin' but breathe hard and deep.

"You a horny boy, Johnny?"

"Yes, Sir!"

"Then how come you just standin' there, boy?"

"Sir?"

"Why aren't your britches down, boy?"

"Sir—you told me not to move, Sir."

"That I did, boy. Well, whataya waitin' for? Pull your pants down, boy—now!"

"Yes, Sir!"

With that shavin' blade still stickin' in his throat, Johnny grabs for his belt, and slowly unbuckles it, tryin' not to make any sudden moves that would make that blade go any deeper than it already has.

"Hand me that belt, boy, I'm gonna be needin' it later on to warm up those pretty baby cheeks of yours."

Johnny obeys his Daddy, and then drops his jeans down to his ankles. Franky grabs him by the back of his neck, and pushes him to the hay-strewn ground. So there's Johnny on all fours now, with his naked asscheeks high flyin' in the air, waitin' for Daddy's Dick again. Waitin' for that Daddy Dick to ride his puckerhole like a rodeo rider on his bull, just a buckin' and buckin' away at it.

Then Franky starts his mutterin' again, mutterin' somethin' about somethin'. See, Franky just can't make sense of why he loves this boy so dang much, why he loves to plow into him so much, why he loves to make such a hurt on him so. Why is this boy's ass sendin' hot shivers down Franky's spine? It just don't make a hill of sense, but now's sure not the time to be figurin' this all out, either.

Franky shakes his head clear, and looks down at his sweet butch boy. And that hot shiver hits his spine again and doesn't stop travelin' until it's gone clear through Franky. It's gone clear through all his parts, settin' him to near shakin' like havin' a fever of sorts. And he was sure soakin' wet as if he was havin' a fever, too. Poor Franky sure has got it bad for this boy.

Franky reaches for his ol' favorite ridin' crop with one hand, gits a good handful of that butch boy ass, and spreads his cheeks wide open. And then Daddy Dick gets to workin', ridin' his young buckaroo. Ridin' and reamin' that buck's hole right there in the hay, in that cherry-pie-red barn those two built together.

Built together, shoulder to shoulder, strength to strength, butch to butch.

Franky couldn't have been any more proud of Johnny as he was right then. And right then and there, Franky made a promise to himself, and to Johnny too. No more mutterin' somethin' about somethin'. It came all clear like to Franky just then. Don't matter what the ol' gang would think about him and Johnny. What matters is Johnny's love for his Daddy, and his Daddy's love for his boy.

And that ain't nothin' to shake a stick at, neither. 'Cept maybe Daddy's Dick Stick.

Wagons Ho

Fargo Wellington

The covered wagon squeaked and groaned but she doubted even that would give them away. The only sign she knew would for sure, Misty's mouth, was clamped beneath her hand. Misty could scream like a banshee when she came. And she was coming now as Rio's other hand nodded back and forth, sunk to the wrist inside the fiery redhead.

Full lips, made thin under the pressure of Rio's tanned and calloused hand, spread apart for white, slightly crooked teeth to grab hold of their jailer. Rio could have howled in pain, but loved every second that the teeth tore at her flesh in spasms matching those that clenched around the sunken and sodden fist.

Their prairie schooner rocked and swayed into the dawn, creaking and groaning from the thrashing inside. Outside, the early morning sounds of the wagon train waking and readying for another day's trek, another ten slow, plodding miles, leaked into their canvassed hovel like a cold, dousing rain.

"Gotta go, Belleza." Rio spoke around her tongue and through the side of her lips while teasing a reddened nipple, suckling and swirling around its rigidity before having to lumber into the gray of dawn.

"Ugh. Do you have to?" Misty asked. Her freckled white skin instantly began to rise with goose bumps now that the warm cover of Rio's body was gone. She wanted to lie back and relax with the aftershocks of her last orgasm. Maybe, she could finally fall asleep. Neither one of them had been getting much sleep.

"We both have to. Come on. Get up. I will fetch the oxen." Rio said with an accent that confirmed her heritage. The olive-skinned Spanish-Mexican wiped her hands on the outer skirt of her disheveled dress, smoothed the layers down and picked her way precariously over their stored goods to climb out of the covered wagon.

Two yokes of oxen needed to be hitched. The big reds were Rio's pride and joy during the daytime hours. She had raised and trained one of the teams herself, since they were calves. The six-year-olds knew her well and did not need tethering in the night. They would not stray far from Rio. The other yoke of oxen, four-year-olds, were new, feisty, cantankerous, and took careful handling to avoid getting gored, even three months into their northwestward drive. Three months of steady, hard work should have settled the team into quiet routine, but then, their fattened loins did not attest to months of day-in and day-out labor.

"Get up. And get out here. We need to get going," Rio shouted to Misty, dodging a horn as the cranky nigh steer flicked at a fly pestering his massive shoulders. She moved the younger, stouter reds in as the wheel team, then fetched her six-year-olds from grazing.

"Misty, get up. I could use some help. The rest of the wagon train is hitching also. Let's not lose another one. We don't know when the next train will be by." Already she was sweating. She felt her cotton dress begin to stick to her skin, resenting the lag in movement, and the inhibiting weight and length of her clothing. Rio had shed the stickier undergarments at least a month ago. It had helped. Occasionally, she felt a stray draft reach up to caress her muscular thighs and had reveled in the light, cool sensation. But those moments were few and far between in this fickle heat.

Rio sighed in futility as she pinned the bows into place on the six-year-olds and hitched them into the lead team position. Four and a half months at the most during good weather was all it was supposed to take on the Oregon Trail. They had traveled for three months already, losing their first two wagon trains off in the distance.

It wasn't all that bad, even though a solitary wagon was vulnerable to attack by Indian war parties, and many immigrants met with hardship, disease, crippling injury, and death. The two hadn't incurred any major tragedies. And Misty always made the delays...worth it.

"Wagons ho!" The trail boss hollered, and that was that, ready or not. Great ships of the prairie lurched and pitched into place, trailing single file until the line stretched ahead so that the first could not be seen in the kicked-up dry dust.

Wagons ho—and Misty hadn't even picked up camp.

Rio ran about collecting and tossing coffee pot, pan, tin plates, and cups into the back of the wagon. She smothered the low fire with a kick of dirt and a couple of stomps. *Where was Misty? What was taking her so long?*

"Ready?" The fair-skinned redhead came from around the back of the wagon, handing Rio's bonnet to her. The Spanish-Mexican woman wound the length of blue-black hair behind her head and poked it with an extra bow pin before tying the faded, thin, frayed bonnet into place.

"Last again." Rio rolled her golden-brown eyes and took up the goad stick. "We shouldn't be eating their dust. We were out here first and have been out here longest. That should count for something." She stepped up to the left side of the lead yoke and commanded, "Come up here, boys," holding the stick aloft, the wind catching a billowy, full-length sleeve to spread it like a sail.

The teams strained into carved wooden yokes, bows grasping onto pins as horned heads the size of a human torso dropped down to start the load.

Successive thunks sounded from the hard-packed earth. The off side, four-year-old steer skittered sideways, loose. "Whoa!" Rio commanded, dropping her goad in front of the legs of her lead team. "Whoa!" And luckily they did. The wheel team's yoke could have split in two, forcing them to lighten their load by half and probably to butcher the younger pair. She didn't want to think about the harsh repercussions.

"Good boys." She rubbed sleek, red necks and scratched along thick dewlaps, showing her thanks for averting disaster.

Three oxen stood, waiting patiently, the fourth grazing in the near distance.

"Misty!"

Sunlight disappeared into darkness for Rio. A black silk scarf hugged her head with knotted force. As she reached for the blindfold, her wrists were captured in tight, individual nooses, her arms jerked behind her olive-skinned neck. A sharp poke to her lower back told Rio to move. She walked, receiving direction from the twisting of biting ropes.

"Misty?"

There was no answer. She was swiftly secured spread-eagle to a rear wagon wheel, wrists and ankles tied to long spokes, the hub jutting into her stomach, shoving her ass out behind her in an unladylike manner. *If the oxen moved...if her beloved boys grew tired of their waiting and wandered just slightly forward to graze...*

"Misty, this isn't funny! Turn me loose!"

"Shush, *muchacha*." The flat blade of a knife trailed across her cheek and down her exposed neck. "You want for me to fuck you, no?"

"Misty! I'm not in the mood." As she wiggled, the ropes only got tighter and the hub of the wooden wheel jammed even deeper into her stomach.

"You no move, and I no cut. *Sí*?"

The skirts of her blue flower-print dress, dingy-white petticoats and all, were thrown up over her hips. The naturally tanned skin of her buttocks glistened with the sweat of midsummer heat trapped under layers of cloth. A cool morning breeze pimpled her exposed cheeks in goose flesh. Rio stopped squirming.

"Good. Good. Shh...*muchacha*." And Rio's right buttcheek felt a couple of soft pats from an opened hand.

She heard footsteps retreating, petite steps with a pitter-patter actually walking away. Her mind reeled at the realization that she was trapped, unable to protect herself, unable to get free. *What if something happened right now? What if something happened to Misty?*

The uneven three-beat of a horse's lope grew louder, coming closer, until, "No, Mr. Hemphill, we don't require any help. We'll be along by midday after we fashion a new bow pin." The horse stomped with anxiety, Rio could hear, and blew dust from its nostrils. "No, we wouldn't dream of holding you up. Bye-bye now." And the horse was away. Rio heard the animal scramble on the packed trail before leaping headlong into its hurried lope.

As the echo of hooves dimmed in the distance, the sound of distinct footsteps padded closer. Like a mountain lion, the redhead paced back and forth with eyes narrowed on her prey. When she pounced, Misty slapped at Rio's ass and pinched the half-breed's exposed sex.

Before she heard the whisper, Rio felt the tickle of breath on her ear. "I want you to want me. I want you to show how much you want me, and to scream your need for me through clenched teeth until spittle runs down your chin, and down your thighs."

Eyes closed tightly behind the soft, black blind. The trussed woman hadn't meant to, but she squirmed against her bindings once again. They held. As she knew they would. As she knew

Misty would.

Whack. Not only did Rio jump, the oxen started. She felt the wagon shudder and the wheel creep forward inches before settling. *Whack.* And her body jumped in time with the wagon's ever-so-slight movement. *Whack.* And she squeezed her closed eyes tighter, biting her bottom lip.

Already her sex moistened to glisten in the sun. Rio felt wetness drool from her groin, and warmth sink into her bare skin, and the sharpness of the blows from Misty's flat, calloused hand awaken wanton desire.

Pressing into the ties surrounding her ankles, she rose on her toes in anticipation of Misty's next slap. It never came. She ground her toes, curling them inside sensible brown boots, her nails clawing the footpad to find escape...or purchase.

That next blow that never came? Rio wanted it. She *needed* it. And her head spun with the realization.

The cool blade shattered her inner thoughts. How it chilled her skin with its touch, from its pure evil, no doubt. Her nipples rose in response. Rio knew that blade, the pig-skinner that had been her bastard father's, all she had left to remember his thieving hide and blackened heart by. The knife was all that was bequest to his bastard child, Rio, after the hanging.

The handle was plump and flanged into a hook that curled below the pinky. It had a six-inch blade with a four-inch hilt for balance, not too big, not too conspicuous. The flange reached to prod between her greased nether lips, stumping over her hardened clit and riding the swollen ridge of her clit shaft.

Bound, all that Rio could do was tighten the ring of muscles around her sex opening as the hooked handle invaded her slicked folds. She had tried to do more, but the wagon wheel hub thrust itself into her belly, nestling rudely between hipbones, notched into her body as if it were made to prohibit her movement just as well as it allowed the movement of the heavy Conestoga.

Clipped black curls matted in cream clung to her skin in the crevice between pussy and thigh. Her body had betrayed her. It wanted the butt of that knife. It wanted Misty. It needed the redhead. But Rio wasn't going to scream any of it out. Misty was the reason they never got anywhere. Misty could never be serious, could never see a realistic future, never see past the next fuck. And she had constantly wanted to fuck. Rio had wanted more.

She bit until her lower lip bloodied. Scream her need for Misty? No, never. Hands balled into determined fists where white knuckles showed the torment. Then her boys moved forward. Misty had spoken to them. Misty, who was never sure about the big boys, who could never trust nor handle the oxen. But she spoke now and they listened, probably anxious to be on the move, however slightly. One step, then two, the six-year-olds handled the full load, as the lonely wheel ox could not help.

Rio's world turned upside-down. Before she had time to adjust, Misty buried her face in the half-breed's crack, rimming the darker, puckered skin around her anus. A finger slid into her sex, but the knife was not forgotten. The familiar weapon was steadied in the hand that pried open Rio's buttocks, cold blade pressing as if to brand itself on her cheek.

"Ugh. Argghhh." Rio's breathing quickened as she clenched her teeth.

One finger, just one, pried through the strong ring and dove into warm wetness, teasing Rio to pull at the digit like an orphan calf sucking furiously at a makeshift nipple for its life-giving milk. Misty's finger pumped in and out of Rio's strong, slippery hole, muscles grabbing at it to tug the petite pecker back in.

Smack. A hand sounded against her ass flesh. *Smack.* The finger had changed back into the calloused open palm. *Smack.* Rio couldn't take much more. *Smack.* Misty's tongue sunk into Rio's cunt once...twice...three times...

Tiny bites marked a red, blotchy trail away from the center of Rio's lubed snatch, but didn't prepare her for what was next. The blade. The hilt. She didn't know which or what. It didn't really matter. One or the other or some sinister trick of Misty's stabbed and pounded Rio from the inside with striking ecstasy. Her eyes streamed readily and her mouth exuded spittle, but nearly upside-down, the stringy saliva ran the course of a tanned, facial cheek.

"Jeez! Jeez! Holy Mother of Jeez—" Rio panted, writhing, praying that the bonds would hold her fast as she bucked backward against them, squeezing and pulling from the inside out. "Misty! Misty! Stop! Stop! You will kill me!"

"That's not what I wanted to hear," Misty's calm voice

answered. She pumped the four-inch handle of the knife in and out of Rio furiously, torturing the bound woman's G-spot with the flange. And a welcomed finger rubbed circles over Rio's anus until the puckered orifice too was invaded, bringing Misty her sought after prize.

"I love you. I love you! I want you. I need you! *Sí?* Okay! I need you! I really, really need you!"

Spasm after spasm wracked the half-breed as she hung from her bindings. Her body jerked and convulsed to the rhythm of her anguished cries of love and lust. She didn't know at what point Misty had stopped tormenting her. She hadn't been capable of recognizing that she was once again head-up. She had been lost in euphoric waves of release, giving over to whatever ties held her.

They would join up with the next train. Maybe.

Rio collapsed against the ropes that held her fast, spread-eagle on the tall spoke wheel. *Wagons ho,* she thought.

INDEPENDENCE

Caralee Levy

I'd been born to a very good Southern family, but I'd become a very bad girl.

The War of Northern Aggression changed everything for everyone it touched. But when I was eighteen, and Delilah was nineteen, I was aware only of how it affected us.

War brought freedom.

I'd left behind my corset and petticoats. I left behind the engagement my pa had arranged with the neighboring plantation owner's son, who wasn't going to inherit that plantation now. I could spit and drink and stay up all night, playing poker and swapping stories. I could put in a hard day's work and spend my hard-earned pay.

More nights than not, I'd find another woman who liked the same things I did. We'd lie on top of my bedroll or hers, where we'd taste each other's sweat and tease each other's heat. Fingernails would dig into someone's back and teeth sink into someone's shoulder, and we'd fuck until we bucked.

That's what freedom meant to me. Freedom meant all that—and a whole world more—to Delilah.

We adventured our way west until we found ourselves in Austin with guns (but no ammo) and horses (with no shoes). A Southern belle I might have been, but I'd also had five brothers, and I could ride and shoot with any of them. Cecie, who'd changed her name to Delilah by this time (Cecie being the name my mother, her mistress, had given her, but Delilah being a powerful woman from the Good Book), would never sit a horse exactly easy, but she and a gun were friends the moment she laid hands on it. So we figured we'd find an opportunity to ply our skills, or an opportunity would find us.

We led our footsore horses into town, past a big white building on a hill that looked like a castle, but was called the "General Land Office," and down the dusty, sun-broiled main street. Posters were up at every hitching post, seemed like.

Cowboys wanted, to take longhorns north. Delilah could read them as well as I could, being as my mother had turned a blind eye when she'd joined me at my lessons. We stopped in front of one poster so our horses could take a good pull at a trough, and we gave it a good long look.

Delilah said, "We've been riding west. Reckon we could ride north just as well, 'specially if we'd really get a hundred dollars."

"But it says 'cow*boy*,'" I pointed out. "They may not cotton to women who want to work on the backs of horses and not on their own backs."

She sighed. "It'd hardly be the first time."

We looked at each other. There was one kind of work we could always get in any burg big enough to have its own doctor: ministering to "hysterical" women. Back then, see, a woman with cramps or other problems with the moon was considered to need a "release." The cure for hysteria was a good rub-a-dub-dub on the old sweet spot. Doctors and midwives found this a tedious chore and tried to pass it off to an assistant whenever possible. They liked it when a white woman, who could work on their white patients, and a black woman, who could work on black patients, walked in the door at the same time. Delilah and I were experts. The patients were usually so grateful; it was just embarrassing taking their money.

Still, we really needed money.

"Well, lookie at you." The voice behind us was throaty and lilting and could only belong to the sexiest woman alive.

We turned and looked. Oh my, and I looked some more. Those chaps had to be custom-made, to fit those hips. And above those luscious round mounds was a small, tight waist. And above that, her chest balanced her hips just right. She probably didn't stand more than five feet, of which every inch was perfect and she didn't need any more. She wore a Colt revolver high on each hip, but with the haughtiness of those cheekbones and the flash in those eyes, I had a feeling she didn't need to reach for the guns too often.

"You want to drive cattle?" she asked.

"Do we get a hundred dollars?" Delilah asked right back. I just barely managed to close my mouth before I drooled.

"One twenty-five, but once grub and gear get subtracted, you'll clear about a hundred."

She nodded toward our horses. "Can you ride?"

"Yes," I managed.

"Can you shoot?"

"Yes," said Delilah.

"You want to take twenty-five hundred head of Texas beef up the Shawnee Trail to Independence, Missouri? It's dangerous."

I wasn't exactly sure where Independence, Missouri, was, but if this lady was headed there, I wanted to go along.

"Yes!" Delilah and I spoke together. I glanced over and saw that she was as smitten as I was. Hypocrite that I am, I felt a pang of jealousy, but I pushed it down. I'd never put a move on Delilah, nor she on me. We'd never talked about it. It's just that, when one person's been a slave and the other person's been a slave owner, then between them is a barrier pricklier than a barbed-wire fence. It's better not to tangle with it.

"Well c'mon then. My name's Nerieda."

We introduced ourselves, and Nerieda pulled her long, black braid over her right shoulder and led us off the main street. I took my eyes from her ass just long enough to get a sense of the neighborhood. Looked like it was all saloons, cheap rooming houses, and whorehouses, not that you could really tell them apart. As with every other place in the South, establishments were clearly labeled "White" or "Negro," but here, white and black brothels were often right next to each other. Also, some had signs for "Mexicans," and some actually seemed to brag, "Got Girls of All Colors!"

Nerieda pointed to a hitching post in front of one of these places. As we saw to our horses, she went over each one with practiced hands and eyes, taking special care with their legs and feet.

"They're sound," she said, sounding surprised. "You haven't been riding them?"

"No shoes means we don't ride," I snapped before I could soften my tone. Not the way to speak to your new boss. Not the way to speak to a woman you want to fuck. But one of the few values I'd learned from my father was a heart-deep pride in caring for horses. For generations, our family had valued our horses more than our own lives.

A slow grin spread across her face. Her teeth were white and even. I noticed a beauty mark by the right corner of her mouth and wanted to lick it. "You care about horses. That's good. My family owned twenty thousand acres in Mexico, once. I care about horses, too." Her dark eyes held mine for a moment, and my knees went weak.

"We'll visit the blacksmith first thing in the morning. Now, come inside and meet the gals you'll be sharing beans and trail dust with."

We followed her inside. A couple of older white women in low-cut dresses of faded and uncertain colors lounged, bored, against the bar. We ignored them and went through a door hung with a buffalo hide to a back room.

"Gals, let me introduce two new cowboys, Delilah and Moira."

"Hello."

"Howdy."

"And g'day to ya."

"Hiya."

"*Hola.*"

"It's a pleasure, I'm sure."

Ten women in flannel shirts, denim pants, and boots rose from where they'd been playing cards, reading the Bible, or taking a snooze, and greeted us ten different ways. They were ten very different women. Small Wolf, who I found out later was Comanche, was even shorter than Nerieda. Another, a nearly six-foot, bouncy pillow of flame-haired Scottish womanhood, was named Deirdre.

I felt a lot of eyes assessing me, and I was returning the favor, all the while wanting a bath real bad. I hadn't seen a mirror for a long time, but one look at Delilah told me that a long, hot soak would help both of us. It hadn't seemed to matter so much, outdoors with the horses, but now I felt itchy.

As if reading my mind, or maybe she'd just caught a whiff of me and drawn the logical conclusion, Deirdre said, "Welcome aboard, friends. We'll be drawing you a bath, won't we, gals?"

They did. We went into the kitchen, where they shared their jerky and biscuits with us and heated a big cauldron of water. When steam started curling off of it, they poured it into a cast iron tub. A cake of soap and two towels appeared, and then they excitedly urged Delilah and me to get in. Deft fingers removed my clothes, and out of the corner of my eye, I saw Delilah getting the same treatment. Then we stepped over the edge of the tub and sat down, one of us at either end, with our legs drawn up so our feet weren't touching. Despite having an audience, I couldn't help relaxing in the water's hot embrace.

I saw Nerieda holding straws, and all the women drew one. Deirdre and Elizabeth, a thin woman from West Virginia, got short straws, which I guessed was a good thing in this case, because they smiled and clapped their hands.

Elizabeth knelt down behind Delilah, dipped the rough towel in the hot water, soaped it up, and handed the soap to me, I thought. But as I reached for it, Deirdre's plump hand, pink from the steam, reached over my shoulder and took it instead. Elizabeth sponged Delilah's shoulders and back with the soapy cloth then dunked it in the water and began to scrub her arms.

Deirdre was mirroring her. I let each arm relax in her strong grip and savored the sensation of the sweat and grime sluicing away under her touch. The other women stood in a circle and watched intently. Nerieda's lips parted in a knowing smile.

I saw Elizabeth's hands move to Delilah's legs, scrubbing up the thighs and down the calves, the soap making pearly bubbles in the curly hair there.

Deirdre did the same to me. My hips relaxed, and my knees fell apart. Then our "washerwomen" picked up our feet and scrubbed hard at the dirt ground into the calluses. With only one foot down to brace ourselves, both Delilah and I slipped forward in the tub. My toes wedged under her right buttock, round and hard from months of riding and walking and hard labor.

Her eyes were closed, and I felt uncomfortable looking at her, so I gazed over her shoulder instead. My eyes met Nerieda's, and neither of us looked away. She wet her lips. Then Deirdre began to soap my breasts. The heat I was feeling became a need, and I let my head fall back against her own soft pillows and my eyes closed. Her full lips came down on mine, her gentle tongue parting them. As if from far away, I heard a murmur among the watchers. Most of all, I was conscious of Delilah's rough, callused heel pushing into my sex.

Nearly out of control, I thrust against her foot and felt a shiver start. Delilah's buttocks moved. My feet, lodged under them, slipped. I scrabbled for better purchase. One foot found again that wonderful home beneath her hard, round muscle. The other cast about, and for a tantalizing moment, I felt her dark, curly triangle tangled in my toes. I squeezed my foot down between her hard thighs and probed her soft spot.

She shouted. Her heel pushed hard against my sex, one, two, three times, pushing me right to the edge. Deirdre bent low, nibbling my nipple. Her beautiful, full breasts pressed naked against my face. When had she unbuttoned her shirt?

Delilah's heel withdrew from my aching sex. I tried to follow, but Deirdre held me fast. There were splashing sounds. Delilah was standing up, done. I wasn't done, but Deirdre's fingers found my sex and danced there. I stretched the length of the tub and surrendered to her beauty in a long, shuddering climax.

Several pairs of arms half-lifted me from the tub and wrapped me in a soft, clean-smelling blanket. They led me to a bunk against the wall, where Delilah was already sitting.

Maggie, one of the other black cowboys, was picking out her short hair and applying some kind of oil to it. "You gotta use oil, or it just keeps breaking off and matting," she was saying. I was glad Delilah was finally getting some advice about her hair from someone who seemed to know something about it. I'd never been able to help her with it, but Maggie had gorgeous, long, shiny cornrows that set off her round cheeks. I pictured Delilah in cornrows, imagined them cascading over my face and chest, as her mouth moved down my stomach toward my sex.

"Welcome," said Nerieda, interrupting my fantasy. "You fit right in. We'll get you outfitted and your horses taken care of at sunup, then hit the trail directly. Get plenty of sleep." She left then, presumably to take care of some last-minute details.

That night was hot. The blanket was scratchy against my naked body. We'd washed our clothes in our bathwater, and they were still drying. Several of the women snored. And my body hadn't gotten enough.

I could hear Delilah's even, deep breathing within easy arm's reach and could picture her beautiful breasts rising up and down with each breath. I remembered the way her triangle had felt against my toes and the quick grind of her callused heel against my sex before it moved away. I nearly reached for her but touched myself instead.

It was wet fire down there. I made it burn brighter, and brighter, until I bit my lip to keep from moaning. I shuddered over and over, until finally my fingers traced a sticky, lazy path back up my stomach, my hands relaxed, and a deep sleep held me close and rocked me.

After a couple of weeks on the trail, our bath seemed like a pleasant dream of Paradise. Working the rear of the herd was the worst, because the cattle kicked up great clouds of dust and insects. We rotated that duty.

Flocks of birds followed the herd to eat the bugs, and I got pretty good at imitating their calls, there being not much else to do. Saddle-soreness—for none of us was used to riding twelve hours a day—abated after the first week or so. In fact, when we got off our horses, we started to walk with a wide, rolling gait, as if our legs thought there still was a horse between them.

The streams were running full, so water for the livestock wasn't a problem. Even so, a couple of cows collapsed, no knowing why, giving us two orphan calves. Delilah and I pretty much adopted the dogies, carrying them across our saddles to save them some steps and giving them our own water midday so they could drink more often.

We were making good time, Nerieda told us, about twelve miles a day. Purple black thunderheads hurling jagged spears of lightning appeared and disappeared on the western and northern horizons, feeding the streams we drank from but not bothering us.

We reprovisioned in Dallas, Nerieda taking Deirdre, who was our cook, and two white cowboys with her. Elizabeth, our wrangler, and the rest of us stayed behind to keep a sharp eye out. Rustlers liked to stampede cattle in these parts. One long, hard drive north would get them to Indian Territory and a wide choice of trails. If word had gotten round about a bunch of women taking cattle north, some rustlers might think we were easy pickings.

Delilah and I cleaned our revolvers, determined that there was nothing easy about us. Turned out, we didn't need them. We were a little disappointed then, although later on we were to get our fill of gunplay.

Nerieda brought a couple of bottles of whiskey back from town. Deirdre added molasses to our bacon and beans for a good supper that night. Not having ridden that day, we weren't all tuckered out. Instead of curling up in our bedrolls right away, we put extra wood on the campfire and stayed up a bit. We sipped whiskey and sang songs; Irish and Scottish songs that I knew but also Indian chants, shape-note gospels, slave spirituals, and Spanish *corridos*.

Delilah was on the other side of the circle from me, with Maggie and the other black woman, Mary. When they taught us "Lay Down My Burdens," their voices blended so beautifully, I had to pretend to retie my bandana to wipe away a tear.

As Deirdre shared out the last drops of whiskey, Nerieda stood up next to me. She'd been drinking all evening but was as steady as a rock.

"We've had it easy so far, but it gets more difficult soon. Ahead of us is Indian Territory, and then we'll have to get these longhorns into Missouri. That'll be hard, because longhorns carry Texas fever. They don't get sick from it, but Missouri cattle do, and Missouri ranchers don't take kindly to it. It's a wild place anyway, with what they call 'reconstruction' going on." She threw down her tin cup and unbuttoned her blouse. "So to give us strength, I say we all get to know each other just a little better." With that, she unbuckled her belt. We all cheered.

I have to say, just the sight of those proud breasts over that tiny waist would cheer up any cowboy. When she wriggled her hips free of their well-worn denim, we were all feeling mighty happy to be on the trail at that moment.

"C'mon, gals," she said. "We're already in a circle. Let's get naked." Clothes began to come off quicker than a cow could stampede.

"Pay some loving attention to the gal on your right, and the gal on your left will take care of you," Nerieda instructed us.

The woman on my right was Deirdre. I slid my hands up the wispy red hair on her wide calves, laid down between her long, full thighs, buried my face in one beautiful, moonlike buttock, and slipped a finger inside her sweetness.

Breasts, Nerieda's breasts, rubbed against the back of my own thighs, and teeth sank into my right buttcheek. I clenched tight against the pain, but without preamble, she shoved her small fist up my best place. It hurt like hell but at the same time released my juices like a dam breaking. As she worked me, I felt myself melt into a river. I would be saddle sore in a whole new way tomorrow, but I didn't care.

It was hard to concentrate on Deirdre, but my hands, blessedly, seemed to know what to do. I added another finger and another and worked my thumb against her sweet spot. With my other hand, I pressed down on her buttocks and she moaned and writhed between my hands. Around the circle, moans and whimpers in different languages made counterpoint to the surrounding crickets. The campfire flickered against sweat-slick skin of a dozen hues. The stars watched.

Then the first orgasm started. Maybe it was mine. That cry of surrender opened a torrent in me, and I came and came against Nerieda's fist, begging her to bang me harder and loving the way the tough prairie grass scraped against my skin.

Deirdre throbbed heartily then eased herself away from me, and I let her go. If I came again, I was going to die. If I didn't, I would die. Nerieda withdrew. I cried out, but she ended my ecstatic agony with a sharp crack of her riding crop against my buttocks.

I never would have thought I could be so grateful for a large welt on my seat, especially when I'd be on a horse all the next day, but without it, I don't know how I ever would have gotten any sleep.

Sweaty bodies rolled off each other. A few partners exchanged kisses. Across the campfire circle, Delilah was kissed first by the woman on her left, then by the one on her right. I had a terrible feeling then that I was losing her, and I hoped that Independence was still a long ways off.

Nerieda didn't kiss me but whispered in my ear, "As trail boss, I can't form special attachments, but once we get where we're going..." She gave my hand a hard, clawlike squeeze.

A moment ago, sex with Nerieda seemed worth dying for, but as I saw Delilah embracing Maggie and Mary, I felt something die inside me. No amount of sex would ever make up for that.

In Indian Territory, we had no more than the usual troubles. Thunderstorms stampeded the herd a couple of times, but they stayed pretty much together and didn't go too far. Water stayed plentiful. Even our dogies put on some weight.

Delilah and I still laid down our bedrolls side by side, and we still rode together, but when we weren't riding or sleeping she spent time with Maggie and Mary, and I mostly ended up with Deirdre. The other cowboys were jealous of me, because Deirdre was the cook and she'd give me candy now and then or fritters with wild berries in them. Sometimes we'd have sex behind the chuck wagon, and it was delicious in a mellow way, like a well-buttered ear of sweet corn. Deirdre was a very beautiful, very nice person. She just didn't have the wild side that I really responded to in a woman.

I overheard Maggie and Mary talking a few times about collecting their hundred dollars in Missouri and using it to set up a storefront farther north, in Chicago maybe. They wanted to do hair and such. With all the time Delilah was spending with them, I thought maybe she'd go north, too, but she didn't say anything about it and I was too chicken to just up and ask her.

We'd followed a chain of lakes in northeastern Indian Territory. Now we were at the Missouri border. We stayed put all day and prepared to move that night. We could have just stayed on the Kansas side of the border, but there was less water, and the Jayhawkers and Bushwhackers were rumored to be more active there.

As the sun went down, Delilah and I rode with Nerieda at the head of the herd. The cattle didn't want to move, so we whooped and hollered at the leads, flapping our hats and charging with our horses, until we annoyed them into a trot.

Clouds moved in from the west. A slight drizzle fell, and the only light in that vast sea of grass was the occasional beam from one of our dark lanterns, searching ahead. Nerieda had a compass that she'd consult, then tell us to change course.

Sometime after midnight, Delilah said, "Psst! Moira, ten o'clock! Is that a farmhouse?"

I lifted the brim of my hat, peered through what had become a windblown curtain of rain, and saw a light. I raised my own lantern and shone the beam behind me so the others could see the signal to stop.

Delilah and I rode ahead of the lead cattle and stopped. They were glad enough to come to a standstill. As soon as you stop a herd, they start to spread out. We had to make a decision fast and get them moving again.

"What's happening?" asked Nerieda, a sound of hoofs and a

husky voice in the dark.

"We see a light, ahead to the left." I kept my eye on it. "I think it's moving."

"It's definitely brighter than it was a minute ago," Delilah confirmed.

Not a farmhouse, then, but other folks out on the prairie at night. The odds that they'd be friendly were lower than my chances of marrying that neighboring plantation owner's son back home. What was his name?

"Get them moving. Turn them to the right. Take them straight away from those lights. We can't outrun them, but the visibility's bad enough, we may be able to hide right out in the open. After you get them moving, line up with the rest of us behind them. And draw your guns."

The cattle made more noise than we would have liked, and it seemed to take forever, though I'm sure it was only a moment. We got them walking south and east, away from the oncoming lights. Eight of them. From the height and movement, their bearers were probably on horseback. Not some lone, loco hunter then, looking for whatever might be caught on such a night.

Delilah and I rode to the end of the line of cowboys and waited for the shooting to start.

We didn't have to wait long. The approaching riders could probably hear the herd and didn't know we were waiting for them. They moved their horses into a canter and started shooting, most likely up into the air, trying to stampede the cattle back toward Kansas.

The first part of their plan worked great. Cattle bellowed and started to run, all except for our two dogies. They stuck right by Delilah and me.

The second part, dealing with us, didn't go so well for them. Thing is, when you're a woman who ain't womanly, you're used to people picking fights with you, and you get tougher than a hickory stick. Even Deirdre, who liked to pass out candies from her secret stash and fuss over the two dogies like they were pet kittens, had a rifle on her shoulder and was taking aim as steadily as any veteran.

The oncoming riders charged their horses right into our line. I don't think they even knew we were there until we started shooting. Several slumped from their saddles, their horses running by us, still chasing the fleeing cattle. A few managed to turn their horses and get away. One tried to turn his horse, but the animal reared and dumped him on the ground instead. Delilah shot the man in the stomach as he tried to scramble to his feet. Served him right for trying to gallop a horse in the dark over wet ground.

"Hold your fire!" Nerieda shouted. We did and waited. The enemy seemed to have turned tail. Little Wolf let out a war cry, the kind that would continue to terrify Americans in north Texas for several more years.

With the rustlers, farmers, or maybe just general hell-raisers gone back into the prairie dark, I became aware of how electric I felt. I had energy coming out all over me, like a lightning bolt. I felt like I could do anything. I wanted to knee my horse into a gallop, wet ground and darkness be damned, and just chase those fellows into the next county and beyond.

Delilah sidled her horse over to mine and slapped me on the back. "Well, would you look at that!" Delilah shouted. "We won! We won!" I'd never seen her so excited. Hell, *I'd* never felt so excited.

And I guess it took the thrill of gunplay to clear my mind so I could see the obvious. This was the high point of Delilah's life so far, and she was sharing it with me. Not with Maggie or Mary, but with me. All giddy from the fight, I asked the question I had wanted to ask: "When we get our hundred dollars, do you want to head up north? Throw in with Maggie and Mary maybe?"

"Maggie and Mary? What would I want with a hair salon in Chicago? They're not having adventures like this in Chi-town. I figured maybe you and I would head out to California, or down to Mexico. Something fun like that."

"Oh," was all I managed. I reached out, found the edge of her sodden poncho in the dark, and pulled her to me. I leaned over and kissed her full on the lips. Her own lips froze beneath mine, but only for a second. Then they parted, and she kissed me back as passionately as I ever could have wanted.

I felt a huge grin spread across my face. Tonight, my fingers were going to explore the area only my toes had gone before, and we were going to look straight into each other's eyes as we sought the ultimate place, a place we could go together: Independence.

SQUAW, 1863

Anonymous

He pulled me up to my knees by wadding the hair at the nape of my neck into his fist. I tried to collapse back to the gritty, rock floor but his fingers opened and slid the length of my black tresses, clenched, then wrapped my thick hair around his hand like a rope. The snug blindfold slid cockeyed, allowing a flickering glow to taunt my sight through a wedge-shaped slit along the bottom of my right eye.

Hanging by the fiery pull to my scalp, I struggled less, until finally giving in to remaining upright on my skinned knees. I heard the ching-ching-ching of his spurs moving around to the front of me as he loosed my hair.

The blindfold was ripped away. The gag in my mouth remained, as did the twisted bonds about my wrists behind my back.

I bobbed my head up and down, side to side, squinting as my assaulted eyes became accustomed to the quivering lamplight that danced upon red rock walls.

He stood in front of me, square and confident and powerful for his smaller frame. The scent of horse-sweat and leather and cooked game wafted from his earth-encrusted clothes to invade even my nostrils. I would have spit at him, if I could have. Or her? *He was a she!*

She tore into a strip of trail jerky; rolling the dismembered chunk over her pink, wet tongue before closing her mouth to devour the piece. She lapped at the thick stick and sucked its length in and out of her mouth with the noise of ten babes at the breast.

I stared up at her, looking boldly into steely eyes. This amused the hardened woman. She grinned, showing feral teeth slathered with saliva, prepared to shred their next prey.

The dry gag was snagged from my mouth and gruffly shoved down around my thin neck. Coarse knuckles scraped across my cheek until calloused fingers dove through the hair at my scalp and gripped. The stumpy strip-jerky traced the outline of my closed lips until it pressured the sensitive skin against hard teeth.

The thick, dried stick of meat was pushed forward and twirled between my swollen, cracked lips, in and out, in and out, softly, slowly at first as she watched with glazed gray blue eyes.

Lowering the prong of meat to fit against her flat crotch, she stepped to my face, thrusting the stick at my parched mouth while shoving my head forward to meet it. Watching, staring at my puffy lips, she humped and pumped with leisurely deliberation.

I bit the protrusion, tearing off a chunk. Then spit it at her. "*Wasichu!*" White! It was most blasphemous. "*Wasichu!*" A curse.

The strike of her fearsome backhand twisted my head to the side, ringing in my skull. I smiled a toothy grin tainted crimson by blood. I had been given worse, captured in a battle of tribes at twelve winters old by the Sioux, and taken at fourteen as third wife by an aging, wrinkled brave who had had trouble breeding me.

I smiled at the *wasichu* woman in man's clothes.

The look of insolence got me hauled by the knotted gag, sitting patiently at my neck, into the air until I gained my feet. My mind swam in euphoria for a brief, breathless moment.

The meat stick was thrown down, exchanged for a Bowie knife, and I was thrust harshly against a red rock wall. Air rushed from my bronzed body. The *wasichu* cut the sinew strings that had held a hide dress at my shoulders, only to find that the supple deerskin could fall no lower than my tied wrists, exposing my ripe body only to the waist.

Breasts sprung forth for attention like wiggly wolf pups; soft, plump and needy. Puckered nipples grew in hardness. A forearm across my throat barred my movement. Nips and tugs and pinches from lips and teeth peppered my brown nipples to painful engorgement. The pointed tip of her honed blade felt its way to my raw wrists and sliced the layers of scratchy rope in one motion.

I snatched up the pistol that hung low from her thin, rangy waistline, resting against a hardened thigh. With the speed of an osprey snatching trout from the rivers, the *wasichu*'s talons grasped my fingers enclosing the weapon's butt. She leaned into me, pressing her length against my own, making her lean frame seem grossly heavy. "I am not the enemy," she whispered in perfect Sioux.

A twisting wrenched the gun from my hand. I steeled myself for violent reprisal. But her streak of lips pressed themselves against mine, not hard, and not soft.

Wanting. There was a wanting, a desire, almost a need in her kiss that lingered to tease my mouth, swelling it with saliva that drowned its dryness. She brought the gun to point between our faces. A calloused thumb hauled the hammer back, and I watched with widened eyes as her pointer finger caressed the trigger's housing. Her leaden weight lifted from my body, leaving a deadly space between us.

With a flick of her thumb the barrel popped open, and she tipped the gun up to drop every last bullet from its chamber in a spinning, clicking movement, then snapped the round drum closed.

The business end of that revolver traced a line down the length of my torso and through my cleavage without a scratch, the gun's sight having been lovingly filed away to smoothness. It went no further than the trapped, bunched hide at my full hips. I couldn't help but wish it had. The act was familiar, a game that had been in my dreams for many long years, a game once played for real, and just for play. Then I knew.

This time, when I reached for the cumbersome pistol, the woman pressed it into my palm. Her empty hands caressed the sides of my ribcage, venturing softly, lightly to fondle my hanging breasts. She kissed me again.

A familiar hunger for the *wasichu* flared in my belly. It was I who forced our lips to part so that our tongues could battle for what they truly wanted, and our mouths could feed greedily on what they needed.

The summer of my thirteenth winter, I had shared much more than a kiss and a promise behind undulating herds of grazing, breeding horses. This *wasichu* would be mine, no longer the white captive slave belonging to my brother in my blood tribe. I had sworn to that much with my words and my body. Until I had been taken as a captive by the Sioux.

I remembered the battle. Women ran for the hills in the gray dawn, clutching cradleboards and dragging toddlers as the small children screamed and cried. Braves, abruptly awakened, stood their ground outside of teepees, down to the youngest boys with toy bows. In the bloody raid young girls were scooped across galloping war-ponies. The *wasichu* stood among the braves, my last sight of her.

That had been ten or more winters past. And slaves had not been allowed to take names, so I had not even that to remember her by. But with my eyes closed at night, every night, I knew her feel and her touch. I knew her bony pointer finger tracing a straight line from my neck to my navel. I knew her scrawny hands entangled in my grass-littered hair as she roughly kissed me and made me hers. And I knew her lips. These lips.

I wrapped my fingers around her white throat and shoved her face away from me. Her eyes had that soppy, milk-fed look to them, full of softness and lust. I tugged at her jaw to force her mouth to my pert nipple. "*Wasichu*," I whispered with longing.

She trailed to my belly, leaving reddened pockmarks, nipping harshly, biting my full flesh. Her tongue darted out to stab at my navel and turn little circles inside its well.

I mashed my pelvis to her chin, asking, begging, for what I knew she would do next. Her calloused hands plowed the folds of supple hide around my hips, tugging, then retreating to hoist the leather-length from my adorned ankles.

Black curls sprang into sight. The *wasichu* woman fell to her knees, grasping for the curly short hairs, parting them. Dark pink skin glistened in creamy folds.

She ran the calloused pad of her thumb along their length, staring with the longing and recognition of an old lover. I jumped, slamming her back and shoulders with the pistol fisted in my grip.

Her tongue stung my swelling flesh, lapping, tasting, eating. Her teeth bit me, ecstasy. And my cunt crawled with hunger.

I laced my fingers into her wool shirt's collar to steady myself. I brought the barrel of the revolver to my moistened lips, licking its length and shoving the steel rod in and out of my drooling mouth. I wanted more, needed more. I squeezed my thighs to her cheeks and rubbed and humped my pelvis against her captured face and the handholds on my short hairs.

I rubbed the steel pistol over my tits and across the exposed cheeks of my ass. It was perfect. The gun was long and thin and smooth. The metal was chilled to the initial touch and slippery with saliva. From behind, I worked the barrel into my dripping hole, squatting onto the metal shaft and opening my thighs.

She pulled away to watch. The rod slicked in and out of my twat. The blue gray steel became coated with translucent white cream that ran deliciously onto my hand gripped around the weapon's butt.

The scratchy, rough tips of my *wasichu*'s fingers probed and poked the tender nodule within the red pleats of my nether lips. Her ministrations sent me low against the red rock wall and deeper onto her pistol as I panted and shuddered through gritted, clenched teeth to a shattering orgasm.

The gun clattered to the dirt-covered rock floor, my body attempting to follow. Arms caught me, held me. Familiar lips flickered over my neck and cheek. And in my ear, her whisper, "My squaw."

MAIL ORDER BRIDE, CHAPTER 11

Rakelle Valencia

"Someone's been raiding my traps."

Austin slapped the empty iron-jaw hanging from her packhorse. A worthless walk for empty traps had made for a long, cold day. The bundled woman trudged to the hogan, lured by the smell of smoky heat escaping as Sahara met her in the frigid evening air. The sigh of frustration formed crystals in the blistering chill.

"Coyote? Mountain Lion?" Sahara inquired. The pale, freckle-faced girl pulled on her stiff new coat to follow as Blaire Austin towed the horse to the rock overhang.

"The most dangerous of predators," the rugged woman said through blue-tinged lips while yanking at her collar. She tucked her nose into the woolen thickness allowing the captured warm, moist breath to thaw her lower face. "Man." She finished answering with a snarl.

"How do you know?" Sahara struggled to button her canvas, blanket-lined winter coat.

"The ropes were cut. And whoever did it wasn't careful. They left footprints. There was a single pair of boot prints at most of the traps. But several sets of prints met up at one. There were two of them. Maybe three." Numb fingers untied then dropped the traps from the horse's packsaddle. Chains clanked. Metal banged on the hard ground. The packhorse skittered to the side unaccustomed to the clunky iron killers. This horse was young yet. Caught from the box canyons, this one had been wild.

The colt was a small, stout horse of Spanish descent; his body showed its ancestry by performing in a gaited fashion. The young, yellow-colored stallion was a buckskin, blending well with the canyon walls. His band's lead stallion had run him off. That's when Austin had happened upon the animal. She had roped him with ease because the yellow horse had been lame.

When Austin tracked him into sight, his sweaty body had shown pockmarks from fresh bite wounds. The three-year-old had been considered, by his father, old enough to move away from the herd. Nature insisted that the burgeoning colt find a new band. It was Nature's way that he should win a herd of his own or join a bachelor band if unworthy or unfit.

Wild stallions drove out their offspring as each one became of breeding age. Mother Nature's helping hand in this way prevented inbreeding. The problem was, this youngster hadn't wanted to leave. It had taken much convincing, as evidenced by the angry, reddened marks on his body and his three-legged lameness.

Austin pulled the packsaddle from the colt's back and rubbed the sweated areas. The yellow horse tilted his muzzle into the air. Black mane fell away from his head. His forelock drifted to one side as he curled and puckered and twitched his lips in approval of her scratching.

"Good hands. Most everyone around here enjoys your touch. The pup hungers for it when you're gone and won't be pacified by my own," Sahara said as she retrieved a set of figure-eight, braided, leather hobbles from the ground near the traps. The girl fondled the supple shackles in blotchy red fingers before handing them to Austin who made no response.

"Did you lose much in the traps?" Sahara blew into her fisted hands while rocking from one foot to the other.

"Hare. Rabbit. Lost them to whoever raided the traps. Would have been good winter fare. And they were in full winter pelts which are the best for curing." Austin turned the hobbled stallion loose to graze, tossing him an armful of stored hay. Before heading to the warmth of her home, the tired woman hoisted her saddle onto the hanging rope, out of the reach of wilder animals.

"Will you set the traps again?"

"I'll set the traps. I wonder though, will I catch a four-legged or two-legged?" Austin walked off. She headed to the hogan stiff with cold and angst. In her mind she had calculated that there wouldn't be enough winter food stored for the two of them at this rate. No winter supplies meant someone would starve.

Helping herself to the simmering stew, Austin ate with haste. In a foul mood, she stripped off her clothes and collapsed onto the straw pallet rolling into several wool blankets. The pup scurried over to the heap, curling submissively against her stomach.

Austin wanted to be alone. The homesteader was frozen, frustrated, and tense. One hand slid between her thighs for warmth, the other draped over her pup. She drifted into a light sleep, aware of Sahara, and listening to the unfamiliar, soft sounds of domestic chores.

When she awoke in the night, Austin's vision filled with Sahara. The redhead's skirts were hoisted to her navel. Pantaloons slouched on the floor as the girl's bare legs splayed apart. The paisley shrouded figure sat on the course wooden stool meticulously placed in front of a blazing fire. In her tiny hands were shears.

The shears had arrived with packaged goods from the general store. Austin had seen the silvery shears and recalled wondering what they were for. Long, thin, knife blades seemed more practical. But she had gotten distracted and hadn't asked of their use. Now she was to find out.

With disbelief, she scratched and rubbed at her eyes, closing only one at a time for the ministrations, so as not to lose sight of Sahara and the shears. The bright blue eyes watered with burning, tired sensations adding a fogged outline to her view.

Set in the meeting of Sahara's porcelain white thighs, a blazing thatch of red pubic hair leapt forth as if made of flames. Austin was intrigued at the sight. *Was Sahara's mound that red or had the glow from the fire tainted the color of the soft patch making it appear to be ablaze?*

The girl ran petite fingers through her wiry muff. Curly hair sprung back into place as digits passed by. Tiny fingers disappeared from sight in the plush pile. Austin could only imagine the feeling of its crinkly softness.

The glint of the shears captivated Austin. Sahara snapped the silver scissors shut, opened them and snapped them shut again. The swish and click of steely metal played in harsh contrast to the quiet, pale, softness of its victim. Austin focused on those shears with mounting curiosity and tension. The tool had been cold and clumsy when the Navajo-raised woman had plucked them from the table for examination the other night. She thought it odd how the bitter metal daggers could be thrust destructively together in partnership with a mere snap of the fingers.

Imagining the sting of frigidity landing upon its fiery victim, Austin shuddered under heavy blankets. She nestled her hand further between her own thighs, perhaps in protection. Sahara brushed the metal cutters sideways over soft curls. The pile once again folded under pressure to jump back into place as the threat passed. The pale, freckled lass took the scissors away momentarily and crammed her fingers into the red orange lushness. Sahara choked curly strands of pubic hair bringing the shears back to sever the strangled victims.

Austin wanted to cry out "No." She wanted to feel that furry pelt. Run her fingers through its thick, lush curls to caress an animal the likes she had never touched before. Her own brown muff jerked under her hand. Her thighs squeezed convulsively with the clicking of metal rhythmic in her ears. Austin rocked against her palm. A brown crinkly pelt nestled shaggy and crisp between calloused fingers in contrast to the red thatch that she couldn't tear her widened blue eyes from.

Lower lips now showed through the fine hair. Lips reddening to a different shade, brighter than they had begun. The crease between those nether lips filled with another redness still, glinting with moisture, and stealing the show from the shears. Austin saw Sahara's wetness as she felt her own. The moist, slippery feel filled the furrow between the trapper's legs.

Turquoise blue eyes watched Sahara dip a finger into slickness then run the tip of that digit along the crevice. Glinting moistness smeared the entire length of the crease. The petite girl then plunged the shears toward the saturated source, never really contacting the skin beneath. Sahara continued to snip the red orange tendrils from the slick area. Incising its covering, the shine was more exposed to the dancing reflections of the fire and to Austin's watchful eyes.

A groan escaped the frontierswoman, but she squeezed her eyes shut and bit her bottom lip to gain self-control. It was no use. Lying on the straw pallet she silently rocked onto her palm. Spittle drooled to her chin from between white front teeth clenched onto a rolled lip. Brown muff slid along fingers with an exuberant wetness.

Austin bit her bottom lip even harder lest she cry out. Grunts were silenced in her throat. Moans that echoed in her head never reached her lips to escape. Her body arched into her palm seeking relief from inner torment. Tense and tortured she couldn't hump her hand any faster or harder without Sahara noticing. Austin stilled her body with difficulty, changing tactics to work two fingers in tiny circles over the protruding nodule that had arisen.

The other hand fell from the dog to grasp at the blankets and at the covered straw of her pallet. It wasn't enough. Two hands. Austin needed two hands. She slapped the other to her crotch. There was a moment when her body jerked of its own volition from a loose spasm. There was that promise of delight yet to come niggling at her insides. And there was a craving to find release from an unfamiliar powerful takeover of her body. She squeezed her eyes shut.

Struggling within, Austin writhed and convulsed searching for the peak that would end the misery of her teeth-clenched bottom lip and sweetly agonized body.

There was more Austin needed to get there, so much more. As if it would never be enough, the lone woman pumped at herself, pressuring the entire outside of her crotch and vaginal lips. She seared a path with those little circles using slippery fingertips on and around her hardened nodule. It still wasn't enough. She didn't know what she needed. She only knew that what there was wasn't enough.

Her body rocked. Her hand beat a faster rhythm than she could stay with in undulation. Austin searched for the sight of Sahara from tense, slit eyelids. Focus fell first on the red fluff lumped on the floor then followed a porcelain foot, to a calf, to knee, to thigh...

"Mmm...ohh...oh." Silently crazed, she cleaved her lip between strong, healthy teeth. A metallic taste assaulted her tongue.

Those slit eyes stared, watched, and devoured the sight of the trimmed, wet nether lips across the room. Flames danced lights and shadows on the glistening form. It took Austin a moment to recognize that Sahara too was working at herself. The girl caressed and cajoled slippery moistness along the inside of her swollen, pouting lips.

Sahara slid a finger down the crevice. It disappeared somehow, somewhere, to emerge again and repeat the magical act. Austin watched mesmerized and tore her pressuring hand away to probe with a long, thin middle finger. There. There. And her finger too was swallowed. Delight rang in her ears, engulfing her brain.

Austin thrust once...twice. Her body humped with force to meet her finger. The wild woman wanted to scream, to rip the air vocally with her need and her hunger. Tensing, she tore her head violently to the side. Her back arched. She moved over the straw pallet in restrained torture. From the back of her mind her head cautioned. She would draw attention to herself. But it felt too good. Austin didn't care. She didn't care.

She looked over at Sahara to find a face mirroring her own; contorted, lost, unhearing, and unseeing. The redhead leaned backward, reaching for the table to steady her seat. Sahara's pale, petite body lunged at the sunken, busy hand then twitched with spasms.

That was Austin's undoing. In near blackout, Austin's body took on a life of its own, thrashing and traveling the pallet beneath. Wave after wave of delicious release besotted every aching pore of the wilder woman's body. She seized, her body jumping until her muscles burned afire, drowning her in new sensations and forcing her to succumb to a new power and a new desire.

THE FLIGHT OF THE PRAIRIE LILY

Sacchi Green

The staircase rose up from Miss Lily's plush and gilded parlor in a curve so sweeping, so elegant, I doubted there was another such thing between Chicago and San Francisco. Miss Lily herself moved down it like she'd invented the whole notion of elegance, along with all the earthier charms of a woman's body. I doubted whether you could see another such sight as her, either, closer than San Francisco, and likely not even there.

Some sort of satiny dressing gown, open a good way down the front, clung to all of the curves it managed to cover. I supposed I shouldn't have called that early, without taking into account the hours people must keep in such an establishment, but my embarassment was not enough to make me regret getting so interesting a view. While the pretty girl who'd fetched her had surely stirred my pulses, I was happy enough to see the back of her as she left, and not just because the sight of her rear end was mighty appealing.

Miss Lily looked me over real slow, like I might be a saddle horse she contemplated buying. I was all too aware of how tight my brother's britches fit me in the butt. No hope in hell that she'd mistake me for him, even with my hair that same sun-bleached wheat color, and chopped just as short. When her gaze lingered briefly on my crotch I figured it was just as well I'd decided against the rolled-up sock I sometimes use to augment my privates with, in private. I had a notion she'd seen me before, stealing sidelong glances at her in the street, and like as not knew just who I was.

"Miss Lily," I said, trying to sound as cool and unflustered as anybody could in such a circumstance, "I'm Maddy Brown, and I'm here to discuss a business matter."

The arch of her brows heightened. The corners of her red lips would've twitched if she'd let them. After a pause long enough for me to curse myself for how that might have sounded, she said, "And just what kind of business did you have in mind, Miss

Brown?" She sank down onto a plumply cushioned settee, leaned forward, and motioned for me to take a chair.

Well, what I had most urgently in mind right then was finding out how much farther down into her low-cut satin bodice I could see if I moved a step closer, but I sat down. She leaned back, an arm raised along the back of the settee, which lifted one full breast until it seemed like its nipple would surely spring free from the barely confining cloth. My own modest nipples tingled under their homespun binding.

I cleared my throat. "Well, Ma'am, what I need is to purchase a large amount of silk fabric. I was told by Miss Ballingham, the seamstress, that you order bolts of cloth direct from your own source in San Francisco, and then she makes it up to suit you and your—your young ladies. She doesn't get much other call for silk around these parts."

"Very true," Miss Lily said. "But now you feel the need to...to expand your wardrobe? Quite extensively?"

Her eyes gleamed with amusement beneath lowered lids. She knew well enough, I guessed, that dresses were not what I had in mind. "It's not my wardrobe that needs expanding, Miss Lily," I said coolly, damned if I'd let her fluster me any more than I could help. "Do you know anything about hot-air balloons? Montgolfiers, some folks call them, after that Frenchman."

"Ah," she said, sitting up straighter and looking more alert. "You're Teddy Brown's niece, aren't you, God rest his soul. You do favor him considerably—although I must say he'd never have done such justice to those doeskin trousers." She leaned far forward to lay a hand on my thigh, and, between the heat spreading from there to my belly and the truly remarkable view I got of her splendid bosom, I came close to forgetting what I'd come for.

Then she stood up. "Well," she said briskly, "if you're planning on launching Teddy's Prairie Lily, you'll get all the help you need from me, for old time's sake."

I nearly knocked over the chair as I lurched to my feet. In all the time I'd known Uncle Thaddeus, which was roughly the first fourteen years of my life, it had never occurred to me that his airship might be named for anyone, much less the madam of the most elegant whorehouse between Kansas City and San Francisco.

"Come along," Miss Lily said, a touch impatiently, as she moved toward the stairs. "How much silk do you need? Just for patches, or major reconstruction? I suppose the poor thing has been jumbled up in the corner of some barn for the last six years, since Teddy died."

"No Ma'am," I said indignantly, "not jumbled. I did my best. But he didn't use it much those last few months, or fix it up after the barn roof caved in on it during a blizzard." Uncle Ted had finally succumbed to the recurring fever he'd got while he was away at Mr. Lincoln's war, flying airships with Colonel Lowe's aeronauts and keeping the Rebel troops under surveillance. "And then my Pa made me promise I wouldn't try to launch it myself till I turned twenty. Which I just did." I followed her up the stairs, my breath coming a bit faster by the top, not so much from the climb as from the tantalizing effect of satin sliding over well-rounded buttocks just inches beyond my nose.

In the upper corridor, a row of female heads poked out to watch us. Some were two to a room, and the girl I'd seen downstairs, a tousled redhead, had her arm around a taller, copper-skinned girl with long black braids. When she grinned at me, and winked, I found myself giving a moment's thought to the benefits of working in such a place.

Then I followed Miss Lily into the front bedroom, all rose and ivory and crystal, and couldn't think of anything except the fact that she was untying the sash of her dressing gown.

"Well, Maddy Brown," she said, gesturing toward a little room opening off to the side, "I don't suppose you'll mind if I take advantage of my bath water while it's still hot. You caught me just as I was about to step in."

I was amazed she'd agreed to see me at all, in that case, and even more amazed at what she was letting me see. Her rose-and-ivory body was reflected in two long mirrors, but I kept my warm gaze on the real thing and watched sharply for some cue as to what was expected of me. At the very least, I might learn a thing or two of use in the future.

When she raised her arms to pile her red gold hair on top of her head, her breasts lifted and bobbled and seemed to challenge my hands to weigh them. The curve of her rounded belly led my gaze downward to the darker gold cluster of curls at the junction of her thighs and, as she started to turn toward the waiting bath already afroth with rose-scented bubbles, I had a startling urge to catch her round the hips and press my face into those musky curls before she got too clean. I stored away the thought to dream on.

She stepped into the big copper tub and settled languidly into the steaming water. "So, Maddy," she said, spreading soap froth over shoulders and breasts getting rosier by the second from the heat of the bath—and just maybe, I hoped, from the heat of my gaze—"why do you think I brought you up here?"

"To scrub your back?" I asked cockily, if a bit breathlessly.

Not many could look severe in a bubble bath, but Miss Lily managed it. She sat up straight and water sluiced over her curves like syrup over preserved peaches. "Just you turn yourself around, girl," she said, so sternly I obeyed without a murmur. I could feel my face glowing pink as her soap-slicked flesh. "Now open the bottom drawer of that chiffonier."

I did as I was told, feeling, when I knelt down, as though my brother's britches had grown even tighter than before. I had to tug to get the drawer open. Then I saw the folds of ivory silk, and reached out to touch the smooth fabric with something like awe.

"Sheets," Miss Lily said behind me. "The finest quality, never used. Teddy always preferred the French weave, on the bed or in the air. How many do you need?"

I most definitely did not want to imagine Uncle Teddy sprawled on Miss Lily's sheets, touching her silken skin, but I surely wished I could be there in his place. Which reminded me what else I was determined to do in his place. I wrenched my mind back to business.

"I can get by with three or four, depending on how much they cost," I said. French weave might be beyond my means, but I recognized by the feel and heft that this silk was the perfect match for what was left of the Prairie Lily.

"Take six," Miss Lily said. "I'm willing to barter."

So I filled my arms with folded sheets, stood, and turned back toward the tantalizing vision of Miss Lily in her bath. She was sponging her shoulders and breasts; and then, eyelids half lowered as she watched me watching her, she dipped her hand beneath the water and reached down between her thighs. "Set them on the bed, girl, before you drop them," she murmured in a low, purring tone. I stumbled into the bedroom, dumped my load, and couldn't keep from touching myself some before I turned back, which made my borrowed britches feel all the tighter. And damper.

"All right," I said, when I was back beside her. "Let's barter. What's your price?" I knew by now she was toying with me, and I wasn't quite cocky enough to think that what she wanted was what I'd have paid half my savings to provide, and let the Prairie Lily wait another year or two to fly.

"Take me along," she said, no hint now of seduction in her voice. "Take me up with you when you fly her." She stood right up in the bath, looking like that picture of a goddess standing in a seashell, but even more bountiful. When she gestured toward the bucket of water for rinsing I hustled to lift it and pour it over her, struggling to keep a steady aim at her shoulders while my gaze followed the downward flow of the water over the ins and outs of her lush curves.

She stepped out onto a fleecy sheepskin mat as I was bending to set down the bucket, so that for a moment my face was on a level with the triangle of wet curls between her thighs. I came close to falling to my knees to explore those glimpsed delights, and maybe even to rouse a muskier aroma to spice up the scent of roses rising from her skin, but she took down the biggest, softest towel I'd ever seen from a nearby hook and wrapped it around herself. I stood up and stepped back.

"Well," I said, struggling to remember what we'd been talking about. "So that's all?" I wiped the sweat from my forehead with my sleeve. The little room had got mighty cussed warm. "You want to go up with me? You're that sure I know what I'm doing?"

"You just run along now, Maddy Brown, and don't worry," Miss Lily said, turning her back to me and letting the towel slide away from her fine, round, taunting buttocks. "I know enough for both of us."

I had no doubt of that at all.

It turned out Miss Lily knew a good deal about ballooning, too. She loaned Miss Ballingham two of her girls who were good hands with a needle, and drove the three of them out to the ranch in her own wagon when the seamstress had finished as much stitching as could be done on her treadle sewing machine. While they worked to insert new panels into the huge silk bag spread out on the carefully swept barn floor, Miss Lily grilled me on the rest of the project. When she'd inspected the wicker gondola and the heating device, mounted on steel rods in a way that let it swing to stay level, like a lantern on a ship, she seemed satisfied. I was relieved she didn't question the necessity of using buffalo chips for fuel, charcoal being pretty much out of the question out here on the prairie, and tanks of gas even less affordable.

"You must have flown a good deal with Uncle Ted," I said, for conversation, as we leaned against the paddock gate outside. I tried my best not to be too obvious in how I was looking at her. Ranch hands kept finding excuses to wander by, and I figured it was none of their business if my eyes devoured her with the same avid hunger as theirs. Her severely cut jacket and no-nonsense skirt just made my memories of her naked, glowing flesh all the more vivid, and the row of tiny buttons down the front made me itch to undo them, very slowly, and find out what she wore underneath. If anything at all.

"Just a time or two, since I came West," Miss Lily said. She looked past the colt being schooled on a long rein into some far distance of her own thoughts. "I don't suppose Ted ever told you that we knew each other before, in the war. I was a nurse in a field hospital."

Now I could guess at some of what she saw in that distance. Uncle Ted, like so many others, had caught his fever in a hospital tent, where he'd gone for a simple broken leg after a wind-botched landing. "So you flew with him some back then, too?" I asked.

"Oh, that would have been against regulations!" she said solemnly, but a smile twitched at her carmined lips. Then I started, as she reached out a gloved hand and pinched my butt cheek firmly. "Don't think you're the only girl who's ever borrowed a pair of trousers," she said, with mock severity.

I wanted to ask more, but she started back toward the barn. I watched her undulating walk, and speculated on whether her fine wide hips had been less bountiful back then. It was pretty common gossip that Miss Lily had come West to be a schoolmarm, and decided she might as well make men pay for what they were bound and determined to have anyway. Some still referred to her as the Schoolmarm, in fact, which might have had more to do with her expertise with the customized whip she wore now coiled at her waist than with any actual schoolroom. Gossip also had it that there was no limit to what some men would pay for. I preferred to imagine her soft, and alluring, and naked, but the notion of watching her lattice some whimpering cattle baron's pale hairy butt did have a certain amount of appeal. I was speculating a bit on being the one holding the whip—and then, just outside the barn, she stopped and turned to me.

"So, Maddy Brown, what are your plans for the future? I'll wager you have more on your mind than just getting the Lily in the air."

Well, I did. More even than getting this original Lily right up naked against me, though that part seemed mighty urgent whenever she got close. And when I lay alone in the middle of night. And whenever I had a moment to daydream.

"I plan to move on," I told her, "to someplace with more people, more sights, more choices. San Francisco, for starters. Around here there's a few folks might pay to fly in a balloon, like the hunters who come by train to shoot buffalo, but I'm not of much mind to help them find what few herds are left. In San Francisco, though, folks are always coming and going, some with plenty of money, and there are fairs and celebrations of all kinds. Could be a living to be made by an experienced aeronaut, and plenty of other work besides. And more to see than there is here, and more kinds of people."

Miss Lily nodded, knowing well enough what I meant, what kinds of people I hoped to find. "So you've no ties keeping you here but family?" she asked. "No young man?"

I could tell she thought she knew better than that. "Oh, I've had one," I told her nonchalantly, "a time or two. Just to try him out. But I made him let me tie him to a fence post first, and not interfere too much. That first time he sputtered a bit, but by the second time he was all for it. After that I figured I'd learned pretty much all he had to offer, and sent him on his way."

She laughed so hard she had to lean against the barn. I thought I might have to open up her clothes and loosen her stays so she could catch her breath, but that was mostly wishful thinking. "Maddy, Maddy!" she said, when she could finally speak. "If ever you want such employment, at my place or in San

Francisco, just say the word!" And she tweaked my butt again and sailed into the barn to gather up the seamstresses for the ride back to town. I firmly resolved that the next time she laid a hand on me—and I'd surely give her every chance—my own hands would get busy, too.

But Miss Lily was all business from then on, right up until the still, chilly dawn a week later when we met for our first ascent. Her approaching carriage was visible between wisps of mist rising from prairie grasses silvered with dew, as I made sure of all the final details. The chase wagon was ready to follow where the wind took us and retrieve us when we landed. Ranch hands stood beside tethers staked to the ground, ready to add their weight when the slowly swelling silk envelope reached positive buoyancy.

My body felt a slow swell of anticipation, too. It was a good deal similar to when I was twelve, and Uncle Ted had first let me soar aloft with him, but now my senses had learned vastly more about how intensely my flesh could react. Miss Lily's approach made me tingle with awareness of how much more I might yet learn. She reached me just as the balloon jerked, and lurched, and rose erect to quiver above us, straining at its tethers like a colt born to run.

My blood quickened. Something deep inside me lurched and quivered too, and I could swear my private parts rose just as full and erect as the balloon, and strained as hard to run their course. Flying and Miss Lily were all bound up together in my elation, and from the way excitement glowed in her eyes and made her face seem near as young as mine, I knew she understood.

Face to face in the wicker gondola, a few feet above the ground but still tethered, we both said at once, "Are you sure you're dressed warm enough?" or some such thing. Then we both laughed. I knew how cold the air would be up high, but at that moment I couldn't imagine feeling anything but heat in her presence, all the more so when she turned her back to me and lifted the skirt of her woolen dress up so far I could see her knit silk long johns all the way up to the curve of her buttocks. She had sent me a similar set of underwear, and I knew Uncle Ted had considered knit silk the warmest for the weight, so I was wearing mine too, and had been savoring the smooth friction as if it had been her touch. Now I didn't miss the chance to savor her flesh through both her underwear and the rawhide of my glove, and, far from objecting, she pressed backward into my touch.

"Let 'er rise," I called down to the men at the ropes, and reached overhead to feed more buffalo chips into the burner. Heat rose in flickering waves to fill the envelope of silk, and seemed to ripple through me as well until my body was just as gloriously taut. The earth sank gently away beneath us—and we were aloft, free, rising almost straight up until a light wind at a thousand feet caught us and swept us slowly toward the distant Bighorn Mountain range rising abruptly to the east.

To the west the prairie seemed endless, the high Rocky Mountains only a long blue smudge along the horizon. Far, far, beyond, to the southwest, the earth curved onward, I knew, to San Francisco and the sea. But for now there was nowhere I'd rather be than drifting above a sea of grasses licked with the flame color of Indian paintbrush, Miss Lily beside me in our own private universe.

By the time we'd reached two thousand feet, the wind had dwindled until we were barely drifting eastward. A hawk soared just above and to the side, riding the same air current that bore us. Miss Lily watched with interest as I reached into a sack and brought out the precious store of high-grade charcoal I'd managed to trade for; enough, arranged just right amidst the ashes, to keep us aloft without much effort or attention for at least half an hour. She knew just what I had in mind.

"I suppose, you young vixen, you think you've got me at your mercy up here," she said, looking not the least bit reluctant.

"What's mercy got to do with it?" I sounded a bit more cocky than I felt, but entirely determined. She hadn't brought her trademark whip, which was just as well, considering the close quarters and the burner overhead. "But I do feel responsible for keeping a lady warm enough when I take her for a ride."

"Why, Miss Maddy," she said teasingly, "I do believe I'm so warm now that I must have a few buttons loosened, or I shall swoon," and she raised a languid hand to her high collar.

That was all the encouragement I needed. I moved close against her, shucked my rawhide gloves, spread her warm cloak, and embarked on the glorious task of unbuttoning every last pewter button down the front of Miss Lily's dress. And the shell buttons down the front of her silk underwear, too.

Every few inches I paused to explore the territory revealed, slipping my fingers under the fabric to feel, at first, her smooth shoulders, and on down to generous breasts that filled my hands to overflowing, and then filled my mouth, too, with demanding nipples. Wordless sounds of approval vibrated through her flesh into mine to let me know just what my lips and tongue and teeth were doing right. I might never have proceeded onward if the warm scent rising from her nether regions hadn't grown more and more insistent. When I first tried to move along, she moaned and held my head tightly at her breast for a long further minute; then she urged me downward.

I bent and savored the soft flesh of her belly with such fervor that I left marks. Her long underwear, like mine, was open at the crotch, a construction I had noted with interest. I slid my hand along from silk fabric to silkier skin until short curls coiled around my fingers, not obstructing my progress but rather luring me farther into her damp, musky heat.

My probing was met with great enthusiasm, and thrusting forward of hips, but I wanted more. I wanted to see Miss Lily, in all her naked glory, in the clear light of a prairie morning. The hand that wasn't deep between her thighs had a firm grip on her luxurious hindquarters, and neither hand was inclined to shift position, so, with a quick assessment of altitude and the balloon's state of inflation, I dropped to my knees and applied my teeth to the problem.

The few remaining buttons gave way with a series of soft pops. If Miss Lily's gasp was of indignation, it surely wasn't reflected on her face. I glanced up, saw her head thrown back and her arms raised so that she could grip the ropes connecting basket and balloon, her cloak spreading to the sides like wings. Then I glanced back down, looking my fill at the deep, glistening pink of her nether lips. A demanding wriggle of her hips inspired me to look closer, and closer, until taste took over from sight.

Glory beyond imagining, to be high and free and pressing my mouth into Miss Lily's musky heat! I licked the salt-sweet tang of desire from her crevices, probed and sucked at flesh both rigid and tender, and felt my own flesh tauten still further and my juices flow. Her voice rose, her breathing quickened into a storm of rough gasps, and, though I yearned to see her face in such extremity, I kept at her and at her, until a cry so long and keen it could have come from the hawk cut through the air, piercing through her body into mine.

Much later, skin chilled but still warm at the core, we waited on the prairie for the chase wagon, wrapped close together in Miss Lily's cloak. "I suppose you feel pretty cocky just now, young Maddy," she said, which I surely did. "Ready to prance and paw at the ground, feeling like you know it all, and want it all." She leaned her red mouth toward me, and her bountiful breasts pressed against my shoulder. Her hand rested on my thigh, then slid slowly, slowly toward my crotch; my wetness grew, and my tender parts throbbed and tingled. But her hand stopped just short of glory.

I tried to grasp it and help it along, but she drew away with a sudden strength that startled me. I made a sound somewhere between a groan and a whimper. "There's still plenty more to learn, and more to want, too," she said, with a touch of schoolmarmly severity, "if you're willing to take instruction before you fly on to conquer new worlds."

"Yes, Ma'am," I muttered.

"For now," she went on, nodding toward the expanse of deflated silk pooled on the grass, "just imagine you're the Prairie Lily, all primed to fly, heated up and filled to bursting, surging and bucking and straining at the tethers holding you down."

Well, it was a new point of view, but I could get my mind around it, and was working up some enthusiasm, too, when the chase wagon came in sight. While it still took a fair while to reach us, privacy was clearly at an end. Still, though our clothes were demurely rearranged and pinned and tidied, some lessons in the subtler aspects of seduction went forward, and I paid close attention indeed.

Later still, I knelt beside the copper tub of steaming water, this time free to let my hands slide over Miss Lily's rosy flesh wherever my fancy led; and to join her, at last, in the bath, which was a deliciously close fit indeed. The bed in the next room waited with silk tethers bound to its posts. A contraption of harness and padded leather cock was draped across its rose satin comforter, teasing me with intimations of how much I had yet to learn; but the intoxication of skin on skin, of Miss Lily's gloriously naked body entangled with mine, kept me from being in a hurry to move on. Until suddenly, urgently, I was; and so began the next lesson.

THE COAL MINER'S OTHER DAUGHTER

Amie M. Evans

Where I grew up in Coldwater, West Virginia, boxing and riding in the rodeo, like the prom queen's smooth inner thigh, were strictly men's territories. Girls just didn't go there. Coldwater was like any other small mining town in the 1950s. Business was good, if you owned the mine. Folks got by on credit from the local one-stop store when things were tight and ordered from the Sears catalog when they managed to scrape together some extra money. Everybody planted kitchen gardens with potatoes and tomatoes in the spring to can in the fall and had a few chickens in their yard. Clothes and pickup trucks were handed down and nothing went to waste.

Most folks had lived there for generations. No one moved into Coldwater unless they had kin there already. Everyone except the town drunk went to the one Methodist church on Sunday mornings where the social pecking order (which was repeated by who sat where in the pews) was neat and clean. Everyone knew everyone else's business and exactly where their place was in society, as well as their row in church. Usually no one stepped out of line.

I was the only child of Paul and Ethel Bramley. She was an only child like me. Her parents were both dead before I was born. Pa had an older sister, Belle, who raised him after their mother died. We lived in the Bramley family farmhouse on the last few acres that hadn't been sold off by the eight or so generations that came before me.

We had a barn with a single horse, Lightning, that I loved. Pa took her as a foal in exchange for some carpentry work he'd done and gave her to me as a birthday gift when I was ten. As soon as I laid my eyes on Lightning, I knew I wanted to be a rodeo star. I dreamed of riding out into the arena and doing tricks on Lightning. I practiced rope tricks with a piece of leftover lariat I found in the barn and I taught Lightning to come with one sharp whistle and to go in an endless circle if I whistled twice. I rode her bareback and after almost killing myself, I learned to stand on her back while she circled. She was black and white; not fast at all, but sure of foot and loyal.

Pa worked in the mines like most everyone else in town who didn't work for the mill. He was a foreman, like his father before him who died of black lung when I was three. Ma did odd jobs like sewing wedding dresses and making bread for the store to sell. Aunt Belle's house, a "newlywed rental" meant as a one-year stopover between the wedding day and the arrival of the firstborn, was small even by Coldwater standards. When her husband was killed one week after their wedding in a mine cave-in, she got a lump-sum settlement from the insurance and a regular monthly pension from the Wentworth Coldwater Mine Company as well as a death benefit, from some fancy company out of Texas, that he had purchased before the wedding. She bought the house they were renting from the mine company and still worked at the mill running a fabric-weaving machine.

When I was seven years old, I took my Ma's sewing shears and cut off both of my braids. Ma screamed up a storm but my Aunt Belle said, "She'll just cut them off again if you make her grow 'em back. Best to let the girl be the girl she is."

Aunt Belle immediately became my favorite person in the world. It was Aunt Belle who convinced Ma to let me start wearing dungarees or overalls instead of calico dresses to school. It was Aunt Belle who bought me my first cowboy hat made of woven tan straw with a thin strip of red leather and a metal clasp around the crown. Aunt Belle would become the single most important person to influence who I'd become in my lifetime—even more important than the prom queen with the smooth inner thighs the color of fresh warm cream.

I started boxing in 9th grade. With my hair cut short and my overalls, the boys figured I was fair game. I looked like them, but they knew I wasn't one of them, wasn't as strong or quick. Because I was different I was outcast, and as pack animals, the boys knew they could test their manhood on me with little-to-no fallout from their folks.

I had one friend until 11th grade and that was Kelly Gardener. In 10th grade, she still had two braids with red bows just like the grade-school kids, and poorly mended hand-me-down calico dresses. The youngest of seven girls with not a boy in the family—much to Mr. Gardener's distress—Kelly was just overlooked by her parents.

Everyone in Coldwater was poor except the Jamesons who owned the mill and the Wentworths who owned the mines, but the Gardeners were the poorest of the poor. Mr. Gardener refused to work in the mine and instead eked out a meager income farming his land, and Mrs. Gardener worked at the Wentworth's as the only house maid in town. Kelly's parents were just too concerned with clothing and feeding seven girls to pay much attention to her.

So it was by default that Kelly and I were friends. No one else would talk to either of us all through grade school, me because of my short hair and boy's clothes and her because she was dirt poor and looked it. But I didn't mind at all. I liked Kelly. She was smart and sincere and I thought her braids were cute and practical. We filled our free time together on weekends with adventures in the foothills where we shared our deepest secret dreams with each other. Her skin was soft like I imagined silk was and creamy white, and when we held hands my heart pounded in my chest. But, while she never betrayed my secrets, Kelly's loyalty ran only so deep. The third time the local bullies decided that I was their target, and threatened to get her too, she took off, leaving me to defend myself without even so much as a witness. I'd gotten away the first time with little damage by throwing dirt in one kid's eyes and the second time by running when Kelly screamed and distracted them. This time I came out of the encounter with my first bloody nose, black eye, and tender ribs courtesy of Larry Foster, the ringleader of the schoolyard bullies and future star football captain.

Ma sent my Pa over to Mr. Roy Foster's house. Mr. Foster told Pa if I acted more like a "real" girl maybe I wouldn't get beat up by the boys. Pa must have agreed since he didn't punch Roy's lights out, as was his normal style when one of his own was verbally attacked. While Ma and Pa sat around the dinner table in silence picking at their food and contemplating my future, Aunt Belle spoke up and offered what would become the first brass ring of what appeared at the time to be my hopeless life.

"Paul, teach the girl to box." She said it like an order as she slapped her hand palm down on the table. No one moved as she looked from my Ma, to my Pa, to me. "You hear me or you gone deaf? Teach the girl to box, I said."

"Girls don't box, Belle," Pa said, wiping the back of his hand across his forehead.

"Girls don't get beat up by boys—least not *before* they marry 'em."

Ma giggled at Belle's off-color joke. "Paul, she's right. Jessy ain't like other girls. Maybe we've got to teach her to defend herself like a boy."

That Saturday my boxing lessons began. They consisted of Pa showing me how to stand and how to hold my hands. He taught me to shadowbox in the barn and pretty much left it at that. He would check on me when Aunt Belle was visiting, demanding I show my form, upon which I'd put my legs in position and dance around jabbing at and weaving from blows of an imaginary opponent. For two months I shadowboxed in the barn with only Lightning watching me until Aunt Belle showed up with a punching bag. Not just any punching bag, but a real leather one with padded gloves.

Pa built a makeshift stand from some spare wood and hung it in the barn. He showed me how to hit the bag without breaking my fingers, and how to wrap my fist with the bandages and use the gloves. I spent the rest of the school year doing reps on the bag and running from Larry and his gang. It took a while, but by the time I was seventeen, I'd gotten Larry Foster back for that first bloody nose twice over.

On weekends, Kelly and I would pack sandwiches and ride Lightning bareback into the hills behind my house. I'd wear my cowboy hat, wishing it were made of felt or leather. Kelly would put on a pair of my jeans under her dress and we'd both bundle up in winter coats, gloves, and scarves. Lightning would carry us up the familiar winding path through the pines and leafless maple skeletons outlined in snow, past the swimming hole covered with glistening ice, and up into the foothills above town. Patches, my dog, would run ahead of us pouncing and sniffing at the snow. We'd eat the sandwiches, cuddled together under a pine tree on the edge of a field overlooking the valley, while Lightning turned up the snow looking for any remaining grass blades and Patches patrolled for rabbits.

From where we sat in the cove, it was a breathtaking view that made the dirty little town of Coldwater look like a Christmas-card village even to our knowing eyes. When we were done eating, I'd take Lightning's wool saddle blanket and throw it over us. Kelly would read aloud from whatever dime-store novel we had about the adventures of cowboys and Indians or murder mysteries with big city detectives and femme fatales. We never talked about school or the other kids, only about what we would be when we grew up and how we'd leave Coldwater and have adventures together—me as a trick rider and rodeo star and her as my fancy assistant in a rhinestone cowgirl outfit.

Every Saturday all winter and spring we'd follow the same path into the hills, watching as the snow melted and the plants sprung buds that turned into lush green leaves and obscured our view of Coldwater.

One sunny afternoon in the early summer before our junior year started, we rode Lightning past the swimming hole, barely visible from the path through the leaf-covered trees and bushes, on up into the cove. Little did I know that this would be the day I received the second brass ring of what appeared at the time to be my hopeless life.

We stretched out in the sun on the green grass in the cove that now felt protected from the world by a wall of foliage. I placed my head in Kelly's lap, looking up into the clear blue sky, while she read aloud from a dime novel about Butch Cassidy and the Sundance Kid. At some point she ran her fingers through my hair. The smell of her fresh, clean sweat filled my nose, mixing with the scents of the earth and grass of the early summer hillside. My head still in her lap, she traced with one nail, then two flat finger tips the curve of the muscle of my upper arm.

I rolled over so I was facing her and she set the book down. I lifted myself up so that I was resting on my elbow. Our eyes were locked like two alley cats wondering if it would be a fight or flight. Our breathing grew heavier. I thought about lifting my head closer to her mouth. I imagine her leaning down and kissing me. Then from somewhere deep in the silence, I playfully pushed her onto her back, straddled her, pinned her arms to the grass, and looked into her eyes. I wanted to kiss her. I wanted to know what kissing her felt like.

I lowered my upper body so my face was close to hers and she closed her eyes. I froze. I stopped breathing, paralyzed by the tingling between my legs and the silence that seemed to surround and engulf us. I pressed my lips against hers and kissed her with a closed mouth. She kissed me back, and then opened her lips ever so slightly. I let go of her wrists, letting the full weight of my body concentrated on my pelvic bone press against hers. We kissed again this time allowing our tongues to explore each other's mouths. Her hands ran over the muscles of my arms and shoulders, and down my body to the tight compact lines of my hips and thighs. Finally, she clasped my ass and pulled me toward her. Our mouths locked in an embrace. Our breathing grew heavy. Our hearts raced in excitement and fear. Hips moved rhythmically against each other. I put my hand on her breast and rubbed it through her dress, and an almost inaudible moan escaped her and sent chills down my spine to my crotch.

I wasn't sure what to do next. I'd thought about kissing Kelly, but never about what would happen after I kissed her, especially if she kissed me back. I wasn't sure what to do or what she'd let me do.

Patches barked. I rolled off Kelly. Both of us turned to look. The dog stood five feet away with a stick in her mouth. A long whine came out of her when she saw us watching. Kelly and I exhaled deeply at the same moment, then laughed. I got up and threw the stick for Patches.

"We should get back," she said, adjusting her dress.

"Yeah," I agreed, not really wanting to let this moment end but not sure how to return us to where we just were.

Two days later, Kelly went to Atlanta, Georgia, to visit her mother's sister who had married a college professor. Kelly came back in August with a stylish haircut and a suitcase full of new store-bought clothes that emphasized her budding figure and ended our friendship. It wasn't just the clothes and hair; she'd been to Atlanta. She'd learned to walk and talk fancy, but not sound fake, and she'd learned (what I'd later call the "femme's lethal secret") how to use her eyes to turn a guy to butter or sear a brand into a catty gal's forehead. Kelly came back so slick that she was like a movie star in a magazine and the "popular" kids now embraced her as one of their own.

I'd changed too. With help from Aunt Belle, Ma had finally accepted that I wasn't going to turn into the girl she wanted me to be and had made me some nice button-down, Western, yoked shirts just like the rodeo stars wore and bought me some real jeans from the Sears catalog. Aunt Belle got me a black felt cowboy hat for my birthday and my folks gave me cowboy boots with real metal buckles. My wardrobe started to fill up with items my dad no longer used that Ma altered to fit me. I got a suit jacket and the pants that had been bought and worn only for their wedding day.

Every now and then, I missed Kelly, but I knew from the start that our friendship was based on mutual social rejection and not on any real bond. I couldn't blame Kelly for taking the offer of popularity. I didn't mind not having any friends. Most of the boys just left me alone and some of the girls would talk to me when no one else was around. I spent most of my free time with Patches and Lightning in the hills reading books about great adventures, practicing boxing, or hanging out with Aunt Belle.

Our 11th grade class had twenty-five kids in it. I figured I was just the odd girl out since best friends travel in twos and so do couples. I was happy for Kelly—most of the time. But sometimes I'd see her in the cafeteria talking with the same boys who two years earlier had mocked her and beat on me. She'd have on a cashmere sweater that clung to her breasts and a straight skirt that showed off her thin waist and her firm ass. A pink hue on her smiling lips caught the light as she put a hand on one of the boy's arms, laughing at his joke or story. Once in a while, our eyes would catch each other's across the room; she'd nod and give me that look—that look that even today turns me to butter. Then I'd miss her something fierce and wonder if I'd missed my chance in the foothills.

The summer before our senior year, I spent a lot of time in the hills with Lightning and Patches, riding around, swimming if no one else was at the hole, and thinking about what I'd do after school was over. One hot day in late July as I came around the curve near the swimming hole, I saw Kelly standing there looking out at the water. She had a pair of pink Capri pants on and her hair was up in a ponytail. Patches ran up to her before I could think of what to do.

"Patches, you old beast, you." She squatted down and petted my dog as she spoke then looked up at me. "Hi." Her eyes dropped down at the end of the word then slowly returned to lock on mine.

"Hi," I said back, feeling suddenly awkward.

"Are you going swimming?" She stood up and started to walk over to me. "Hi, Lightning." She cooed as if speaking to a baby and stroked the soft damp face of my horse.

I had actually planned on taking a dip. "No. You meeting someone?"

"No. I'm here alone." She stroked Lightning's mane, then looked me in the eyes and said, "Everyone went to Wheeling for the day." Her eye held mine and I was grateful she didn't add "so it's safe here at the swimming hole for you." But I could tell she was thinking it; she'd been with me a hundred times when the other kids would drive us away from the hole.

I broke eye contact with her and looked up the path as if I didn't know how long it was and said, "I'm going to the cove."

"Jess." As she said my name she put her hand on my thigh. "Can I come with you?"

I could feel my crotch get wet and my heart started to pound. I felt like I was being given a second chance. "Sure," I said, attempting to not sound excited.

I moved Lightning over to a rock so Kelly could climb on to it and get behind me. She wrapped her arms around my waist so she wouldn't fall off and then rested the side of her face on my back as we started up the trail. "You smell good," she whispered in my ear.

"I smell sweaty," I said, but inside I was on fire.

At the cove we sat under "our" tree looking out into the valley now green and full. Patches looked for rabbits and Lightning ate freely. Kelly and I sat in silence, awkward in the familiar place with the distance that had grown between us. I wished I had brought a sandwich and a dime novel.

Kelly pulled grass out of the ground and made a pile of the blades in front of her. "I miss it here," she said. "I miss you."

I swallowed hard, wondering if I'd misheard her, then turned toward her. Her eyes were warm and open and she was smiling. "I...I miss you too." As the words left my mouth I felt naked and vulnerable in a way I'd never felt before.

She reached for my hand and I gave it to her. She scooted over so our legs touched and put her head on my shoulder. I put my arm around her and looked into her eyes, then kissed her. Fireworks went off. I felt like all the problems of the world were lifted away and everything was right again. I realized as the warmth in her mouth spread through my whole body in that kiss that I was in love with Kelly. Not friend-love or a crush, but real love. We'd leave for the rodeo after graduation and have all those adventures. But as soon as our mouths separated, she ripped the brass ring I thought I'd caught out of my hand before I had a firm hold on it.

"Jess, I have to tell you something." She moved away a little. "Larry Foster and I are seeing each other." She said it to the ground, not looking at me.

I could feel my heart pounding and the sting of tears in my eyes. I pushed her away, causing her to tumble over onto the grass, and got up and headed for Lightning.

"Jess! Wait. Talk to me, okay?"

I got on Lightning, whistled for Patches, and road off down the trail. The tears poured out of my eyes. I felt betrayed and foolish. I didn't talk to Kelly again until prom night.

Coldwater High School held its senior prom the night before graduation in conjunction with Driftwood and Townson Place High Schools at a community barn centrally located about twenty-five miles from each school. On prom night, I put on my suit with a pressed blue button-down, a bolo, my prized cowboy boots, and felt cowboy hat. I took Pa's truck into town. I didn't have a date to the prom but I planned on driving over and watching everyone go in. I wanted to be there, dancing in the barn with Kelly. Part of me thought if she could just see me dressed up...

Instead of going to the dance, I went over to Aunt Belle's for some dessert and comforting conversation. "What do we have here?" Aunt Belle said, looking me over. "Are you going to the prom?"

"I thought I'd go over. Kelly's the prom queen. Maybe go see what she wore and..." I shrugged, feeling the flush of embarrassment come to my face. "I mean...no, I'm not going. I just wanted to dress up, is all."

"You know, Jess," Aunt Belle said, putting her hands on her hips and leaning in really close like she was going to tell me the latest gossip about some important person in town, "there are places where people would like you just the way you are." Her eyes held mine while she stood there silent. "And there are women who'd think you are mighty fine." The muscle in her left cheek flinched before she smiled and straightened up. "Yep. Mighty fine."

She turned her back to me and walked the few steps from the door to the stove, giving me enough time to wipe the tear that had escaped from my stinging eyes. She put her hand on the kettle, then faced me. "So, you want tea or you gonna go to the prom?"

I took a deep breath, unsure what to do or what I really wanted. I knew the decision I made at this very moment would affect the way the rest of my life went. I just didn't know what the right answer was for me.

"Come on, I don't want to waste a match if you're gonna run out before the kettle boils. What'll it be?"

"I'm goin' to the prom." I nodded as I spoke. "Yep, I'm goin' to the prom, Aunt Belle."

"Good, then I won't waste a match." She smiled and winked at me.

The rush of pride and courage I'd felt standing in Aunt Belle's doorway left me as soon as I started to drive down the dirty road. I drove slow and took the long scenic route to the barn so that by the time I'd arrived everyone had already gone inside. A few couples were wandering out to get some air or sit in their trucks and make out. A group of boys were by the barn doors smoking cigarettes and laughing.

Inside, the barn was brightly lit. Colorful streamers and big flowers made of paper hung from the rafters. Couples danced to the country sounds of the Dixie Boys while singles mingled by the refreshment table. Boys drank punch and ate homemade cookies as they tried to build up the courage to ask the unescorted girls to dance. Some of the girls had on dresses of taffeta and illusion made just for tonight; others were in their best Sunday dresses. The boys had on suits—some new, some hand-me-downs. Everyone sparkled. This was the end of one life and the beginning of a new, as of yet unknown life.

I parked on the edge of the field at the end of the neat rows of trucks and cars, turned off the engine, then wiped my sweaty hands on a bandanna and checked my face in the rearview mirror. "What am I doing here?" I asked my reflection out loud, then shrugged and got out of the truck.

I'd just take a look, see Kelly's dress, and get out of here before anything happened. Most likely, I told myself as I walked through the rows of cars toward the dance, everyone would be having so much fun they wouldn't even notice me.

"Stop it!" I recognized Kelly's voice. I looked toward the direction of the sound.

Inside Larry's truck, two cars from me, Kelly's back was against the passenger's window and Larry had her by the wrists. Without an idea of what I'd do or say, I walked over and opened the door. "Hi, Kelly, there a problem here?" The authority and confidence in my voice shocked me.

"Yeah, you're the problem. Shut the door," Larry yelled from his side of the truck, but he let go of her wrists.

"Thanks, Jess," she said. I offered her my hand to help her out of the truck and she accepted and stood next to me. Her light blue dress was rumpled and part of the illusion was ripped. Her corsage was smashed flat, petals fell like rain drops as she moved, and the rhinestone prom queen tiara sat cockeyed on top of her head. But she still looked like a movie star to me.

"Listen, Jess." Larry hissed my name as he spoke. "*We* are the prom king and queen, so just get the hell out of here."

"Kelly, you want a ride home?" I said, ignoring him.

I put my hand on Kelly's arm at the elbow to lead her to my truck. Her skin was damp and cold and she was shaking. "Here." I slipped my jacket off and put it over her shoulders. She smiled at me, her eyes full of fear and thanks.

Larry had gotten out of his truck and yelled at our backs as we walked toward my truck, "Listen, Jess, she ain't going anywhere with you." He shoved me from behind, causing me to stumble forward a few steps. He grabbed Kelly's arm and pulled her over next to him. Larry's yelling caught attention.

I turned around, not entirely sure what to do but knowing that I had to take Kelly home. Larry stood about three feet from me with Kelly, panic in her eyes. A small semicircle of boys and girls was forming behind him. Kelly walked toward me. I kept my eyes on Larry.

"Jess, let's go," she pleaded, pulling on my hand.

I indicated with a nod she should start toward the truck, and she did. Larry took two steps forward and yelled, "She ain't going with you, freak."

My plan had been to let her get a head start, then run after her, hoping we'd make it to the truck before he caught us. My body snapped into the boxing form my Pa had taught me—feet spread and fists up.

Larry stopped in his tracks, then laughed. A few of the boys in the semicircle laughed too. "Jess is going to hit me. This will be fun." He spoke to the crowd, not to me, and then took another step toward me.

I let two quick jabs go to his face and followed them with a left to the gut, putting everything I had into those punches. Larry doubled over with blood coming from his face. A girl from the crowd yelled, "That boy just beat Larry up!" Another voice said, "That's no boy, he's a girl."

We broke for the truck, got in, and pulled out before anyone realized we'd left, sitting in silence for part of the ride. I had no idea what would happen tomorrow, but figured there would be a price to pay for what I'd just done.

Halfway home, Kelly said, "Thanks, Jess. I don't know what would have happened if you hadn't shown up." She looked out the window then down at her hands.

"No problem. You okay?"

She nodded. "Hey, mind if we stop at the pond?"

I turned off onto the dirt road that led to the pond and parked the truck next to one of the best bass holes in the county. The sky was clear and full of stars with a big ol' full moon. All the sounds of late spring by the water were in the air, and it was as if nature was singing just to comfort us. I looked out over the water as the reality of what had just happened started to sink in. My knuckles hurt, but I was so full of fear and pride, not to mention surprise, that I didn't care.

Kelly sighed then looked over at me. "What a mess."

"Yeah, maybe I shouldn't have hit him."

"God, Jess. Not that." She put her hand on mine. "You *should* have hit him a long time ago. I should *never* have dated him. I should never have tried to be someone I'm not. Mostly, I should never have given up you for *them*." She shook her head. "They're horrible people. Can you ever forgive me?"

"Forgive you? Hell, Kelly, I..." I wanted to tell her that she'd broken my heart in a hundred pieces twice over. I wanted to say that I was in love with her. I'd forgive her if she'd run away with me. But I said none of it. I was more afraid of her rejecting me again then I had been of standing up to Larry.

She squeezed my hand. "Jess, I understand if you're mad, but will you at least give me another chance?"

"Kelly, I'm not mad." I could feel my heart pounding in my chest and my mouth was dry. "I forgive you." She squeezed my hand again and slid closer to me on the seat, cuddling against me. "I love you." I felt like the words were hanging in the air between us.

"I love you, too, Jess," she said, turning her head toward me and slipping my arm over her shoulder. "I think I knew that for a long time and was just afraid to admit it."

I kissed her, soft at first, then harder, wrapping my arms around her and pulling her close to me. She lay back on the seat and I maneuvered to get on top of her, allowing our legs to interlace, and kissed her again. Our hips started to move, rubbing against each other. I let my hands run over her breasts, then grabbed the flowing skirt of her dress.

"Jess," she gasped, and pushed me down. "I want you."

I slid down—kneeling half on the floor, half on the seat. I lifted up the fluffy layers of light blue illusion that made up her dress. It was like digging my way through soapsuds to uncover her. A garter, stockings, and a pair of white panties greeted me. I lowered my face to her inner thigh. Her skin was soft like velvet, smooth and warm and the color of fresh cream. And she smelled of clean sweat.

I pushed the crotch of the panties to the side and slid my face up her thigh. With the tip of my tongue, I searched the folds of her outer labia, grazed over her clit hood then plunged into her wet pussy. She moaned as my tongue entered her and pushed against her vaginal walls. Kelly tasted like nothing I had ever imagined: salty and sweet. Her hips bucked forward. I licked straight up from her opening to her clit and worked it in a tight circular pattern. Her body jerked. She moaned.

She groaned, moving her hips to follow my tongue. I slipped my finger inside her. She was so wet. Her hips now met my pumping motion. She rested her hand on top of my head. I slipped another finger inside her and concentrated the friction of my strokes against the top while I continued the force of my tonguework on her clit. She moaned, clasped her hand into my short dark hair, and whispered my name, "Jess," into the air. Our breathing, heavy and rhythmic, was in time with the thrusts of my fingers into her cunt. I could feel a wetness pooling between my legs. I never wanted to stop licking her pussy. I wanted to capture this moment in time and keep it forever.

"Jess," she said again, louder, as her hips bucked against my mouth. Her vaginal muscles tightened, then spasmed around my fingers as the waves of orgasm flooded through her.

I took a final lick of her sweet juices before pulling myself up, kissing her neck and lips. We cuddled together leaning against the truck door, Kelly between my legs, head on my chest, and the illusion of her dress like a sparkling blanket covering the seat.

I looked out into the starry night sky, in awe of everything that had happened. I didn't know what tomorrow would hold for me, if Kelly would go away with me or if she'd act like this had never happened. But I knew at that moment I was a different person than I had been four hours before. I could see my future before me. And while I was sure it would be difficult, I also knew my life wouldn't be hopeless. This was the brass ring, the real one that I got to keep and wouldn't trade in for any prize.

SPANISH SILVER

C.A. Matthews

The farm came closer with each pace of the horse. Becky ran her fingers inside the collar of her blue-checked shirt as she rode, tossing back red hair that would have hung to her shoulders if she hadn't bound it tightly back in a ponytail. In the heat of high summer sweat stuck the thick cotton clothes to her body.

Becky was heavily built, large-breasted and broad-hipped, stocky, but not fat. The heavy routine of daily work burned off any excess weight she might have carried if she had been born to a pampered city life. A petite, frail female wouldn't have been suited to her hard farm life.

High up on the hillside the ground was baked hard, and the brush beside the trail had been burned brown. A trickle of sweat ran from Becky's hairline down her tanned face, tracing a random path through the dust and inside her open shirt collar, but the feel of a very different collar filled her thoughts. A broad silver collar fastened with a heavy clasp.

The work had been hard when she and Rachel had first moved into the old hacienda. The place had been almost a ruin, and Becky remembered days when the strain of struggling to make their dream come alive had almost broken them apart. The stables had been in a particularly bad state, and the days of digging out the floors of the stalls and the nights of nursing blistered hands had been some of the darkest they had shared. Just when it had seemed impossible to hold things together, they had found the kettle.

Together they had lifted it out of its hiding place in the floor of one of the stalls, rusted through and fragile enough to crumble in their hands. As it fell apart on the earthen floor, the old iron pot gave up its treasures.

A couple of silver picture frames; a varied collection of beads, their threads long since rotted; gold earrings and other small items of jewelry; and, kept pristine by the soft cotton cloth it was wrapped in, a heavy silver collar.

Formed from two flat bars of silver bent into semicircles, it was two inches wide, a quarter-inch thick and very heavy. Joined at one end by a pin style hinge and at the other by a simple clasp, the entire outer surface had been beaten into tiny dents with a small hammer to give texture to the metal. It had been lovingly wrapped to protect it while it was hidden and on the inside there was an engraving in Spanish. Becky couldn't read it, but Rachel had translated it as "Until the stars no longer shine".

There was nothing in the kettle to say who had buried the trinkets, nor when, nor even why. There was just the jewelry and the mystery. The rest of the antiques had sold well enough for them to finish their dream house, but jointly they had chosen to keep the collar as a gift from the hacienda's mysterious past.

The recollections made Becky's mind race ahead of her horse's steps. She drew a deep breath, raising her large breasts against the thick cotton shirtfront. Her pulse thudded in her temples. She leaned forward in the broad saddle, pressing into the heavy, darkly polished leather. Braced in the stirrups, she let the steady rhythm of the horse grind her pubis into the hard pommel. Inside the restriction of her plain work bra her nipples hardened, straining for release.

Becky's big bay stallion Muerte clattered loudly into the stable yard, iron shoes ringing on hard stone cobbles. Rachel looked up from sweeping the yard. She was shorter than Becky by perhaps a hand, but put together just as solidly. Her thick black hair, cut short but refusing wildly to lie down, gave her a punkish look, an image she'd reinforced by dyeing the ends a deep scarlet.

Rachel leaned the stiff-bristled broom against the wall of a stall as Becky halted Muerte. The thin T-shirt worn for yard work clung to her body as she straightened up, emphasizing the fact that her ample breasts were unrestrained. Her nipples were clearly defined but not as erect as Becky's. Not yet.

Becky caught Rachel's eyes and held the stare until Rachel lowered her glance deferentially toward the floor. Her dark head fell forward in submission. Becky took in the anticipated sight of the heavy Spanish silver choker around Rachel's throat, and smiled to herself. Not an entirely pleasant smile: one with something wolfish and predatory in it.

Becky swept a muscular leg over the saddle and swung to

the ground in one smooth movement. Muerte stood like stone as she tossed the reins casually into Rachel's outstretched hand.

"Make sure you treat him well," Becky snapped.

"Yes, Ma'am." Rachel turned to lead the stallion away to walk him until he cooled down.

Becky watched the way Rachel's full buttocks moved. Stained and faded blue denim stretched taut over Rachel's asscheeks. A heavy cowhide belt pulled the trousers in tight around her waist, their middle seam dividing and defining each plump globe and showing off the muscles. Rachel certainly knew how to walk, Becky reflected.

Becky bent over the wooden horse trough and splashed water onto her face and over her hair. As warm as the water was, it cooled her still-warmer skin. Droplets clung to her hair and lashes as she finally followed Rachel into the cool of the stable.

Muerte was already tied to a post beside his stall, his saddle and bridle removed. As Becky came in, Rachel's broad back was to the door, her muscles moving and flexing as she groomed the big bay with a rough cloth, rubbing him down to remove the lingering traces of sweat from his hide before it could cool and chill him. Becky moved up to stand so close behind her that every sweep of her strong arm made Rachel's back brush against Becky's breasts, teasing her already hardened nipples.

Becky reached up and gently unfastened the clasp of the heavy silver collar from around Rachel's throat. Her pupils were dark and unfocused as she snapped the collar shut around her own neck. Gently she took the towel from Rachel's hand and moved in front of her to brush Muerte's glossy hide. She could feel the heavy pulse in her throat beating against the silver collar, still warm from the other woman's skin. With long, steady strokes she swept the cloth over the horse's flanks.

Suddenly strong fingers twisted into her thick red hair, jerking her head brutally backward. Rachel's face, transformed from its previous deference, snarled into hers from inches away.

"I think," Rachel grated through clenched teeth, "that you have been a poor servant."

Sweat sprang deliciously from every pore of Becky's skin, and she felt a sudden rush of wetness between her legs. Her nipples sprang to attention even harder than before, painfully desperate to be touched. Bent backward as she was, her large breasts strained against her clothing.

"Sorry, Mistress," Becky gasped through the pain from the savage grip on her hair.

Suddenly Rachel sent Becky spinning to fall heavily. She glared down in fury at Becky, sprawled on her side in the corner in a thick pile of hay. The red hair had torn loose from its band and spread in complete disarray, sticking to her face, held there by sweat.

"Did I give you permission to speak?" Rachel hissed. At Becky's mute shake of the head, she pointed imperiously at the side of the stall. "Get the crop!"

Becky leapt to her feet and dashed to the stable wall where a broad-strapped crop hung. It might never have been used on a horse, but it had seen plenty of other use in its time. She dropped to her knees on the cold, straw-strewn floor and offered the crop up on open palms. Rachel took it and stared down at the submissive woman, desperately eager to please, on the ground in front of her. On her knees in front of her mistress, Becky waited quietly, her breasts rising heavily as she tried to control her excited breathing. Her head bowed between her arms, her empty hands still raised, she was passionately conscious of the thick metal of the hammered collar, its weight heavy against the strong muscles of her neck.

"Strip!" Rachel ordered, circling her victim as Becky hurried to do as she was told.

"Faster!" she commanded, slapping the crop against Becky's thighs and buttocks as the woman struggled to remove her clothing quickly. Her fingers pulled at the buttons of her heavy woolen work shirt, jerking as the crop cracked against her legs. Then, as she struggled to release her breasts from her bra, the crop snapped across her buttocks, stinging so hard that she leapt away from its kiss. She pulled wildly at the metal buttons on her jeans, bending to push the heavy material down below her knees. The crop fell on her bare ass with a loud slap, leaving a broad red stripe across her pale cheeks.

Her clothes lay in an untidy pile in the hay. Becky cowered away from more strokes of the whip, crossed hands covering her breasts and arms rising and falling as excitement shortened her breath.

Rachel circled her, brushing her skin ever so lightly with the head of the crop, watching wolfishly as Becky jumped at each unexpected touch. Coming to a stop in front of the naked woman, Rachel tapped the insides of Becky's thighs with the head of the crop, gently but insistently, forcing her to spread her legs apart.

Rachel leaned forward and touched Becky between the woman's wet, swollen pussy lips. Becky groaned, pressing herself toward the invasion. Rachel drew the wet, glistening finger to her lips and held the other woman's gaze as she sucked Becky's juice from her hand.

Rachel's nipples stood out proudly through the thin cotton of her T-shirt. She tucked the handle of the crop into her wide rawhide belt and pulled the shirt off over her head. Her full breasts lay heavy against her naked chest and her skin shone with a layer of fresh sweat. She retrieved the short whip from her belt and cracked it loudly against her denim-clad leg.

Becky immediately moved closer in response to the unspoken command. Rachel grabbed her long red hair roughly and pulled the other woman's face hard into her exposed bosom. Becky's mouth closed over one of Rachel's hard, engorged nipples and she began to suck furiously, her hands coming up to press the rounded flesh even harder against her face.

Becky sucked harder on the swollen teat, her teeth grazing the darker skin around Rachel's nipples. Rachel's eyes closed and her breath became hoarse. She thrust one leg between Becky's thighs, forcing the other woman to spread her legs, pressing her own thigh against Becky's wet mound. Rachel clasped Becky close to her body, her left hand gripping her lover under her thick, red hair, pressing the solid silver collar into the back of her neck. Becky clenched her legs against Rachel's jeans. She began to roll her hips, grinding her pussy over Rachel's muscular thigh through the thick, rough denim.

The heat in Becky's belly matched, then overwhelmed, the stifling atmosphere of the stable. Her breath rasped through her nostrils. Her breasts heaved as they were pressed against Rachel's strong ribs. As Becky rubbed her body hard against Rachel's thigh, her clitoris pressing roughly against the harsh jeans, she could feel her juices soak the cloth until each movement was a wet squelch.

Rachel groaned and moaned as Becky brought herself to a

climax on her thigh. Then, with a deep, involuntary shudder, she pushed Becky brutally away. All down the right leg of her jeans the long, wet trail of Becky's juices turned the faded blue material a much darker shade. Quickly she struggled out of her trousers and boots, dropping them, forgotten, to the stable floor. Completely naked, she threw herself down onto the pile of hay, pulling Becky on top of her in a tangle of tanned, muscular limbs.

Wrenching Becky's face to hers, Rachel claimed a deep kiss from her submissive, shoving her tongue into Becky's mouth, not permitting her lover any other response than full submission. Then she pressed Becky's face to her body, forcing the sweating woman to slide down, down, past the sensitive breasts, over the full swell of her belly. She cried out sharply as Becky's mouth made electric contact with her swollen vulva.

Tongue probing, mouth sucking the clitoris from its hood, Becky rolled the sensitive bud between sharp teeth, always threatening pain to go with the exquisite pleasure. She drove first two and then three strong fingers furiously in and out of Rachel's soaking cleft while her mouth worked its magic on the clit. Suddenly Rachel bucked hard. With a wordless shout, her hands buried deep in Becky's red hair, Rachel came and came again as her lover ate wildly at her wide-open pussy.

As the spasms subsided, Becky unfastened the silver collar from her own neck and closed it around Rachel's with an emphatic snap of the clasp. Then she stood up and kicked her recumbent lover.

"Muerte still needs grooming." Becky's voice was suddenly harsh again. "And make sure you do an excellent good job, if you know what's good for you."

"Yes, Ma'am," Rachel replied submissively, not meeting her mistress' eyes. She gathered up her stained, hay-littered clothes. As Becky left the stable, Rachel reached up to touch the heavy band of silver around her neck and smiled to herself. Her pussy throbbed pleasantly after its hard workout and the blood still roared through her veins, flushing her naked skin with its heat.

As she finished grooming Muerte she wondered once again about the collar, who had ordered its making, what woman had worn it and when, who had buried it for them to find generations later. Its weight bound them together, a shared secret and a symbol of their love and dark passion, a wedding band with more meaning than any exchange of rings. Brushing her fingertips across its antique surface one last time, Rachel bundled her clothes in her arms and ran on naked feet across the yard to the hacienda where Becky would be waiting for her.

Tether is the Night

Stephen D. Rogers

On the advice of my analyst, one evening I stopped to smell the roses, a bunch of wild roses that grew along a stretch of wooden fencing. Flower scent. Big deal. I got to have the same experience thumbing through a magazine while prospective clients kept me waiting. It didn't thrill me then. It didn't thrill me now.

I straightened in time to see a throwback twirling a length of rope around her head. Another loser decked out in leather, boots, and ten-gallon hat that didn't realize the West had been won, and the spoils subdivided into commercial, industrial, and residential zones.

Cowgirl turned to see me and must have read something in the expression on my face, because the loop of rope suddenly sailed through the air to encircle my shoulders. So what? My last girlfriend had been a kickboxer, and she'd left me for a man.

"Nice trick," I shouted. "It should come in handy if the circus ever comes to town. Or is there still such a thing as a rodeo?"

She gave a quick yank to the rope, pinning my arms to my sides, and then reeled me in until I was pressed against the fence at a break in the rose bushes. She smiled as she ambled over, gathering the rope effortlessly and folding it into perfect coils. "Did you say something?"

"I was just complimenting you on your trick. It's a good fallback in case the mime lessons don't pan out."

"Thanks." Cowgirl continued to close the distance until she was standing only two feet in front of me. Her eyes were a piercing blue, her gaze holding me captive until I finally managed to look away. The embroidered shirt, Western cut presumably, revealed nicely muscled arms, glowing with a sheen of sweat.

I cleared my throat. "At least throwing a rope around appears to be good exercise."

"Roping's just what I do to warm up."

Not daring to follow that trail, I slipped into business mode, ignoring the fact that she was the one in control. "You own this land?"

"Everything you see is mine. Even if it's only reflected in my eyes."

I made the mistake of glancing up again. The blue was speckled with gray. Fine wrinkles fanned out from the corners, proof that she'd weathered naturally. I imagined her low in the saddle, pounding across open fields, squinting at a sun that couldn't make her change direction.

My thoughts allowed me to break eye contact. Her nostrils, flecked with dust, flared as though she could smell my loss of composure.

She grinned. "Now that I've caught you, all that's left is the branding."

My heart thudded in my chest.

Her hands moved left and right, fast but slow, and suddenly I was tied between two fence posts, my body held in a bond that I didn't want to test, just in case it broke.

Cowgirl hung the remaining length of rope on one of the posts and then vaulted over the top rail, easily clearing the thorns. She paced back and forth behind me until she settled in my blind spot. "Eyes front."

The sun, red and swollen, was dropping toward the horizon so fast that I could almost believe it was at her command. Despite the ringing in my ears, I heard insects come to life, the sound of a million tiny hands applauding the view.

Cowgirl grabbed me by the ankles and lifted. I pivoted against the fence, holding my body rigid because I knew that's what she wanted. She then moved to the side, gripping my legs with one arm while she popped off my shoes and socks with the other.

She shifted again, changed her grip until she was clenching the fabric of my pant legs. I didn't know how much longer I could keep my back straight, but I was afraid to discover what would happen if I disappointed her.

She tugged. I felt the waist of my pants catch and then she yanked, shucking me in a single motion like an ear of corn begging to be exposed.

My bare feet hit the dirt.

Cowgirl tossed my pants onto the fence.

A single hand massaged my panties, ranging over my buttcheeks. She placed her hat on my head and leaned forward to whisper into my ear, "Yes, you're mine now."

The hand disappeared and then came back with a quick slap.

I jumped.

She traced the edge of my panties and then slapped me again.

I bit my lower lip, riding the tingle.

Cowgirl pulled my panties down to my ankles and ordered me to step out of them. She kissed my ass before standing and I rotated it toward her.

Now the spanking began in earnest. The branding, she'd called it.

I bucked against the pleasure. If Cowgirl hadn't secured me properly, she'd just have to try better the next time. The rope held.

The fence rocked a little but I was confident that Cowgirl knew what she was doing.

She stopped.

My ass ached, both from what she'd done and a desire for more. I toyed with the idea of asking for a double branding but decided that strong and silent was the way to go.

Her hand caressed me, her fingertips rough where I was most sensitive. A finger rolled underneath me, parted my hair, and rode up over my clitoris.

I opened my eyes to see that darkness had fallen.

The finger traced a few lazy circles and then lowered, slipped inside me, made me groan. Cowgirl withdrew it and pressed my thighs further apart.

She shifted again, moved beneath me, and then her mouth was covering my pussy. She nibbled and sucked, drove me crazy with her tongue.

This hadn't appeared to be a widely traveled road, and I could only hope it remained that way. Heck, I was so oblivious to everything but what Cowgirl was doing that there could have been a traffic jam ten feet behind me, ranch hands leaning out of pickup truck windows to whistle appreciation at the Wild West show. Rodeo, indeed.

As she concentrated her tongue on teasing my clitoris, she pushed one and then two fingers deep inside me, beckoned me to come closer, or at least to come.

She paused whenever she brought me to the brink, kissed my thighs while she twisted her fingers. If I hadn't been tied in place, I don't know what I would have done, but it sure as hell wouldn't have been practicing my knots.

She replaced her fingers with her thumb and then slid her wet middle finger along my crack, cooling my still throbbing ass, the skin prickling in the night air.

As Cowgirl resumed licking me, her middle finger found my puckered hole, danced around the edges, popped inside with a single, tender thrust.

I was out of my mind.

Cowgirl ran her other hand up and down my right leg, stopping to wind circles behind my knee, cup my ankles, and separate my toes. I couldn't understand how she was capable of doing twelve things at once. It was all I could do to remember how to breathe.

That said, my nipples wished Cowgirl had even more hands, more lips, more teeth. If only there was some way she could lash my breasts with her tongue while she continued working her magic elsewhere.

Perhaps Cowgirl had some hired help waiting back at the barn for the boss to return with her latest acquisition. My analyst had suggested I try to meet new people to help me get over what's-her-name.

I wasn't allowing myself to be fucked by a total stranger. I was following doctor's orders.

Cowgirl slowly pulled her finger from my asshole. My muscles clamped down hard to no avail. She then filled the need with her thumb and stuck three fingers of her other hand into my pussy while raking my clitoris with her bare teeth.

I started to pant, knowing I was going to require all the oxygen I could get if I was going to survive this orgasm.

She slowed and then went wild on me.

I exploded, holding onto that fence for dear life.

As soon as I stopped seeing stars, I saw the stars, brighter than I ever imagined they could shine. Cowgirl untied me before retrieving her hat from my head. Even though there was no other source of light, I had no difficulty finding my clothes and slowly pulled up my pants as Cowgirl watched, hands on her hips.

"You belong to me now."

"In case I wander off by mistake, I don't even know your name."

"Just ask for Lariat."

"You're joking." I sniffed as I finished dressing. "Honestly, what is it really, Cindy Lou? Aunty Em?"

Lariat shook her head as she measured out a length of rope. "Somehow I don't think that branding took."

Grinning wickedly, I leaned against the fence and kicked my shoes off into the darkness.

Ridden

Crystal Barela

I could feel her pubic hair. Back and forth, the silky roughness teased its way across my body, up my leg, over my thigh, past my steaming cunt. Could she see the heat rising from me into the still night air? Don't move. She wanted me to be still. But how could I? I squirmed as desire licked at my insides, and my hands ached to caress her breasts. I wanted to feel her nipples in my mouth, hard pebbles beneath my tongue, to bite, to play, to tease.

She had pulled into the drive four days ago in an old and rusted pickup, leaving a trail of dust along the gravel road.

"Hear you're looking for a handy...," she'd smiled, one lip curled slightly, as she took her hat off and squinted into the sun, "man." Her face was tanned, fine lines like rays of sun framing her eyes. Her hair was short, with gentle waves softening her face. She'd stood on my porch, low-riding denim looking as though it belonged to every curve.

My tongue had stuck in my throat, suddenly dry. I'd felt undressed, as if my sundress and sandaled feet exposed my inner self to the world. Was it the heat that had caused that bit of perspiration to pool between my breasts? Or was it her eyes, brown and warm? All-seeing eyes?

"Yes. I am."

Now she rose up over me, a silhouette in the darkness, her cowboy hat framed by the night sky. Her teeth flashed as she leaned forward and grabbed my wrists, rolling us across the ground, dust rising, hat flying. My heart raced against her breasts as her lips came in for a nibble and traced their way along my jaw, sending chills along the length of my body.

Her lips were near my ear. "Is your pussy hot?"

"Yes," I gasped, but she wanted to find out for herself. One gloved hand trailed down my quivering stomach to the place in question, and I felt the rough leather skim my clit. Once, twice—

I shivered. She ran her hand the length of my slit, tracing, teasing. Then I gasped as her finger dove into my wetness. She stroked steadily into me. My hips rose to meet her. The leather was deliciously rough in contrast to her lips, soft as air on my neck and collarbone. I was begging for her to fuck me. She took her time.

She brought her hand to my breasts and circled my nipples, leaving a wet trail before tracing it along my lips. My tongue stole out for a taste. I had to taste pussy, hers, mine, I didn't care. Her eyes gleamed as I licked the glove clean, and she leaned in to taste with me, our tongues tangling against the leather.

That second day I had watched her walk across the field from the bunkhouse, laughing with some of the other men I kept on for seasonal work. This life suited her. Tanned skin, calloused hands and instincts. She'd made her way over to the house where I had set up breakfast for her and the others.

"Find everything you need?" I'd asked as she took a seat at the table and I set a mug of coffee in front of her. "Sugar, milk?" She'd answered in the negative, eyes squinting in the early morning sun from under her cowboy hat.

"Bunks are comfy."

"I'm glad to hear it."

She'd nodded and lifted the coffee to her lips. I'd watched her swallow, the gentle rise and swell of her smooth throat, soft skin, warm skin. She'd met my eyes. Hers were very warm.

Now she released my hands. They went to her hair, the short curls clasping my fingers in a soft embrace as our lips married, tasting and drinking each other in. Her hand found its way out of the glove and into my hot cunt, pushing and pushing, one finger, two fingers, three. Her thumb was circling my clit. I began to plead and whimper.

She was riding my leg like a horse, the hair and wetness streaking across my skin as I begged her to fuck me harder. Three fingers, then four. The pressure built. Her lips left mine and she licked her way down my neck. My eyes squeezed shut. Her hand worked faster.

"Look at me!" she growled. I did. She smiled and went lower, playing with my nipple, tugging it to rock hard attention.

Her tongue journeyed down my stomach, leaving a wet trail in the dust. Her eager muff took a similar journey down my thigh and over my knee. Just as her lips found my clit, she eased herself onto my foot. I could feel her hot juices coating my toes, the sensation making me even wetter. She pumped on my foot. Her dripping pussy clenched around my toes in time with her hand. She rode my foot like it was her horse, fast and hard.

She began to ball me. Her fist strained against my opening, pushing in, overflowing with my juices, my insides ripening like a melon. Her fist flew home, making a place to move and expand. I cried out in pleasure as it worked, and felt my walls spasm. I was begging again, "Please...please."

Her tongue swirled around my clit, once, twice. My insides quivered. She lapped quickly, like a cat. I closed around her hand like a vise. Her name was a prayer on my lips as my legs clenched, my calves knotting in pleasure, my center imploding, sending a ringing through my head and under my skin.

A stream of wetness covered my foot as she sank toward my ankle. She worked herself faster and faster, grinding, calling me names against my quivering pussy.

My body pulsed, my skin felt on fire. The sucking sound as her hand left me made my muscles clench again, but before I could absorb the sensation she rolled me roughly over on my front. I could feel her weight on me, pressing my sensitive parts into the dirt as she massaged my ass.

"Like that, cunt? You're my hot little cunt, aren't you?" Her voice was husky. I gasped as she slapped my ass and ran her fingers, still wet with my juices, along my crack. Her fingers circled my anus. *Oh my God*. I tried to turn over but she held firm, massaging and circling my back door, pushing, probing. Her mouth trailed along my neck, calling me her dirty little cunt.

I pictured us as we lay in the field behind the barn, dirt and sweat and bits of grass sticking to our bodies. Her fingers probed into me. *Yes. Yes I was. I was her dirty little girl*. She pushed a little further. The pressure, the thrill as it sunk home, made me close my eyes tight, absorbing. She licked my neck, bit gently, and moved her finger, softly, softly—then faster. The pleasure was intense. My nerve endings writhed as I ground myself into the earth, into the rocks, wanting that friction. My hands pulled up weeds. Dirt caught beneath my nails. I pushed against the ground, needing, searching—must find it—until her other hand found its way back to my clit. With one thrum I was gone. I couldn't breathe. My legs tensed, the muscles moving under my skin. I wanted more, and I wanted to get away. It was too much, and not enough.

"Want more?"

She knew I did. I wanted her.

"Why don't you just take it?" she'd said this afternoon, not stopping her work, the hammer sending the nail through the wood like it was butter. I couldn't take my eyes off her bare arms, the toned muscles dancing as she worked.

"Take what?" I'd backed away nervously, my hip hitting the stall door.

"What you want." She'd stood, hanging the hammer from her belt as if she were a gunslinger. Her walk was cocky as she'd come toward me. Sunlight streamed through the dusty darkness in patches, highlighting her eyes, and the gold and turquoise buckle just below her navel. My senses had quickened. I could smell damp hay, and the sweat on our skin. The air had seemed to crackle as the hairs on my body rose to attention. She'd leaned in close, denim touching denim.

I had tasted her breath, hot and sweet, with cinnamon. Her face had swum out of focus as she'd leaned in closer. "Are you gonna take me?"

I turned over in the dirt, my breathing erratic. She sat, her chaps modestly covering her legs and nothing else. Somewhere she'd found a cigarette and was blowing smoke in the darkness. I crawled on hands and knees to her, coming up between her legs and nuzzling her neck. She smelled of horses, earth, and sex. I kissed the taste of cigarettes off her lips and licked her teeth, smooth in contrast to her tongue. Her smile brushed my mouth.

"You *are* a little cunt."

I laughed and straddled her legs. I ground my pussy against hers, getting wet again, rocking gently, resting my arms on her shoulders, looking down into her rich brown eyes. If only I had my dildo! But it was on my bedside table, where I'd left it after fucking myself senseless the night before, her ass in low-slung jeans the catalyst of my fantasy.

A rock, long and smooth, lay in the dirt beside us. I reached for it.

"Nasty, bitch!" Her voice ended in a gasp as the cold, heavy hardness came between our wet pussies. We ground against each other, the friction making us hotter. Our tongues danced together, licking and sucking.

I pulled away slightly, holding her head close. My tongue traced her lips slowly as I pressed myself against her. Skin met skin, making sticky sucking sounds as we moved. The music of it pulsed in rhythm with her breathing. My hand found its way down between us, snaking toward its goal, the hard rock filling my fingers as it was about to fill her needy hole. I rubbed her with it, getting it wet, feeling it slip in my fingers, slip against her.

"What do you want?" she asked, as I pressed the rock into her, her insides clinging to the smoothness. We rested our foreheads together, eyes closed. I began a gentle rhythm. "What do you want?" she asked again, her voice catching as our eyes opened.

"You."

OFF HER HIGH HORSE

Bryn Haniver

"I don't like horses," I said, struggling to keep my voice calm.

She looked down at me sympathetically, which was frustrating enough. I was five foot ten barefoot, and right now I wore heavy leather hiking boots. I should have towered over her, intimidating her petite femme soul with my hard body, jade green eyes and spiky blonde hair.

Instead I was backed nervously against the rock, waiting for her and her high horse to pass by on the narrow trail. My only other option was a whole lot of empty space. We were on a steep, narrow descent in Utah, a half day north of the overcrowded Grand Canyon: similar scenery without the masses.

Normally I was a lean, mean, solo hiking machine, used to man, woman, and child getting the hell out of my way. On narrow trails it didn't work like that when horses came by. I'd hiked the Grand Canyon just once. A hiker couldn't descend without numerous mule trains passing by, a bunch of lazy asses on their way down and back. Even though most of the time I could sit on a boulder a respectable distance away and scowl at the soft, wannabe cowboys who stared a bit long at my sweat-soaked sports bra, I still didn't like being near all those mules.

This was worse. There was no room to back away, just cliff and empty space interrupted by a narrow ledge. The horse came closer, eyeing me now. My fear of the damn things overcame my usual bravado and I pressed hard against the cliff.

"Just relax," she said. "It's a bit tight here, but I know what I'm doing." As she got even closer she added, "If you're too tense it'll upset the horse."

I tried not to look at the horse. The rider was much easier on the eyes, a pretty young woman with curly brown hair tucked up into one of those Forest Service Stetsons. A cowboy. A danger ranger. She was easy to focus on, even with the horse breathing down my neck.

She had big brown eyes that were concentrating carefully on

the trail and me. It was hot, and there were sweat stains on her green uniform shirt in the pattern of her bra. Her breasts were large, though her waist curved in beautifully before flaring out to wide hips. Those leather chap things, dusty and worn looking, partly covered her legs, and I could even see broken cactus spines protruding from the bottom of them. She was short but curvy. I found myself imagining her naked: soft, sweet and submissive.

"That's better," she said as the horse passed, jolting me out of my fantasy. She moved down the trail a short ways and then looked over her shoulder. "You okay?"

I got mad. In what kind of sick world did this petite femme ask *me* if I was okay? She should be on her knees, begging to touch me. She should be open and quivering, waiting for me to take her. She should be...

"'Cause you look a little flushed," she added. The horse started to turn.

"I'm fine," I blurted. "Really. Thanks."

"Great," she said. "Maybe I'll see you down at the river."

I shook my head as her horse disappeared around the bend.

"Fucking cowboy," I muttered.

I was thinking about what my friends back in the city would have made of that little encounter when I finally reached the river. At the low elevation of the canyon bottom it was hot, though the water was moving quickly and looked cool. I set up my tent at the far end of the camping zone, as far from the hitching posts and her horse as possible.

Back in the city, they'd have laughed their asses off at my fear. Which meant I'd tie them up and yell, spank, and fuck them back into order. Which might be worth it.

I heard the horse whinny as I was heading for the river and actually shuddered. No, it wouldn't be worth it.

A short way upstream from the camping area I found a great little swimming hole, a beautiful blue pool where the water slowed, surrounded by warm red sandstone. On the rocks was a Stetson and dusty green uniform. In the water was a spectacularly naked ranger.

She was floating on her back, those big breasts at the surface, nipples pointed to the sky as they dipped in and out of the cool water.

I peeled off my sweaty bra and shorts and stood tall on a flat rock at the water's edge. As the current spun her slowly around, her eyes widened at the sight of me.

She stood, and I tried not to stare at the rivulets of water running down her breasts.

"I'm glad you made it...," she began brightly, but I interrupted her, using my voice like a whip.

"Quiet. Come up here," I said, nodding at the bare rock in front of me.

Those big brown eyes looked spooked but curious. She waded forward, not shy about her body at all. She got out and stood a foot in front of me, her head now coming to my neck, which was a bit different than on the trail.

I held my left breast between thumb and forefinger. There was dust on my neck where the collar of my shirt had been, and salty sweat over much of my chest.

"Lick it," I said firmly, my voice brooking no argument.

She didn't argue. Eyes still wide, as if she was amazed at herself, she leaned down just a bit and tongued my nipple. It immediately began to grow. I have small breasts but long nipples. She moaned softly and took it between her lips, but knew better than to put her arms around me.

"Harder," I whispered, struggling not to shudder as she sucked away the salt. When I couldn't take any more I grabbed her head firmly and moved her to the other side. She sucked hard right away, and before long I had to stop her. The trail had made my legs wobbly.

I stepped into knee-deep water, sighing at the cool swirls around my sore feet. I handed her the small sponge I'd brought, and then turned to admire the scenery upstream. Without a word she dipped the sponge into the river and began sluicing the dust and sweat off me.

You can't use soap in these backcountry rivers, but she was especially thorough with a sponge. By the time she finished she was kneeling in front of me and I was soaking wet. When she gently found my clit with her tongue, I clutched her head and flew up to a fierce orgasm, my legs finally giving out and depositing me into the cool embrace of the river.

A short while after I'd come, I leaned her forward and slipped two fingers into her sopping pussy from behind, holding her long wet hair with one hand while stiffly finger fucking her with the other. She came right away, thrashing about in the shallow water, coughing and sputtering even as her body shuddered and relaxed.

That evening we spread a blanket on the still-warm sandstone, sprawled out together facing the star-filled sky, and just talked.

"It was so nice to let go," she said. "To let you call the shots."

I grunted an affirmative, remembering her tongue.

"On the trail, being in uniform, people always expect me to take charge. I don't mind, I like it actually, but still, it was nice to let go." She nestled her curly mane into my shoulder.

"Most of my girlfriends have been in business, or academics," I said. "I guess they like to let go too."

I sensed her studying my profile.

"Do you ever let go...," she began, but I cut her off.

"No."

The next morning she asked if I wanted to go up to an overlook hardly anyone knew about. I agreed until I realized she was talking about riding up.

"It's no problem," she said. "My horse is used to packing in supplies and stuff. He can take the two of us for a couple hours. I'm short and you're lean after all."

I'm not worried about the fucking horse, I thought, but decided against saying it. I really did want to see this overlook, and I damn sure wanted to spend time with this lovely young ranger. Or I did, until she became a cowboy again.

I found myself staring as she saddled the horse and put on her chaps. They weren't frilly at all. They were salt-stained, dusty and worn-looking. Still, from behind they framed her ass beautifully.

She finally talked me into the ride with some soft, sweet kisses. Despite my penchant for domination, I'm a sucker for soft kisses. If a horse could deposit this sexy femme and me at a beautiful viewpoint, it couldn't be that bad.

I'm not sure how the hell she rigged things but the ride was not comfortable. Most of the time I felt like I was going to fall off and had to cling to her like some pathetic biker bimbo. Every time I screwed up enough courage to lean back a bit, the horse would jolt and I'd be clutching her again. A couple times I swore she was doing it on purpose. Not that I minded holding those lush curves, but I hated feeling so helpless.

When we finally got to the overlook, I was pale and sore and overwhelmed, a ghost of my usual self. I actually let her help me off the horse—glad to be back on my own two feet, but not happy at how close to us the big beast remained. The day was already hot and we both peeled off our long pants. I had jockeys on. She wore black thong underwear.

The view was breathtaking, jagged fins of colorful sandstone sliced by deep canyons, all descending sharply to the rushing waters at the canyon base. We were at the top of a massive cliff, with no signs of civilization anywhere, including railings. Staring out into all that empty space I felt my stomach pitch and my knees grow watery. I didn't object as she grabbed my elbow and walked me back from the edge.

I stood for a while, breathing deeply and trying to regain my poise, until I heard her say, "Stand up straight."

I turned. She was leaning against her horse, idly rubbing its thick neck. Still wearing her shirt, she had removed her underwear and put the leather chaps back on. She looked so sexy it took my breath away. Her eyes were intense and the tone she used must be her ranger danger voice; firm and confident.

"What did you say?" I tried, but my voice sounded meek and I was appalled to notice I had straightened up like I was told.

"Now take off your top," she said.

I was flabbergasted. "Who the hell do you—"

She firmly patted the horse and it whinnied, loud, and lifted its head. The cliff edge was behind me so I couldn't retreat. Fear shot through my already rubbery legs. Before my brain even realized it I had my shirt and sports bra off.

She looked at me and nodded appreciation. "Sun feels good, doesn't it? Pinch those long nipples of yours."

My hands moved to my breasts. The sharp sensations made things even more surreal; hot sun on bare skin, tingling nipples, empty space behind me and this cowboy and her horse in front. As I squeezed and whimpered she stared at me. I felt totally exposed.

Finally she spoke again, saying only, "Kneel."

I knelt. Her horse seemed even bigger, but the low perspective helped with the vertigo I was feeling.

She stepped toward me, just a couple of paces from the horse but close enough that I could smell her musky scent in the dry air. Salty leather surrounded her bare thighs and trim pussy. I found that concentrating on her glistening labia helped calm me. When her hand touched my head, I leaned forward and began tonguing her with firm, slow strokes.

I forgot about the cliff, the horse, forgot everything but her taste and the slick feel of her. I clutched her bare ass and slid my tongue ever deeper, hardly noticing as she had orgasm after orgasm.

Finally, when her legs were wobbling and my jaw was sore, she whispered, "Great view."

I barely remember the ride down or the long hike back out of the canyon. I felt humiliated, angry, and a bunch of other things I couldn't explain. When she told me to come visit her trailer after I'd hiked out, I'm not even sure what I said.

I wasn't too surprised to find myself there the next night. Before getting out of my car, I dug through my stuff, coming upon the harness and dildo with a feeling of relief. I put it on right there. The apparatus was familiar even in the dark desert night. Pulling on tight pants and a top that was more corset than blouse, I strode up to her door and knocked hard.

When she opened it and smiled at me I pushed her inside. Her eyes went to the bulge in my pants.

"Uh-oh," she said. She was wearing a sundress. It made her look very feminine, and made my whole body tense with lust.

Her trailer was small but well decorated. I motioned to the beautiful Navajo rug in the center of the floor. "Hands and knees," I said.

She got down on all fours and watched as I unzipped my pants, those big brown eyes getting glassy when she saw the strap-on.

"Turn around," I said. She spun slowly, remaining on her hands and knees. I flipped her sundress over her hips, revealing her wide, bare ass. She moaned softly and arched her back, a smorgasbord of soft skin and delicious curves.

"If I knew anything about saddles, you'd be wearing one for this ride," I said softly, moving behind her.

"Remind me to teach you sometime," she said, the words trailing off as I pressed the head of the dildo into her pussy. She flattened those big breasts against the floor and lifted her ass even higher, allowing me to slide all the way in.

I did my damnedest not to yell out any cowboy clichés. My longer legs allowed me to get up high and settle onto the top of her ass as I drove in and out with increasingly frantic thrusts.

She stayed below me, lurching straight backward for deep penetrations without throwing me off. She knew how to provide a good ride. She came quickly once but barely slowed down.

When she came the second time things got rougher. Her bucking and squirming ground the harness into my clit and swept me along for the ride. In the midst of it all, her knees finally gave out and we collapsed into a slick, writhing mass on her rug.

"That was different," she said after our breathing had calmed somewhat. She reached down between my legs. "Hmm," and she stroked the slippery dildo. "Do you think someday I might try—"

"No."

She nestled her mane of hair against my chest. "Hmm...," she said again, and outside in the night, a horse whinnied.

Ranch Hands...and Tongues

C.B. Calsing

When I'd signed my contract with a major metropolitan Texas newspaper as their first female sports writer, I'd thought I would be covering the big stuff: Wimbledon, the Pro Bowl, and the Final Four. My credentials were impeccable, and the newspaper appreciated having a token woman on this traditionally male staff.

It didn't help my case much, though, that I've been called a luscious brunette. The editors brought me out at awards ceremonies and conferences, but when it came to assignments, I was screwed. I don't think it was just because I was the junior staffer, either. Even if they had hired me, they were still reluctant to give me the really big stories. What I got was worse than varsity girl's sports (which, from a personal standpoint, wouldn't have been that bad, but death to my career): I was stuck with the rodeo circuit.

Now, don't get me wrong. I'm Texan, born and bred, and, like any good girl down here, I love the rodeo. But I was raised up with it. I didn't need to spend my professional life following it around like I did when I was a kid. A job was a job, though, and I was stuck in a contract that I couldn't get out of, required to write a column a week on the WPRA.

There was one upside: most of the girls who hung out around the rodeo were pretty hot. They had tight jeans and strong arms. Feminine athleticism has always been a real turn on for me. All of that horseback riding builds great thighs!

So, I was assigned to go to some backwater rodeo and cover an up-and-coming female bull rider. She'd shown a lot of promise as an amateur and this was going to be her debut in the professional circuit. I'd read all the articles on her published previously. There was something about the girl that I found appealing, like the way she smiled through all her injuries and victories; how her embroidered cowboy shirts, sporting piping and big roses, pulled tight across her breasts; and how her long, blonde hair was tied in girlish braids.

I pulled my rental car into the dusty lot and parked among

the F-150s and Suburbans. The smell of manure and barbecue filled the air as I made my way to the stands, equipped with beer, camera, and notepad. I snapped a few pictures of the arena, of cowboys leaning against fences spitting tobacco, and horses tossing their heads while they waited in the pens.

My subject would be riding with the men. There weren't enough female riders to make it a separate event. She was third up and I watched with interest, managing to snap off a few pictures and take notes. She stayed on for the full eight seconds and had a bull with good action, but her total score was in the low 80s. That was good, but not the exceptionally high score I had hoped would pad my story.

I watched the rest of the event with little interest, already starting my article in my notebook. She knew I was there and, when she'd cleaned herself up after the ride, made her way into the stands and introduced herself.

"Julie Montgomery," she said, handing me a strong, calloused hand with short-clipped nails. I gripped it from my seat and smiled at her. "I recognized you from your picture on your byline. Mind if I sit?" she asked and I shook my head.

She was a lot cuter in person, wearing red jeans and boots and a black tank top and black straw hat. I realized how out of place I must have looked in my Capris and cardigan set.

Of Julie's attire, most notable was the large silver belt buckle that drew my attention down to her slender waist. It was a best all-around buckle from an amateur rodeo. The silver plate winked at me in the bright sunlight, almost slyly, begging to be undone. I sighed lightly.

"Nice ride," I commented, forcing my eyes away from the buckle and back to the arena. Julie shrugged.

"I could have done better," she said, a bit wistfully. "I was hoping to blow them away, ya know?" I nodded understandingly, making a couple notes as I did. She'd certainly blown me away, but that had nothing to do with the ride.

"More events this afternoon?" I asked.

"Yeah. Listen, if you want to continue this, there's a roadhouse with great steaks down on the highway." She took my notebook out of my hand and scribbled an address on the cover. "Can you meet me there for dinner tonight, maybe around seven? You could have more of my attention then." She winked at me. I smiled and nodded. When she got up to walk back down to the arena my eyes followed her tight ass.

I sat at the bar and drank another margarita. I started to think I had been stood-up, but, at seven thirty, looking exceedingly flustered, Julie finally rushed in through the front door of the roadhouse. I waved from my seat at the bar and she joined me. She was wearing a white dress shirt, tied under her breasts, a tight blue-jean skirt, and her red boots. Her legs, though a little bruised, were slim and muscular. She ordered a beer and took a second to catch her breath.

"I'm really sorry I'm late.

"It's all right," I replied. I was happy she was there. We took our drinks to a table and ordered up a couple of steaks. We chatted, and I made notes about her life, her interest in rodeo, and the history of her family. The steaks were pretty good and, afterwards, we shared a slice of chocolate cake.

"Where are you staying?" she asked. I told her the local motel and she sneered.

"That place is disgusting. You could come stay at the ranch, and get some great pictures of the place for your article. And, I make a great omelet."

I raised an eyebrow at the offer. I was very interested in Julie, but I couldn't tell whether she was into me, or just being friendly. Tentatively, I agreed, having not even checked into my room yet.

I paid the dinner bill with my expense account, and followed her old Chevy truck in my rental car until we turned off not far along the highway onto a dirt road. An overhead wooden sign claimed the property to be the Montgomery Ranch.

The old ranch house was illuminated in our headlights as we pulled up. It was two-storied, whitewashed, and looked homey. I pulled in next to the pickup and followed Julie onto the porch with my bag over my shoulder. Inside it was cool and I could hear the hum of an air-conditioning unit. Julie raised a finger to her lips.

"Most of the house is asleep, so you gotta be quiet." She led me up the stairs to a room on the second floor and we crept in, closing the door behind us before she flicked on the lights. I wondered how many people were living in the house.

The room was cozy, decorated in gingham, and hung with pictures of horses. There was a large four-poster bed spread with an inviting patchwork quilt. I smiled at the quaintness of it, a big improvement over the hotel room I could have spent the evening in.

"My room's just across the hall," Julie said. She stepped within arm's length. "Um, I don't usually kiss on the first date."

"Is that what this has been about?" I asked, raising an eyebrow.

"Well, I thought...," she stammered, her coy confidence abandoning her in an instant.

I smiled and took the last step toward her. "You thought right," I said, laughing and lifting a hand to run my fingers through her hair before pulling her toward me. I dropped my bag to the floor. When our lips finally touched, I felt her sigh, and she wrapped her arms around me, clutching the back of my neck and my waist, pulling me firmly against her. When my tongue slipped between her pink frosted lips and past her teeth, I tasted chocolate cake, beer, and tobacco. Her rough scent reminded me of barn wood and hay.

Our tongues darted together, tagging and retreating. We played at this until she pulled away and ran the back of her hand across her mouth self-consciously.

Julie smiled at me, radiant in her rusticity. "I'll, um, I'll see you in the morning, okay?" she said, turning toward the door. I held her shoulder.

"Are you sure you don't want to stay here?" I asked her. She shook her head, then opened the door and left, closing it softly behind her.

The bed didn't look as inviting now, knowing that I was going to do nothing in it but sleep.

Sun streaming through an open window, the smell of coffee and frying bacon woke me. There was no clock in the room so I had no idea what time it was. I got up, found a shower, then headed downstairs to the kitchen with my camera slung around my shoulder, notebook in hand.

Surrounding a huge old trestle table, Julie and near a dozen other women sat eating and laughing like it was a holiday. I found an empty seat.

It wasn't long before a plate of eggs, bacon, biscuits and gravy had been set down in front of me. I hadn't expected so many girls in the house, but the idea was certainly appealing.

Julie graced me with a fetching smile and whispered a comment to the girl sitting next to her. That girl giggled as she eyed me across the table. I smiled in reply, not feeling the least bit embarrassed.

At least two of the other women seemed somehow related to Julie, probably sisters, but the rest were a mystery to me. Seeing the confusion in my face, Julie spoke up. "They're the ranch hands and my sisters."

I nodded in understanding. What a great angle, to tell a story about an all-girl's ranch! There were at least a couple of sets of lovers around the table, by the way they had their heads bent together and ate food off of each other's plates.

I finished breakfast and helped clear the table. Everyone else filed off to do her day's work on the ranch. When all the dishes were done, Julie turned to me.

"So," she began, "what is it you'd like to see? The horses? The bulls we're breeding? The goats? We make our own cheese here, you know. It's good to diversify."

"Whatever," I said, smiling. "Give me that ten-cent tour."

Julie took me by the hand and led me into the bright sunlight. We crossed the yard behind the house and entered a big barn. In stalls on either side, animals were eating their morning meals. In the middle was an old tractor with a wheel off. I looked up at the rafters, where a tire swing had been tied. The hayloft was stocked and tools leaned against the walls here and there.

"Come on," Julie said, leading me to the back of the barn. There, in a pen in the corner, was a regal quarter horse mare with a brand-new colt asleep at her feet. The mare eyed us warily as we approached. I took Julie's picture leaning against the pen with the mare's muzzle in her hands. It was a great shot.

"Want to have some fun?" Julie asked me. I raised an eyebrow as she took my camera away from me, placing it on the seat of the tractor. She looped the tire swing over her arm and climbed up the ladder into the hayloft. From there, she swung one leg through and jumped off the edge. The swing arced through the air with Julie whooping and hollering all the way down as she spun in the air.

When she finally stopped, she brought the swing over to me. I climbed the ladder and looked down from the hayloft. Julie looked back up at me with a wide smile gracing her lips. From my vantage point, I could see the tops of her breasts. I hooked my leg through the tire and jumped. The dusty air of the barn whipped through my hair and I laughed out loud, thoroughly enjoying myself. As I swung to the far side of the barn, Julie caught the tire and jumped on.

The two of us swung back and forth in the barn, the fresh smell of alfalfa around us. We grinned foolishly at each other. My desire for her grew.

"Want to go again?" she asked. I nodded and we climbed up to the loft together. Before I could get hold of the tire, Julie pushed me back into the hay. I quickly overcame my shock as I watched Julie start to unbutton her sleeveless denim work shirt.

Conveniently, there was an old patchwork quilt nearby, and Julie spread it out over a mound of hay.

"You wanna get naked?" she asked, dropping her shirt and teasing one of her gingham-and-lace bra straps off of her shoulder. I licked my lips seductively, kicked off my sandals, and unzipped the front of my jeans. As Julie stared, I peeled the sides back slowly to show the black lace underwear beneath.

"That's a start," Julie said, pouting playfully. "But I want more." She stepped out of her boots, then undid her belt, pulling it out of the belt-loops and dropping it heavily to the loft floor.

I pulled my tank top off over my head and threw it aside, braless breasts bared. With the clip out of my hair, long brunette locks fell around my shoulders. I demurely positioned a few curls to cover my bare breasts.

Julie pushed her jeans slowly down her body then kicked them off. Her panties matched her bra. I, too, sloughed off my jeans and my own lacy underwear.

Shed of clothing, we kissed hungrily. I tangled my fingers in her long blonde hair. The feeling of her weight stretching the length of my body was luxurious. She was bacon-fed and well toned, strong and voluptuous.

The air of the barn was warm against our bodies. Her tongue darted in and out of my mouth teasingly, slipping against my own, retreating. Her bare breasts pressed against mine. A thin film of sweat formed between our bodies letting the nipples slide across each other as we moved.

My nipples were hard and taut, aching to be pinched, sucked, or bitten. I cupped one of Julie's breasts, taking the small nub between my thumb and forefinger, rolling it playfully. Julie hissed and kissed me all the more fiercely.

Wet, my clit crying out for attention, I maneuvered myself to straddle Julie's leg and slowly, delightfully, began grinding against her. The feel of her flushed skin against my hot cunt and rising clit thrilled me.

Julie grasped the opportunity to move herself against my leg. Our tongues still tagged at each other, while one of my hands was clenched in her hair, and another clutched at her breast. Julie cupped my ass, kneading it slowly, digging her short nails into my flesh.

She pulled away from me, stretching her rugged body, snarling at me. Sex seemed to turn her feral.

Julie licked her lips then dipped down, running her tongue from one of my nipples to the other. She was between my breasts and across my stomach, gliding down my body until her pink lips stopped just shy of my cleanly clipped pubic area.

One tanned hand brushed across my short hairs. She parted my swollen lips with soft, confident fingers. Looking me in the eye, she languidly lapped her tongue against my clit. I shuddered. Julie licked again. I moaned.

Her hand slithered further down until I felt a finger slide into my pussy. Another finger unexpectedly slipped into my ass. I gasped, and Julie watched me, appearing pleased with herself.

The mingled feelings were exquisite. Her tongue flicked over my clit, sending shocks of pleasure through my body. Her fingers knew where and how to move to keep me just on the edge without sending me too quickly over.

It wasn't enough, though. "I want to taste you," I said.

Without a word, she turned around, presenting her gorgeous ass to my face before burying herself back in my muff.

Slyly, I ran a finger down the crack of her ass and dipped it into her hot cunt. Julie moaned and rocked her body against me. I pulled my finger out then grabbed her with both hands, yanking her hips down against me, playing my tongue against her swollen clit and dipping my fingers in and out of her pussy.

She groaned and lapped. Her pelvis gyrated against my face as I stroked her flesh with my skilled tongue.

Julie moved even more urgently against me. Quickening the pace, I felt the rush of her breath against my clit as she exhaled.

Her soft whimpers slowly rose to small, sharp cries and Julie was on the verge.

I wanted nothing more than to push her over.

"Oh, God, yes!" she called out at last, throwing back her head and howling at the roof of the barn.

Then she sunk her head back down to my pussy. I spanked her playfully. She moved everything inside me, making the room spin as I lost myself in the gorgeous sensations.

My body arched up against her, trying to take in more of her fingers than was possible, demanding every bit of her. She nipped and licked. I ground my hips against her face, no longer able to contain myself. Her teeth scraped my flesh and the shock of the pain was all that it took.

I cried out, awash in rapture. Chickens cackled and fluttered beneath us. Pigeons flew over our heads and out the barn door, but no higher or faster than the sound waves of my pleasure.

Julie got up and collapsed next to me on the blanket, her blonde head resting on my shoulder. She looked satiated.

"I pegged you for a screamer," she said to me matter-of-factly. "That's why we couldn't, ya know, last night."

We took that final dive on the tire swing together. The sun was getting low in the west. The smell of barbecue was in the air. And another night still lay ahead.

Dry Hearts, Dreaming

Jay Lake

Katherine Dunham found her wedding ring again, gleaming in the stinking green mud at the bottom of the stock tank. She'd taken to walking the bed of the pond once the summer's drought had stolen the last of the water. The water had stolen her husband David the year before, drowned in two feet of it. The day of the funeral, she'd thrown the ring in where he'd died, cursing and crying, then gone back to running the farm.

Now this. The well going dry, the creek running with dust, and Maggie Blaylock coming to haul off her last sixteen head of cattle before they died too, lowing their thirst at the edge of the stock tank. Nineteen years of marriage and hard work, and all she had to show was drying mud in the heart of Caldwell County, Texas. Katherine sat down in the reeking ooze with the ring in her hands and cried as if she could fill the tank.

The heat took everything. With the water went the garden and every growing thing; with the well went the house, so that it stank of dust and compost and hot, resentful cats. Waist-length blonde hair pinned above her head, Katherine lay naked in the empty tub, the porcelain beneath her covered with the op-art Mona Lisa that David had painted in their youth, stealing the last bit of cool from the tub's chipped walls. She stole, as well, the last bit of comfort from her memories in the flooding morning light.

Cicadas buzzed. David had loved her body, saying she had girlish breasts with nipples like cured dates. She ran a hand across her flat belly, teasing the delicate hairs. She remembered his larger hand, still fine even with his rancher's callouses, but strong, the fingers blunt. David's fingers had been unafraid to voyage anywhere across her body, messengers of his passion.

A rusty drip from the faucet landed on her foot, tracing a discolored trail like a line of old kisses. Katherine licked the fingers of her left hand and gently rolled her nipple, pressuring the little raisin to swell into one of David's dates. Her breast shifted under her palm, the tiny stretch marks of age sliding across her hand.

Katherine's right hand drifted below the curve of her belly, the cold tub and the hot sunlight reminding her of making love with David on the roof, in the back of the pickup, on the bank of the stock tank. She rolled the little pad above her labia the way David did before he knelt to his feasting, and she smiled at the memory of being interrupted by chickens in the barn. Her legs slipped open, knees against the scarred lip of the tub.

"Kath? You in there?" It was Maggie's voice, calling from the yard.

"Shit!" Katherine jumped as the screen door banged. Scrambling for a towel, she caught the top of her foot on the old faucet, tearing skin away in a grating line. Her crotch slammed on the edge of the tub, and she rolled down onto the filthy little rug whimpering, staring up at the cobwebbed ceiling. She focused on the metallic reek of the hard water in the toilet tank, trying to chase the pain of her foot and her pelvis away.

Maggie stuck her head in the bathroom door. "What happ... Well. Excuse me." She smiled, shaking her head. "Aren't you a little old for this?"

Katherine realized she was massaging her aching crotch. "Just a minute," she gasped. "I was taking a bath."

Maggie glanced at the dry tub, then back at Katherine, still smiling. "Uh-huh. Take your time. I'll be out at the corral."

Nipples aching in synch with her throbbing crotch and stinging foot, Katherine drew on one of David's old oxford shirts—his go-to-town shirts. She always threw a few drops of his cologne onto the cloth when she hung them on the line. It kept him close.

Katherine stood on the porch and looked out. Scattered clouds lied their way toward the horizon, carrying her water toward Louisiana or Arkansas. Vultures circled, silhouetted in the shining vault of the sky. Below them, dusty live oaks and mesquite and juniper lined the fences, stood behind the rusted roof of the barn.

Framed amid it all, Maggie's curly brown hair was a mop top above a broad ruddy face. She wore a checkered shirt with the sleeves torn off, worn jeans stretched over broad hips that might have brought forth a whole generation, in another era.

She'd known Maggie for years, as close as anyone outside her marriage. Maggie and David had been closer, sharing the secrets of agriculture, home brew, and old pickups, and sometimes even sharing smiling glances at Katherine. No matter how much Katherine liked the other woman, being caught rolling on the floor naked was downright embarrassing. At least it was Maggie. Somewhere inside, she was almost glad it was Maggie.

Katherine watched Maggie among the few cattle in the corral, all that was left of two hundred head of hopes and dreams, before the water failed over the past decade. Maggie knew her work, a cattleman like David had been. She wasn't pretty, Maggie, but Katherine had always loved the way Maggie's smile could leap across a room and seize a person like lightning in the brush.

Maggie noticed Katherine staring. She motioned Katherine over. Katherine had finished dressing in a teal prairie skirt David had loved, and her working boots. She didn't bother with panties, and she only ever wore a bra to go to town. David had liked that too.

"Hey, girl." Maggie stepped up onto the useless rain barrel and hopped the fence, landing on her old shit-kicker boots like a dancer. Katherine admired the way Maggie moved, for all her middle-aged size.

"Maggie, I'm sorry. You caught me at a weird moment." Katherine was blushing. "It's not what you think."

Maggie laughed, her smile flooding her face. "I certainly *hope* it was what I think." She swung her hips and winked as she pulled a sheaf of paper from her shirt pocket. "I've got the contract for the cattle right here. They're looking okay, but I can't get Opal and Earl's trailer until next week. If you want to execute today, I'll pay a per diem boarding fee and drop off some fodder."

Katherine glanced at the fields west of the corral, where the stock tank lay hidden from the house by the rising land. The grass had colored past gold to a dusty, failed tan. Nothing out there now but cow shit and flies. The cattle had been gnawing the bark on the trees along the fence line. The money from the sale of the main herd was almost gone. Katherine sighed. "Keep them here as long as you want. Every bit counts."

"Kath." Maggie looked at her boots. "It's not my business, but what are you going to do? My money will take you through the fall, maybe. But you've got nothing in the ground, nothing left to sell but the land."

"You offering?" Katherine heard the false note in her voice, like a lie told in church.

"That's not what I'm saying."

"I can't sell. Maggie, it's...it's..."

"David," said Maggie.

Katherine started to cry again. She opened her hand to show Maggie the wedding ring. "I can't go."

Awkwardly, Maggie pulled Katherine into a hug, stroking her hair. Katherine's sobs slowed, but she settled into the crook of Maggie's neck, feeling the other woman's breath on her ear. To Katherine's surprise, her nipples swelled under the pressure of Maggie's chest.

Suddenly Maggie let her go, breathing ragged herself. "Sorry," Maggie said. "I've got to go." Her smile was shy, for once. "You smell nice, whatever that scent is."

Sorry for what, Katherine wondered as Maggie almost ran for her truck. Sorry about David? For the hug? Or for letting go? She stood there wrapped in David's scent and the memory of Maggie's hug.

That night there was lightning high in the west, another lie told by the summer. The cats were out administering small, furry death in the darkness. The chickens were up in their pecan tree. Katherine lay almost naked in the old brass bed, wearing only David's oxford shirt, unbuttoned and open against the heat. She watched the flashes in the sky and thought of the drying stock tank and the death of their farm. David. Her fingers strayed to her nipples. Then she found she was thinking of Maggie.

"I've always been with men," Katherine whispered to herself. She remembered her lovers. Danny, in high school, with the crooked, freckled cock. Her first blow job, a prom night gift for him, but they'd never fucked, no matter how hard he begged. It was all dry humping. He'd tried to eat her once, but just made a fumble of it and came all over the carpet in her mom's den.

Ronnie, in junior college. She smiled, gently rubbing her clitoris. Ronnie had known how to do yeoman's work at her genitals—clitoris, vagina, his to command. After her sixth orgasm one evening he'd just, well, slipped on in. Katherine giggled, fingers straying down to begin spreading her labia, opening herself as she dampened.

Then Ronnie had taken her camping with his roommate Butch, and somewhere inside the tequila and the laughs and the skinny-dipping, she'd slept with both of them at once. She didn't feel good about being around Butch afterwards, so she broke up with Ronnie, which meant she was free when she met David.

She smiled again. David. There'd been no one else since they met, no need for anyone. She was his Feast Dish and his Heart's Desire and his Rack of Pleasure and a dozen other names whispered in passion and in lazy love.

David.

Tears stinging her eyes, Katherine paused to slip her ring onto the knuckle of her index finger. The ring was still crusted with mud from the stock tank. Lying on her side with one leg cocked upward, she pushed into her vagina with the ring, using her thumb and middle fingers to spread her labia. Pinching her nipple, lit by summer lightning, Katherine pushed and shoved and fucked herself with the ring, tearing and bruising at her vagina, cutting her nipple with her fingernails, as if pleasure and pain together could draw her husband back from the darkness.

She screamed into the summer night, screaming her orgasm and her pain, bloodying the sheets like red rain on parched soil. Shivering, throat raw, she cried herself to sleep with the thought of a sleeveless checkered shirt.

Katherine woke the next day with her wedding ring loose inside her vagina. She had to limp to the bathroom and work with lotion to remove it, she was so dry and tight. It took a while to clean up herself, her clothes, and her bed, using precious water, but she felt better than she had since David died. Katherine found an old jar of silver paste and slipped the bloody ring into it. She hid the jar in the back of the medicine shelf. Then she went and found a worn flannel shirt, checkered like Maggie's, and put it on, heedless of the heat.

In the kitchen, she checked the calendar, wondering when Maggie would be back. She was glad of the days of waiting, because she needed to heal a little more.

Sunday brought a squall line out of the north, one of those Texas storms that looks like God's fury but turns into sixty-mile-per-hour winds with a trace of rain so light it might be the tears of His angels. Still and all, it was the first real hint of rain the lying weather had brought in three months.

Katherine stood in the cracking mud of the stock tank and watched the black line on the horizon stalking forth on blazing legs of light. She wore another of David's oxfords, with the flannel shirt open over it, flapping in the wind.

"David," she asked the wind, "are you okay?"

Live oak leaves, musty cutouts of brown, swirled around her feet.

"I'm not doing so well, David. I had to sell the last of the cattle. The tractor's gone. I still have your truck, though." She stared into the wind, eyes watering, or maybe crying. It didn't matter which, not now.

She could hear a hail of pecans knocked loose by the wind, rattling on the barn roof.

"I'm going to have to take a job in Lockhart, maybe all the way to Austin."

A few stray drops struck her face. Not rain, but at least the remembrance that water still existed somewhere in the world. Katherine drew a deep breath, smelling the ozone of the storm and the swirling dust driven before it. David's cologne touched her nose for a moment on wind, as the tears of angels wetted her face again.

She sighed and was happy.

Monday her body felt better, but her heart ached. Maggie didn't come. That night Katherine touched herself for hours, but never needed the orgasm.

Tuesday Maggie called, a hurried monologue. "I'm sorry, Kath, the truck's got a flat and Opal said Earl would fix it but Earl's nephew Big Billy has the shop jack down in Fentress and I can't tow with the Pontiac since I broke the leaf springs, and my God, look at the time, I'll call tomorrow."

"Are you okay?" Katherine asked the dial tone.

On Wednesday Katherine wept, and tried to find peace sitting in the dried stock tank, but the squall that had brought David to her on Sunday had taken him away again. The lying clouds changed direction and moved closer together, and for the first time in almost sixty days the thermometer on the porch didn't crack one hundred. Back in the tub, she couldn't come no matter how much she needed to.

The phone rang that night as she sat in the cool, dry bathtub counting cobwebs. It took her a while to get out and answer, but the caller was patient.

"I'm sorry," Maggie said. "I'll come tomorrow."

"Please," Katherine whispered.

She smiled at the dial tone until the operator came on to see if she needed assistance.

Thursday Katherine got the cattle back in the corral for Maggie. Then she ran a full bath for the first time in seven weeks. She was sick of sponging clean, and she wanted to be ready for Maggie. Katherine washed her hair, twice, and shaved her legs, which she hadn't bothered with since David died. Then she did her nails, and added a tiny bit of makeup to her face. She even found a bottle of her perfume, which she hadn't worn since the funeral.

"What the hell am I doing?" Katherine asked the mirror. She couldn't decide if she was worried about cheating on David, or scared of being attracted to Maggie. It didn't matter, she told herself. What mattered was that she might be happy again.

Katherine put on the teal skirt again, and her good boots, brown leather that came up to her knees. In a box in the attic she found an old gauze blouse from college, one that hid the curve of her breast but showed the brown of her nipples.

She left her hair down, brushing it out two hundred strokes on each side. Katherine went out on the porch, smiled at the driveway, and said, "I'm ready."

Katherine waited an hour or more, not enough to sap her contentment but sufficient to put an edge on. The faithless clouds were piling in the southeast. The wind was different, different than it had been in months. As Katherine stared at the sky, she heard the gravel crunch of tires: Maggie's truck, an old navy blue Dodge with dinner-plate headlights, towing a thirty-foot livestock trailer.

Katherine stepped off the porch, walked toward the truck. Maggie smiled through the bug-smeared windshield, then got out.

Maggie's curly brown hair shone. She wore a different flannel shirt, sleeves torn off this one as well, and clean, black jeans with silver-tipped roach-stomper boots.

Katherine's voice was light, like tiny bells. "You going to herd cattle in those boots?"

"Never know what might happen." Maggie extended her hands, palm down, reaching for Katherine's. "You feeling better?"

Katherine took Maggie's hands, pushed them together as if in prayer, then pulled them to her lips. She kissed the fingertips. "Much better, now."

Maggie stepped so they were standing almost nose-to-nose. "I'm sorry I took so long. I had to think."

This is it, Katherine told herself. "Me, too." She laughed. "Thinking, I mean, not being sorry."

Maggie traced Katherine's chin with one blunt finger. "Good thoughts?" Maggie whispered.

"Oh, very good." Katherine took a deep breath, remembering David, and gathered Maggie to a full-bodied hug, kissing the other woman. Katherine meant to go lightly, slowly, like a first date should, but she was betrayed by the hunger of the last empty year. Maggie parted her lips and their tongues slipped together. Katherine shivered.

"I've never...," Katherine whispered, pulling away. She wasn't sure what came next.

"Don't worry," Maggie said. "I have."

Lightning struck the woods, the thunder almost immediate. The chickens shrieked and as the wind whipped up, twirling Katherine's skirt and spreading her long hair like a banner. Leaves whirled, carrying the scents of storm and forest.

It was David, Katherine thought, come back again on the wind and driving the water before him like heaven's cattle. "Yes!" she screamed. "Give me my goddamned water!"

Holding hands, she and Maggie danced in the yard as the giant raindrops fell. It began to pour, a real Texas frog-strangler that would close roads and carry off bridges.

"Come on," Katherine shouted, tugging Maggie's hand. "The stock tank!"

They ran through the gate into the west fields. Katherine skidded them up the little rise to the edge of the dried pond.

It was still baked at the bottom, greenish slime piled around, but already the mud was running with little tiny floods, cracked edges softening and crumbling even as the two of them watched. The feeder creek ran with a strengthening trickle. The heavens dumped water straight down.

Katherine could feel her nipples like giant candied dates. She wanted Maggie, right there, under the falling water, in the pond, where she'd found the wedding ring. She wanted Maggie so she could bid farewell to David. Katherine wanted love to return from its drowning pool. She pointed at the ground, tugging Maggie's arm downward.

"What?" shouted Maggie over the pounding of the rain. "Here?"

Katherine cupped one hand over Maggie's ear, holding her other hand. "No, silly, down in there."

They tumbled down the bank, rolling in the mud. Katherine let Maggie pull her into a deep kiss, hands tugging through Katherine's long blonde hair as Katherine rubbed Maggie's scalp, her back, her broad ass through the jeans. Maggie wiggled downward toward Katherine's dark nipples standing like beacons through the soaked gauze blouse.

She kissed like a greedy child, sucking and gnawing right through the gauze. Katherine hugged Maggie close, face up, drinking the rain as the other woman knelt before her, hungry at her breasts. The gauze itched, tweaked, even burned as Maggie's tongue and lips and teeth worked at Katherine's nipple. Maggie's hand massaged Katherine's right breast, while the other worked up under her prairie skirt, stroking Katherine's thigh, along the inside, up the tendon, across her ass, around to the front, a broken fingernail snagging in a curl of pubic hair, an inviting tension.

Katherine released Maggie's head and unfastened her skirt. Still wearing knee-high boots and her translucent gauze blouse, Katherine lay backward in the mud, the rising water at her ankles. Maggie mouthed loving words at Katherine, unheard over the pounding rain, then gently spread Katherine's thighs, kissed her belly button, smoothed hands over her flanks, began to chew at the top of her pubic hair. The rain fell so hard it bruised them both.

Lightning struck again, thunder crackling. Rain steamed from the parched ground. The mud deepened, smelling green and brown. The cattle bellowed fear in the corral as Maggie licked at Katherine's clitoris, holding back her labia with spread fingers. Maggie's other hand supported Katherine's ass, spreading the cheeks and gently working a muddy thumb into her anus. Katherine breathed hard, missing her rhythm for a moment, but the fingers were damp and gentle, so she relaxed into it and pushed her pubic bone into Maggie's face.

Maggie worked harder in the pounding rain, scraping Katherine's clitoris between tongue and teeth, fingering her vagina with one hand and her anus with the other, all the penetrations in the world at once. Over and over Maggie drove Katherine past the edge of screaming orgasm—three, five, seven times. Maggie's touch kept changing—blowing air, then sucking it in through clenched teeth, kissing, teasing, gentle, rough. Katherine drank rain and shrieked to the sky as water lapped her calves and filled her boots. Her body split open again and again and again.

"Ahhh...my sweet...," Katherine said as Maggie rolled over, almost waist deep in the stock tank.

"Your hair, darling," Maggie began, then laughed. Katherine could feel the weight of the mud.

"You too," she told Maggie. Maggie's boots were coated with mud, her jeans all but ruined. "My turn, now."

Maggie pulled back, just a bit, rolling away. "I don't, I don't look like you. Oh Kath, you're like some kind of goddess. I'm old, and fat, and..."

"And beautiful," Katherine said. She pulled off the drenched, torn gauze, wearing only the tall leather boots now. "With your smile and my hair and juice all over your lips." She crawled through the mud, licked Maggie's face and hands clean of rain and mucus and salt and little curled blonde hairs.

Then she undid the pearl buttons of Maggie's checkered shirt, pulling it open to show the heavy underwire bra.

"Your breasts are so small and pointed," Maggie whispered.

Katherine undid the hooks. "Yours are so large and glorious." She had never kissed a woman's nipple. It was larger and fuller than a man's, and the breast beneath, pressing like a pad against her face, was a completely new experience. Maggie's breasts were enormous. They *were* Maggie.

"I want to taste you, every part of you," Katherine whispered in Maggie's ear. She set to work practicing what Maggie had preached on her.

They made muddy love in the pond, naked but for Katherine's boots, for two hours, crawling slowly up the bank as the water rose, clothes forgotten under the rising tide. As the rain moved off, they lay along the top of the bank. Katherine traced the lines of Maggie's swollen labia and clitoris as Maggie gently ran her tongue over Katherine's inner thigh, and across her genitals. They were mapping, now, studying the territory into which the rain had earlier rushed them.

Katherine adored Maggie's thighs, like tree trunks, the way they had enfolded her head as she went down on Maggie, the way Maggie cracked Katherine's neck when she came, thighs closed and shivering. Katherine adored Maggie's great breasts, could lose herself in their huge pink aureoles and the broad, shallow buttons of her nipples.

Water dripped from the trees, burbled in the grass, changed the smell of the fields as utterly as if it were a different country. Katherine listened to the sounds of renewal for a while, enjoying the warmth of Maggie's tongue. Her world felt right again.

"Maggie," she said.

"Mm?"

"You asked what I was going to do."

Maggie sat up on her elbow, looking Katherine in the eyes. "And?"

Katherine swung herself around and kissed Maggie, pressing their bodies together, her wet leather boots wrapped around Maggie's left leg. "I'm going to remember David, and work at loving you, and accept whatever the rain brings me."

Maggie glanced at the stock tank, swollen full from three hours of hard Texas rain. "Maybe I'll leave those cattle here for a while, now that you've got water again."

Together they swam the stock tank, diving for their clothes

and Maggie's boots. Later, Katherine gave her wedding ring back to the brown water, this time with blessings.

PLEASURE RIDE

Skian McGuire

"Wanna go for a ride?"

My girlfriend grins down at me, squinting into the setting sun. Birds are singing their lazy evening songs across the lower pasture. I inhale the sweet smell of grass and wildflowers, the rich tang of manure, the hot breath of a horse trying to lip a treat out of my shirt pocket. She doesn't mean, on horseback. I fish out the peppermint I brought and unwrap it before I get the front of me drenched in slobber, and consider the proposition.

I don't have anything against horses. Ever since my first and last dizzying attempt at sitting on the back of one, I've maintained a friendly relationship with all the farm's equine inhabitants, both my feet planted firmly on the ground.

I love Lady almost as much as Carlie does. She was a boon companion to the shy and awkward teenager my lover was, before she'd gone away to college. Now Carlie's home again to take over the farm none of her brothers wanted, and we're all getting a little long in the tooth. Lady is safe from having to teach me horsemanship, and so are Maggie and Molly, the Belgians Carlie uses for mowing and tedding and baling. Nor will I ever ride Maggie or Molly's future progeny, the potential for breeding being Carlie's reason for working mares instead of the traditional geldings, practical Yankee that she is. They're so huge I wouldn't think of climbing onto one of them even in a nightmare. No, I'll never be a horseman of any stripe. But luckily, it isn't a saddle my sweetie has in mind.

I stare pointedly at the bulge in her crotch. She must have gone up to the house to shower and change after the evening milking then come out on horseback looking for me.

"Is that a carrot in your pocket or are you happy to see me?" I drawl in my best Mae West.

She laughs out loud and swings herself down. "I'm always happy to see you. Don't you know that?" With Lady's reins in one hand and my hand in the other, she walks us back to the horse barn, and the first pale stars are just visible in the cobalt blue above.

I wait while Carlie unsaddles the patient mare and sends her out to join the big girls. We watch Lady trot out to the small herd, spry as a filly in the cool evening air, in spite of her twenty-odd years.

"Wanna go upstairs?" Waving a hand at stairs that are little more than a wide-stepped ladder, Carlie gestures a gentlemanly "after you," and she doesn't have to ask me twice.

"You do that just to watch my ass, don't you?" I ask when she pulls herself up into the hayloft after me.

She just smiles. Her straw summer cowboy hat has been left down below, or she might have tipped it at me.

"You!" I grab her belt and draw her close for a kiss so long and deep it leaves us both gasping at the end of it.

"What did you have in mind, pardner?" I stroke the hard-on in the front of her Levi's. "Ravishing an unsuspecting girl in the hay?"

She chuckles. I don't know which part she finds funniest, "ravishing," "unsuspecting," or, most likely, "girl." I never was much of one even in my younger days when roles were out of fashion, and now you'd be hard pressed to pick which of us was the more butch, my sweetie or me.

She knows just what I'm thinking. "You go on and bring her here," she tells me, "and I'll be happy to oblige."

"I just bet you would. But you'd better get her yourself or you won't be able to follow her up the stairs."

Her mouth finds my neck, where she's taken to kissing and nuzzling very distractingly. "True," she murmurs. "I'll just have to stay here with the big ol' bulldyke I've got."

"Good thing," I tell her, out of breath, "'cause she's already hot for you."

She tugs the hem of my T-shirt upward. Taking the hint, I yank it unceremoniously over my head. Carlie helps skin off the sports bra that's plastered to me with sweat, then she draws all the usefulness out of me with her mouth sucking hard on my nipple.

I groan. "Enough of that," I finally manage, and get a handful of hair to pull her off me before my knees get too weak to hold me up.

"Ouch!" She says, laughing, "I need a haircut!" Her graying buzzcut is barely long enough to get a grip on. I shut off her words with my tongue thrust between her lips.

My hands work the buttons of her plaid summer shirt, then devote some frenzied moments to yanking out her shirttails while alternately slapping her hands away from my pants button. We break off the kiss, laughing. "Not so fast," I tell her. I grab the hard length of her cock through denim and fasten my mouth on a nipple through her thin cotton wifebeater. She gasps. I push her backward toward the hay.

I don't know where the popular mythology arose from, that haylofts are fun and romantic places to fuck in. Even if it's not the loose-piled hay mow of years gone by, but neatly piled in tight-pressed bales, dried grass is a prickly, poky, scratchy misery of a thing. It sticks to everything. It gets in everywhere. My girlfriend, having been raised on a farm—this very one, in fact—knows this. Which is why she'd come up here earlier in the day and tucked a canvas tarp over the layer of bales, then spread a quilt on it. Like a good Scout, always prepared, she'd carried up a box with condoms and lube and a couple of bottles of water, too.

Carlie sits down hard when the makeshift bed hits the back of her thighs. It hasn't been a hot day, and the air is pleasant on my bare skin, the loft doors swung wide to reveal the silhouette of a plastic owl in the opening. I can hear the lowing of one of the cows from the other side of the field, where a few are still milling about in the yard outside the milking parlor like church ladies after the service. I picture the Jerseys in flowered hats and print dresses, and giggle.

I'm unzipping her fly and hauling out the big brown dick she's stuffed in there. She asks, "Are you laughing at my cock?"

"I would never laugh at your cock." I boing it back and forth a couple times to show her how seriously I take it. "Never," I repeat. "I love your cock."

Leaning back on her elbows, Carlie's eyes narrow suspiciously, watching me play with her prosthetic appendage. Unlike the men I've heard of who give their dicks pet names and refer to them by the masculine pronoun, my sweetie insists that her dick is a girl. She doesn't have a name, but she's definitely of the feminine gender. "I'll show you how much I love her," I tell Carlie, and rip open a condom packet. I pop the rolled-up condom in my mouth.

Carlie's eyes get wide as she watches me work the rubber over the head of her cock with just my lips and tongue. She groans when I unroll it almost all the way down the shaft, drawing her cock into the back of my throat while I massage the rubber over it. "Oh, God," she breathes, "yes, suck it."

I do it the way I know she likes it, whirling my tongue around the head and stroking the shaft with my hand so it drives the base against her, pounding her clit. She can come fucking my mouth if I let her. I stop just before she does.

She's panting, flat on her back. Her eyes open and fix on me pleadingly, so much like a calf I have to smile, but I know just what I want.

"Scoot on back," I tell her, unzipping my jeans while I toe off my sneakers, and she does, digging the heels of her beat-up old cowboy boots into the tarp. She knows better than to take them off. I like to fuck her with her boots on.

Sometimes I like to fuck her in her dusty brown chaps, too, my big butch girlfriend who always wanted to grow up to be John Wayne. I know how much she likes the ladies—always ready to rescue a damsel in distress whether she needs rescuing or not—but a lonely cowboy won't say no to a little comfort and relief from one of his fellows, out where the prairie meets the stars. Sometimes I put on a Stetson myself, just to look at her from under the brim. Sometimes she wears the five-pointed sheriff's star I bought her for her birthday, and I get to be the no-account cattle rustler. I won't begrudge her a night on the town, looking for that whore with the heart of gold, or maybe romancing the pretty young widow woman. Back here on the ranch, I take what I please.

She's smiling by the time my jeans hit the floorboards. I set the pump bottle of Slippery Stuff down within easy reach and throw a leg over her, and she's got a handful of it to slather on her cock before I even settle in.

"Not so fast!" I plant my mouth on her for another breath-stealing, heart-stopping kiss. For good measure, I get a grip on the control knobs and twist. She gasps and bucks her hips, as I knew she would, with nipples wired directly to her clit. Sometimes I wonder if she could come from just my sucking on them, but I've never been patient enough to try. Carlie might fault my impatience in bed, but she also knows she never has to wait very long when she's as worked up as this.

I push the head of her cock just inside my cunt and wait there, letting her eyes focus, letting her get a good look. "Oh," she says, and shifts, impatient herself now.

"Wait!" I command, "Don't move," and slowly, slowly, lower myself on her, watching her face as she watches her cock disappear inside me, all the way to the hilt.

"God, yes," I groan, unable to hold back. It feels so good. I draw back and ride it all the way down, again.

She can't hold still anymore, and her hips are bucking, driving her cock into me with every stroke while I ride her. I can't stay upright on this wild mount, and I have to double over and cling to her while she fucks me. I fuck her right back, slamming down hard enough that I know she can feel it. This is the way I want to make her come, with her cock filling me, fucking me like she was born with it, feeling the wave of orgasm building in me while I watch her eyes glaze over and finally squinch shut, and she's ready to explode with her own orgasm. This is what I want, and this is what I take, riding hell-bent for leather.

In the evening cool, the sweat drying on my bare skin, my sweetie pulls the comforter up around us and cuddles me in the falling dark. A million stars sparkle through the loft door above us, and the chirp of the crickets is a slow song tonight, with fall coming on. We snuggle together long enough to watch the sliver of a moonrise.

At last, I sigh. "Time to be getting back to the house. The dogs will think we've left them forever. And the morning milking will be coming awfully soon."

She laughs and runs a hand down my bare flank under the covers. "I could see about something else coming awfully soon. We have time."

I shiver under her touch, and goofy with sex and laziness, tell her, "It's nice to have time." We do, too—all the years behind us and more ahead of us, knock on wood. It would be a blessing to see our lives together rolling out in such grand measure no matter where we were, no matter what fate brought us. I shiver again, with thoughts of how different everything might have been.

"Besides, I told them..."

After all these years, I know without having to ask that it's the dogs she means.

"...I was going out for a pleasure ride."

"Yup." I snuggle in closer, absolutely contented. "That it certainly was."

PETROGLYPHS

Toby Rider

Something moved among the Douglas firs, where the forest thickened and sloped upward toward burnished rock. The short hairs at the nape of Sigri's neck prickled with the sense of being watched.

Outwardly undisturbed, she went about the business of pitching camp on the open plateau. No staring toward the trees or up at the rocky outcropping whose crevices concealed, she knew, a narrow cave; no pausing to listen for movement; but aware, as always, of every detail of her surroundings.

Copperlode grazed serenely on patches of autumn-browned grass among the gone-to-seed wildflowers, lupine and columbine and monkeyflower. She raised her chestnut head from time to time to cock an ear toward the forest, but without alarm. Sigri pretended not to notice. No grizzly, for sure. Even without the light breeze from that direction the horse would have been aware of danger.

When the mountain tent was firmly anchored and a small fire begun in the old circle of blackened stones, Sigri went to lean her close-cropped head against Copperlode's glossy neck. She murmured a few words, stroking the soft muzzle, until the mare's head twitched and one ear pointed again toward the trees.

Sigri moved away at a tangent to the direction of the horse's attention. When she reached the brushy edge of the woods she drew her knife and hacked away at deadwood. Her only apparent concern was the gathering of fuel for the fire, but tension built in her gut as she progressed slowly, casually, toward where someone waited; a tension that spread in ripples up and down her rangy body. Still she gave no sign of awareness, or of the tingling in her ass whenever her back was to the treeline.

Finally she dropped her armload of small branches, sheathed her knife, and stood stretching and rubbing her back. Stetson tilted against the sun's glare, she gazed out over the plateau and beyond to the mountains and valleys of the Absaroka-Beartooth Wilderness.

Now. At any instant. Now the attack would come.

She would come. Pi'tamaken. Running Eagle.

Only a whisper of sound...Sigri whirled to meet the onslaught, the thought flashing through her mind that twenty years ago Pita would have made no sound at all.

Arms raised, hands locked in each other's bruising grip, they strained together, strength against strength. Pita tried to hook Sigri's knee, but Sigri jerked a thigh hard into her opponent's elkhide-clad crotch. When they fell together her Stetson was jolted loose but she managed to stay on top, her cropped yellow-white head leaning above the other's bronzed face and tangle of long black hair.

Pita tried to twist away. Sigri's head plunged suddenly toward her exposed throat, teeth nipping hard at the salty skin, counting coup according to their private ritual. The familiar taste sent a ripple of heat through her own throat and chest and beyond. Once she wouldn't have hesitated to draw blood, but that had been long ago, and the world a different place. No knowing what might be in blood these days.

She raised her head. Pita glared up at her, eyes fierce in her angular face. Then she grinned, her teeth flashing white. "Good one," she conceded.

Sigri worked her thigh against the elkhide with less violence, or maybe just a different flavor. Pita began to arch toward the pressure. The old, imperative ache hit Sigri's cunt like summer lightning, but Pita lurched abruptly aside and then upward with a whoop of triumph, and suddenly Sigri was on the bottom, needles and twigs prickling into her back and ass. The scent of arousal mingled with the sharp tang of crushed fir seedlings. She could see in Pita's face that the moment had passed.

"Helluva place you picked for bushwhacking," Sigri said. "What were you gonna do if I didn't come close enough and kindly turn my back? Wait to scalp me in my sleep?"

Pita rolled off, leaving Sigri dangling between chill and heat. "Something like that. If the smell of coffee didn't drag me out first. But you knew all along somebody was there. What made you think it was me?"

"What did you expect, fer chrissake? One, you only made about as much noise as a pair of bull elk in rut, whereas most folks would've trampled the place like a herd of bison. I nearly didn't hear you. Two, that's one of my own horses you've got stashed over behind those boulders." They eyed each other warily as they stood up. No need to add that it was twenty-five years to the day since they'd first discovered this place, and the cave beyond. And twenty since the last time they'd met here. Promises had been made. Not counted on, maybe, in recent years, and neither had gone so far as to remind the other; but here they were.

"Your pretty lady back at the ranch seemed to think you wouldn't mind if I trailed you up here. Even outfitted me and trucked me in." Pita eyed Sigri sidelong as they strode toward the campsite. "That's some mighty appetizing armful you've got back there."

"Emmaline been giving out free samples?"

"Just coffee and pie good enough to keep any cowboy close to home. Doesn't seem to have fattened you up much, though." She tweaked Sigri's lean rump. Sigri tweaked right back, harder, finding more to get a handle on. Running Eagle didn't appear to have been doing quite as much running as she used to. Still not that far past slender, though.

"Guess you'll just have to put up with camp coffee for now," Sigri said, ignoring Pita's unasked question as she added wood to the fire and set up the tripod for hanging the pot.

"So does she?" Pita persisted. "Keep you close to home?" The fact that the ranch was two hours of driving and three of trail riding away was irrelevant, and they both knew it.

"Emmaline's got no worries, no matter where I go. Or who I do." Sigri finished messing with the pot and sat down to wait for the coffee to boil. No need to mention that she'd had little enough inclination to wander these last few years. Sending Pita up here had been a generous gesture, and Sigri had no doubt that Emmaline had known just what she was about. Emmaline always did know.

Pita surveyed her closely for a moment, then nodded and went off to bring the hidden horse and gear to the campsite. When they sat side by side at last, devouring hot coffee and cold ham sandwiches, proximity and unresolved arousal went a long way toward restoring the bonds of years long past. But not all the way.

"Haven't heard from you in a while," Sigri commented. Two years since that last brief post card from Durango, down in Anasazi cliff-dweller territory. That had been about the time Emmaline moved in. Sigri'd be damned, though, if she'd let on that she'd kept count. "How's it been going? Still irresistible to all those eager young archaeology grad students? I don't imagine you have any problem keeping your bedroll warm out on those digs."

"Nope. No problem at all. But damn, they get younger every year!"

"What's the matter, Professor, you getting tired of teaching youngsters the same old games?"

"Most of 'em you made up in the first place," Pita said with a reminiscent smile. "That one about buttering the sweet corn always goes over real well, whether they're convinced it's a genuine ritual or not."

"Nothing like getting an ear of corn nice and slippery the natural way," Sigri agreed. Her boyish grin would never grow old, no matter how many lines time and weather etched on her face. "Sprinkling on the cornmeal and licking spirals through it was a good one, too. Can't go wrong with corn when it comes to ritual material." Her tone was light, but the way she remembered it, those things they'd done with and to each other all those years ago had always had a touch of sacrament about them.

Well, maybe not always. "I'll bet they appreciate the hell out of Little Big Horn, too," she added. "But I expect you've gone more high-tech by now, with silicone or whatever they're using these days." Not that Sigri didn't have her own fairly state-of-the-art mail-order equipment stashed in a handy drawer at home.

"Little Big Horn was always just for you," Pita said gruffly. "You made him. " She stared into the fire, which seemed brighter now that the sun had edged below the highest peak. "Like you made me."

Sigri sensed the sudden change of mood and searched to find the kind of words that seemed to be called for.

"Always struck me that was pretty much a team effort," she said, knowing it sounded lame. What was Pita looking for, after all this time? After all she could have had if she'd wanted to stick around for it?

But Pita seemed to have some words penned up that needed setting loose. "So how did it happen," she mused, eyes fixed on the stick she was poking gently among the embers at the fire's edge, "that I turned out to be the college professor, instead of you?"

She didn't look much like an academic just then, dressed in traditional elkhide, black hair streaming wild, her strong dark face needing only a few streaks of war paint across the high cheekbones to strike terror into the hearts of intruding settlers. "I never had any use for books or history or any kind of learning until you dug up those old woman warrior stories and made me read them. Woman Chief of the Crow. Running Eagle of my own Blackfeet tribe, who even took a wife. You gave me my true name."

"As I recall, I had to tie you to a fence post to get you to hold still long enough to listen to me read 'em out loud," Sigri said. "I got tired of the both of us always picking fights just for an excuse to grab each other, not knowing what we were doing or who we really were."

"Hah! You couldn't have tied me to anything on your best day!" Pita retorted. "But you did know enough to look in books, and those hippie magazines later with all those Two-Spirit movement articles."

"I had a little help from that Miss Edmonds who started the library in behind the Post Office," Sigri said. Just knowing Miss Edmonds had understood what she needed and not been scandalized had helped her as much as any book. Not many, she knew, were that lucky, even these days.

"So now," Pita said, as if she'd follow Sigri's train of thought, "I'm the one who passes along the lore, with everything else I can dig up, literally, about the ancient history of my people."

"And I'm the one tied to the land," Sigri said. "These mountains and plains. And the horses. That's all I need."

"And Emmaline?"

"She goes with the deal," Sigri acknowledged. "With the plains, and the ranch, and the horses. All part of the same thing." She flipped the dregs from her coffee cup into the fire and was on her feet before their aromatic sizzling had subsided. "How about you?" she asked, stretching out a weathered hand. "Is Running Eagle still part of the mountains?"

Pita reached up to grip Sigri's proffered hand. "I'm here," she said simply, and yanked herself erect. There was an instant when they leaned apart, balancing each other's weight; and then both arms tightened and their bodies collided.

It was a hug to leave bruises, more like two grizzlies than lovers. There would be finger marks on backs and asses for days. Sigri bit along the side of Pita's neck and stopped short of drawing blood this time only because lips and tongue demanded their turn at the feel and taste of her skin. Pita tore Sigri's shirt open with her teeth and chewed at a shoulder as though softening up the sinews before devouring them. The need rose between them with such demand that gutteral sounds rumbled in their throats.

"Here?" Sigri gasped, "Or up there?" jerking her head in approximately the direction of the rocky cave on the mountainside. Pita's answer was a hand shifted from clutching at Sigri's ass to thrusting against her denim-clad crotch. "Plenty to go around," she muttered, ducking her head against Sigri's tingling chest so she could see to unzip her jeans and get her fingers where they'd do the most good. Sigri got her hand inside the elkhide trousers almost as soon.

It was all hard thrusts and fast reactions, until tensions building for years found sudden, sharp release, as near to simultaneous as made no difference. "God *damn*!" Sigri panted, when she could speak. "We've still got it!"

"And that's just for openers," Pita said, struggling to control her breathing. "I'll meet you up there." She knelt to dig in her pack, then moved off across the plateau, slowly at first, accelerating into a smooth lope that took her swiftly into the forest.

When Pita's lithe form had melted into the trees, Sigri turned away to bank the fire and check on the horses, then followed at her own striding pace.

The trail, such as it was, ran along beside a narrow stream. Sigri was glad to find no signs that any creatures besides wild ones had been this way in recent years, except for Pita, who, at this moment, was as good as wild.

The last stretch was steep. Sigri paused to try catch her

breath where the trees ended abruptly at the rocky outcropping, although anticipation had as much to do with it as exertion.

There were easy hand- and footholds in the stone at first, but higher up it would have been slow going for anyone who hadn't been this way before. Sigri pressed her body close against a vertical rock-edge barring the way and swung one long leg over to the unseen side. Her foot found the knob she knew was there, and her hand reached out to find the slanting finger crack high above; and then she was all the way around, leaping from her tenuous hold into the narrow, gravel-floored entrance of the cave.

Sigri's eyes adjusted to the relative dusk inside. There had been a time when Pita might have lunged at her at this point, but their games had moved on to something more like ritual, and the place had taken on a touch of something almost sacred.

She almost wished Pita *would* lunge. But there she was, several yards inside, waiting as motionless as the stone pressing into her back; and as naked, except for a soft deerskin pouch on a thong around her neck. She had built a small fire with wood gathered along the way, and, though it gave off only a little heat, Sigri felt no chill when she, too, left her clothes at the entrance.

She stopped just inside for a moment to duck her head toward four small dark splotches on the cave wall. Painted handprints, left hundreds of years ago. Had they been meant as a message, or a simple affirmation of someone's presence? Or existence? Twenty-five years ago two girls in need of affirmation of their own identities had drawn wishful conclusions. The prints were small enough, after all, to have been made by women. So they had left marks of their own to puzzle explorers hundreds of years in the future, deeper marks, laboring at them each time they returned.

Sigri moved on in, gripped by the increasing urgency of the present. Pita stood silently, pressed against the rock wall, arms at an angle from her sides, legs slightly spread. Only her black eyes moved, burning into Sigri's pale blue ones. Stifling the urge to lunge herself, Sigri fell into the remembered ritual, lifting the deerskin pouch gently and drawing from it a stick of compressed charcoal wrapped in cornhusks.

"Pi'tamaken," she murmured huskily. "Running Eagle." The roughness of the husks raised a flush on Pita's bronzed skin as

Sigri rolled the still-wrapped cylinder along her collarbones and across her breasts, forcefully enough to scrape against dark, hardened nipples. Then down the curve of her belly, and lower, pausing to thrust a few times between her thighs until wet streaks darkened the pale, dry husks.

Pita stood outwardly unmoved, but a pulse throbbed in her throat and the beating of her heart disturbed the smooth skin of her chest. The tender flesh of Sigri's own cunt and clit swelled and moistened, and she knew that Pita's body mirrored that reaction. The mingling of their musky scents was intensified by the drifting smoke of cedar and sage.

Sigri lifted the cornhusk packet and tore away the covering with strong teeth. Pita's taste clung to her lips and tongue. When enough of the black stick was unwrapped, she splayed her left hand across Pita's belly and traced around it, leaving a five-fingered mark on her skin. Then she drew a line down one side of Pita's crotch until she hit the rock wall. Sigri could feel, without seeing, the shallow groove chipped into the stone years ago to follow the entire outline of Pita's body.

Down along the inner thigh, the muscular calf, the ankle's bones and tendons, she drew the charcoal, following that groove. Her left hand still pressed into Pita's flesh hard enough to leave bruises as she knelt to draw her line along the outer leg, hip, waist, arm, smearing the skin as well. When she stood to trace around shoulder and neck and head, her body was pressed so closely against Pita's that she could feel their hearts pounding in counterpoint.

Sigri switched hands to draw the line down the other side. This time her fingers gripped Pita's flesh lower down, her palm pushing hard against the silent woman's mound.

"Don't move," she warned, kneeling to complete the outline, moving the charcoal inch by slow inch upward toward the triangle between Pita's thighs; but her left hand urged something different, sliding downward and kneading flesh grown hot and slippery. Still Pita was immobile, except for her quickened breathing.

"Almost done," Sigri murmured, so close that her breath stirred Pita's pubic hairs; and then, as the lines met and the pattern was complete, she dropped the charcoal and leaned forward to taste what she'd been hungering for.

Pita still did not move. Her stillness became a challenge. Sigri grabbed at her hips now with both hands and licked and bit at the flesh so clearly eager for what the will resisted. Pita's thighs tensed.

Sigri worked her tongue deeply into Pita's warm, welcoming cunt, then abruptly withdrew, and suddenly Pita's hands were clutching at her short pale hair and trying to force her head closer. Instead, Sigri's fingers took over, thrusting far into the depths she had once known better than her own.

Pita's head tilted back. A sound began in her chest like the low rumble of a cougar sure of its prey. Then, as Sigri pounded into her faster and harder, Pita's voice rose in pitch until her final cries could have rivaled the screams of an eagle.

When the echoes had subsided from both flesh and stone, Pita slid down along the rock wall and slumped against Sigri's shoulder. They leaned together for a few moments, in perfect balance, until Pita lifted her head.

"That's only half of what I came for," she said, not altogether steadily. "Up against the wall, now. If you dare." Some intense emotion underlay the mocking words.

This ritual had always had more meaning for Pita than for Sigri, who looked up now at the cave wall, where the newly-blackened outline overlapped another one. The pair was linked so that the grooves defining arms and legs and torsos intersected as though two bodies stood close together, each with a hand on the other's crotch. Their shapes were curved just enough to show that they were female, which, in Sigri's case, had required a bit of exaggeration of her rangy lines; and, between each pair of hips, a line coiled into a spiral. Future archaeologists should have no trouble interpreting their symbolism.

Sigri did, of course, stand and press her back against her own outline on the rough rock wall. If she didn't get fucked by Pita pretty damned soon she'd be banging her fist against that same wall. And when Pita stood before her, outlined by the glow of the fire, naked and wild as some shamanic spirit from the depths of time, Sigri felt the power of the ritual grip her.

"*Sakwo'mapi akikwan,*" Pita murmured. "*Matsops.*" Boy-girl. Crazy woman. Old words, signifying their connection to those who had gone before.

The stroke of Pita's hand along her side, drawing the charcoal through the stone groove, the clutch of Pita's fingers on her flat belly, heated Sigri's blood to boiling. She needed to move, to thrust her hips forward, to grab at Pita and force her to feed the hunger pounding through her body.

Still she stood, as Pita had, pressed against the stone. Part of the mountains. Part of time. Linked to those who had gone before, and would come after.

Then Pita's hand reached Sigri's wet folds, and probed into her depths, and time and place were swept away by the surging demand of her body. Her final shout of triumph rang out like the bugling of a bull elk in rut.

Like Pita. Sigri slid down the rock wall, ignoring the scrapes its roughness imprinted on her back. They huddled in each other's grip until the little fire was almost out, and then they pulled each other upright.

"We have to go back," Pita said softly. Sigri nodded, knowing that going back meant more than just climbing down to the campsite. It meant Emmaline, and the ranch, and classrooms and archaeological expeditions and nubile grad students.

But there was still tonight. Where the trees met the rock, Pita turned to flash Sigri a grin of challenge. "I'll race you," she said, and then, shouting over her shoulder as she got a head start, "I did bring Little Big Horn, and first one to the camp gets him."

SNOWFOUND

Connie Wilkins

The lights of Dutch Flat shone through the dusk and swirling snow as we rounded the last curve of the Bear River. Old Ulysses picked up his gait, not needing the lights to know that shelter and feed and the company of his own kind lay close ahead.

As for me, hunched against the cold in my sheepskin coat, hat brim pulled low to keep the snow clear of my eyes, I'd be happy enough for shelter, too, and a good meal. The company of my own kind was a more questionable matter. I had acquaintances in town, and some who counted me as friend, but only one who understood the resolve it took for me to put on the face and manner that the rest took for granted.

The early snow lay a foot or more deep in the open, deeper where it drifted against outcroppings of boulders and scrub pine and juniper. Ulysses was the first to notice something different about the long, white mound at the edge of one such thicket, partly obscured by weighted branches.

I might have missed it altogether, being inwardly focused on reassembling my go-to-town identity: Jack Elliott, miner, trapper, supporter of civic projects and worthy charitable endeavors if their proponents could catch him on his rare sojourns in town; a sizable man, good for backup in a fight, known to crack heads together in the quelling of drunken brawls, and a sharpshooter from his days in the Union Army.

All this was creditable enough, and, on the whole, true. A role I could live with. It was the frequent whispers, meant kindly enough, in general, that made my innards shiver. Some newcomer on the porch of the general store or in a saloon would dart his eyes at me while he leaned close to an old-timer to hear about poor Jack Elliott who'd been wounded so bad at the Battle of Chickamauga that his beard never grew again and his voice had gone up to about the pitch of an adolescent boy's.

Then they'd shift uneasily in their chairs until somebody commented that Jack surely had an eye for the ladies, at least, even though nobody'd ever seen him go upstairs at the whorehouse. He'd buy a girl a drink, though, and even dance, with a good deal of enjoyment. That'd bring a bit of a chuckle, and more uneasy shifting, but if I came close enough for hailing there'd be genial enough greetings and invitations to sit in at poker games.

My ruminations had begun to drift back toward the girls in the dance hall, all curls and red lips and waists laced up tight to make their bosoms swell above their low-cut gowns, when Ulysses' sudden halt jolted me. I looked where the horse was looking, and saw a twitch of movement. Just a juniper branch springing loose from its weight of snow, I thought, maybe triggered by some small creature sheltering beneath.

I urged Ulysses onward, and he took a few strides, but stopped again when we'd drawn about level with the suspicious mound. Ulysses was not of a temperament to shy at trifles. Half Morgan, half Clydesdale, he had strength enough to fear little, wit enough to know what needed fearing, and courage enough to face the latter if I asked it of him. From Vermont to the war in the South to the Sierra Mountains he'd carried me, through the hellfire of battle and the solitude of wilderness. It wasn't fear, but more likely curiosity that halted him now, or perhaps his judgment that I ought to take notice of whatever this was.

Another twitch, more shedding of snow, and I saw that he was right. Jet-black hair lay beneath a powdering of white. Ulysses held steady as I dismounted, my Sharps carbine at the ready, and gently prodded a snow-covered shoulder with the toe of my boot. No response. No further twitching.

I knelt, still cautious, and turned the body on its side. The face revealed was pale as ivory, eyes closed, with a knife slash and swelling purple bruises extending from the narrow jaw up over a delicate cheekbone.

A child? A female child? I dropped my carbine and brushed away snow with both hands. She wore a quilted jacket and cotton trousers, much too thin for the weather. I shed one elk-hide glove and slipped a hand under the flimsy covering, looking for a heartbeat. The curve of her breast told me that she was, in fact, no child. I looked closer at her face and realized that she must be from the Chinatown section of Dutch Flat, populated by immigrants who had come first for the mining, then for the building of the railroad.

I touched a finger to her exposed throat. Cold. Cold as death. But not dead, not quite, not yet. A tremor of a pulse still stirred the smooth skin.

Dusk was deepening into night, and the swirling snow had intensified. There was no time for any but the most cursory search for other injuries. I lifted her slight form across my shoulder, retrieved my carbine, and contrived to mount one-handed. Ulysses started forward, needing no more direction than my knees and heels provided.

She was so pale, so cold... With only a moment's hesitation I pulled open my coat and hugged her to my chest, closing the sheepskin around her. She stirred a bit, curling instinctively closer to my warm body. Then, eyes still tight-closed, she slipped her arms around me as far as they could reach and nestled her uninjured cheek against my breast.

Some strange force leapt inside me. Beneath my woolen shirt my flesh stirred and swelled under the pressure of her head. Lust, tenderness, perhaps some vestigial instinct for nurturance, warred with fear of discovery.

In spite of sore temptation I had never trusted even the most appealing of whores with my secret. I knew some would have been as glad of my attentions as of my money; other women had been, from time to time, even in the War. I had not been the only female-born to take on a man's role and enlist. Not all of us had been following male sweethearts, either, and some of us had found each other and taken brief comfort amidst the hell of war.

By the time we reached the town, I had decided that my fears were unfounded. She was still unconscious, and, in any case, might well not even speak or understand English. Once I had taken her to safety, it was unlikely that I would encounter her again. My arms felt strangely reluctant at the thought of releasing her, though, and I began to consider where, after all, she would be safe.

Ulysses had headed out of habit toward the one place where we were always welcome. Doc Warren was the only inhabitant of Dutch Flat, or California, or anywhere west of the Hudson River, who knew my full identity, having nursed me through a fever when I'd first come west. He'd been willing to keep my secret, whether from some sense of medical ethics or an inclination toward solidarity with a fellow soldier. As a military doctor he'd seen as much of the horrors of the war as any rifleman. Maybe more.

We'd become friends, having more in common than not in spite of the twenty years difference in our ages. I often stayed with him when I came to town for supplies. In any case, where better to take an injured girl than to a doctor's house? But the Chinese, I knew, had doctors too, with their own strange medical ways. And someone in Chinatown might well be searching for this girl.

I very nearly turned Ulysses away from his accustomed route and toward the settlement across the tracks, with its Joss house temples, Chinese merchandise stores, gambling halls, restaurants, laundries, apothecaries, brothels, and opium dens. Then I looked down at the ravaged face so close to mine and realized that someone had slashed her, had committed mayhem, quite deliberately. And that either she had been running away, or someone had dumped her outside of town in the bitter cold with night and a snowstorm coming on. I would not deliver her back to that former life without finding out more.

She moved a little in my arms and gripped me harder, though her eyes were still closed. I felt a surge of protectiveness; no more, I tried to tell myself, than anyone might feel for some kitten or pup plucked from destruction. But a tingling in my body, a stab of longing where the weight of her hips pressed against me, told me that I lied.

Doc had rooms and an office at the back of the building housing the post office. To my relief, there was a lamp lit in his window. I'd worried that he might be off tending to injuries or delivering babies.

He was slow to answer the thump of my boot on his door and my shout, though, and once inside I could see by the dilated pupils of his eyes that he had been dosing himself with laudanum or some such pharmaceutical. I'd be the last to blame a man for trying to dull recurring dreams of the horrors of war, or the other miseries doctors must witness, but it was still early in the evening, barely past afternoon, and somebody might have needed him. Somebody *did* need him.

"What's all this, Jack?" he said, his words only a little slurred. I lay my burden on his sofa and turned to see him shaking the fog from his head. An odd look passed across his face as he focused on the girl, and he hesitated for a long moment, but his hands seemed steady enough when finally he bent over the girl to explore her injuries.

"I found her about a mile out along the Bear River Trail," I said. "Or you might say Ulysses found her. She was covered in snow, lying where she'd either fallen or been dumped." The rough anger in my voice might have been roused entirely by those who had done such a thing, or a little may have been aimed at Doc himself.

He straightened up wearily. "You go get Ulysses settled in while I make us some coffee. Might have a bit of tea around here for the girl, too. A hot drink inside her is the first thing she needs."

I nodded, then wished I hadn't when snow melt dripped from my hat. Fifteen minutes later, back from Ed Sawyer's livery stable two streets away, I left my hat and coat on the stand by the door after shaking off as much snow as I could on the doorstep.

Coffee was brewing on the black iron stove, beside a great kettle of steaming water. Doc had spread a blanket over the girl and was kneeling by the sofa applying unguent and bandages to her injured face.

I hauled my gear into Doc's spare room. My shirt was wet from clutching a snow-covered body against it, so I dug a dry one from my pack, and, as was my habit in adjusting to the role of an upstanding male member of the community, I dealt firmly with the most obvious evidence to the contrary by binding my chest tightly with cotton bands.

"Give me a hand here, Jack," Doc said when I emerged. "She's coming around. You sit there and prop her up while I get her some hot tea."

At first glance it looked to me as though she was still out cold, but then I detected a glint behind her long lashes, and felt more than saw her gaze track me as I moved across the room. I edged onto the sofa, raising her shoulders just enough to slide my thighs beneath them. When she didn't seem to object, I pulled her higher against me until she was sitting on my lap. Her uninjured cheek lay against my collarbone and her black hair brushed my throat and chin.

It seemed somehow so natural a position, restful and stimulating both at once, that Doc's return with the tea seemed almost an intrusion. But faint spasms of shivering swept her body every few seconds, and I knew he was right about the need to warm her. Not that alternative methods of doing so didn't occupy my mind.

"Drink this," Doc said with firm authority, but I noticed that his hand holding the cup wasn't altogether steady. The girl's nostrils twitched as she inhaled the steam suspiciously, and her lips remained stubbornly closed. Even I could detect the scent of some herbal soporific.

"Let me," I said, taking the cup. "Open up, now."

Instead, she tilted her head back until she could gaze up into my face. Her dark almond-shaped eyes were intent with some emotion I couldn't decipher, but whatever she saw in mine seemed to satisfy her. She lowered her mouth to the rim of the cup and drank as I tipped it toward her.

"You make a fine nurse, Jack," Doc said. "Now see if you can get her clothes off."

I looked sharply at him to see whether this was some sort of joke. There was a wry sort of smile on his face, but when he went to the kitchen pump to half-fill a copper hip-bath with buckets of water and then turned the contents of the steaming kettle into it, I understood what he was about.

She let me unfasten her jacket and slide her cotton trousers down her hips, not merely placidly, as the herbs might dictate, but with an appearance of languid pleasure. A little smile curved her lips very briefly, though she winced at the pain this caused her cheek, and when she lifted her small round buttocks to let me ease the fabric past them her fragrance was so inviting that I was hard put to resist lowering my face to taste the musky sweetness between her thighs.

Doc Warren kept his back discreetly turned until I had her in the bath, and when he turned back he managed to keep his demeanor professional enough. I tried to follow his lead, though the slender grace of her body and the smoothness of her honey-hued skin had my pulses pounding. Her breasts above the water were small but beautifully shaped, rounder than I would have expected from such observations as I'd made of the few Chinese women seen on the streets of the town.

Doc shot me a sardonic glance, appreciating, I knew, the

irony that my presence bolstered the proprieties in a literal sense, since I had a woman's body, but smashed them to bits in terms of a lustful gaze.

"Is she going to be all right?" I asked gruffly. "No frostbite?" Her feet had been blue-tinged, but were now turning bright pink in the hot water, and her color in general seemed to have improved.

"I'd say you and Ulysses found her just in time," he said. "I think she'd been running away, not dumped, and had fallen not long before you happened by. The snow was building up fast just then. She'll do fine in that respect."

His tone warned me of some deeper concern. "How about her face?" I asked. "She'll be scarred, I know, but..."

"The face will heal, more or less," he said. "The slash isn't all that deep. But yes, there'll be scarring. She'll never work again in Madame Yee's House of Flowers, or any other."

Well, I couldn't say I was much surprised. "So you know she worked in a brothel?"

"Jack, I know all too much about her, and you'd better know it, too." Doc rubbed his face wearily. "It was a fine thing you did, saving her from freezing to death, but I'm not sure you did her any favor at all."

He reached for a blanket left handy over a nearby chair and unfolded it. "Let's get her dried off and bedded down. She's about asleep as it is. Then we'll talk." As I rolled her in the blanket and then unrolled her into dry quilts on the bed, I saw half-healed lash-welts and other marks across her back and flanks, and wondered angrily how any brothel proprietor could have allowed such damage, if only because it would decrease her value.

When we sat by the stove with cups of hot coffee and a plate of cold ham and biscuits, Doc was silent for a while. I was on the verge of pushing him impatiently for an explanation, but he said abruptly, "Did anyone see you carrying her through town?"

"Not that I noticed," I said. "Ulysses did all the navigating. If there were folks about, they'd have had their hats pulled down against the snow just as far as I did. And if they did see me, I'd guess I only looked about as bearlike as usual, hunched against the cold and wind. I had her close inside my greatcoat."

"That's just as well, then," Doc said, "or she'd be lucky to see another dawn. And so would we, if I'm any judge of how you'd react when they came to get her."

"Who'd be after her?" But I thought I knew part of the answer. Someone who had hated her enough to try to ruin her face.

Someone who wasn't going to touch her again without going through me first.

Turned out, of course, there was more to it than that. The Tong Wars of San Francisco's Chinatown had spread to the Sierra gold fields. Business owners in thriving towns like Dutch Flat could be coerced into paying "protection" money as readily as those in the city, and, since one brand of corruption begets others, a town official might take the opportunity to get his share of what was going in return for turning a blind eye toward illicit activities.

Hong Lian, Red Lotus, had been part of one such arrangement, a "gift" from a Tong chief to the sheriff who had taken a fancy to her at Madame Yee's. Reportedly he'd taken a few other things to her as well, and when it came to spurs she'd rebelled. Doc Warren had spent the day working on the sheriff, trying to repair injuries caused by sharp fingernails and teeth so savage they'd come close to inflicting the kind of wounds rumored to be the cause of my own minor deviations from standard manhood.

"So both the law and the Tong are after her," Doc said. "The Tong has already marked her, as a lesson to others, but they're by no means finished with her. Running may have been her only chance to choose the manner of her death. She might even try to run again."

"Then I'd better watch close to be sure she doesn't," I said curtly. Mind and body too tired and conflicted for useful thought, I went and lay beside her on the bed, fully clothed. I woke near morning to find that a blanket had been laid across me, but I was still cold, so I burrowed as quietly as I could under the rest of the quilts, and when sun slanted through the window I found a slim, naked body wrapped in my arms and a knee nudged against the damp crotch of my Levi Strauss canvas trousers.

Doc had left coffee and cornbread in the kitchen, along with a note. "Think hard and fast, Jack. And keep her quiet. We're in deeper than a bull in a heifer."

I blessed him for that "we're" and for his wry humor. I'd brought trouble to his doorstep, and he'd taken it in, both as doctor and as friend.

A tin of tea leaves sat on the table. I did my best to brew a cup, thinking to take it to the invalid, but before I got to the bedroom door she was standing there, wrapped in a quilt, long dark hair tousled about her face and shoulders.

"Jack?" she said experimentally. Her voice was high and sweet, and this was the first time I'd heard it.

"Jack," I agreed, nodding.

She put a hand to her own chest. "Hong Lian," she said, or at least it sounded close enough to the way Doc had pronounced the name last night. I didn't think I could get my mouth around either version just yet.

"Red Lotus?" I asked, and she nodded back at me.

"Lo-tus," she said, and came forward to take the cup from me. For all that she drank daintily, and was somewhat impeded by her injury, the tea seemed to disappear in a flash. She walked to the kitchen table, set down the cup, and turned back to me, loosing her grip on the quilt a bit so that it fell open to show her nakedness.

Thinking what to do—thinking rationally about anything at all—was about to get harder than ever I'd dreamed. And the voice in need of quieting would turn out to be my own.

Lotus raised the edges of her covering like wings, and came toward me. Her warm scent flooded my senses. She got so close she had to tilt her head back to look into my face. "Jack," she said again, and raised a hand to my cheek, letting go one corner of the quilt. Her stroke on my skin felt like the taste of warm honey. "*Mei-lai*," she whispered.

I had no time to wonder what the word meant. Her hand descended over my jaw, my throat, across my breasts, making them surge as though they'd burst their bindings. Then she was kneeling before me, both hands on my belt buckle, murmuring more words I couldn't have understood even if blood hadn't been pounding in my head so loud I could scarcely hear.

A few panicky thoughts still pierced through the turmoil. What was she expecting to find? Did she know by now who, or what, I was? Or did she plan to use me as she had the sheriff, in order to escape? The thought of her sharp little teeth in my flesh made me wince even as my wetness flowed.

Then her fingers slid inside the unbuttoned fly of my trousers, and found me, and I barely stifled a yelp. The busy post office was a thin wall away, and the clop of hooves and stamp of boots, slightly muffled by last night's snow, came in from the nearby street. I could hear an indistinct buzz of voices, and mine would surely be heard as well if I raised it.

But her fingers moved more insistently, and her little red tongue thrust its way in beside them. Her other hand still worked at my belt buckle, and any minute I would be in a state of helpless glory, hobbled by pleasure and my own trousers about my ankles.

With a low growl I lifted her to her feet, and then so high along my body that her soft throat was against my hungry lips. Her laughter vibrated right into my mouth. Her body wriggled, but not in resistance, as I carried her back to the bed.

My clothes were off before I knew it, and we were rolling naked together. She looked so small and fragile, in spite of her full round breasts and gently curving belly, that I was afraid I might crush her with my bulk. But she seemed infinitely resilient, thrusting her hips upward toward the pressure of my thigh between her legs, arching her neck to grasp one swollen nipple and then another in her hot mouth. When she sucked hard, then harder, with a hint of grazing teeth, I groaned, and bucked until the creaking of the bedstead might have been heard in the street. It took only a few thrusts of the fingers she had worked between us to send such stabs of pleasure coursing through me that my teeth clenched in my own forearm to stifle cries that would have resounded like the roar of an angry grizzly.

In a state of gasping collapse I rolled from her body, and suddenly she was on top of me, and all over me, kneeling astride at one moment to streak my belly with her juices, then sitting beside me, leaning to plant little kisses all over my body from knees to swampy crotch to breasts and chin and lips.

"Mei-lai," she murmured, again and again. I wondered vaguely whether it was some former lover's name she chanted, but then all thought fled as she shifted her body upward and straddled my face. I steadied her small round buttocks with hands that encompassed the whole of their curves and thrust my long tongue up into her streaming heat. My lips worked against

her nether ones, and her hips wriggled wildly around the probing spear that was my tongue, until the spasms sweeping her shook my head from side to side in the fierce grip of her thighs. Her voice, in rapid cries no louder than a mewling kitten's, still pierced me to my core.

We had barely time to recover before Doc Warren returned from his rounds. We were clothed, but the very air must have reeked of what we'd been up to, even though we'd managed to heat water and wash up a bit.

"No need to ask," Doc said dryly, "what kind of thinking you've been doing." He went to the cupboard for sticking-plaster to repair the bandage that had loosened a bit from Lotus' cheek. "Whatever you're going to do, you'd better do it fast. Snow's not all that deep from yesterday's storm, but Many Bearclaws over at the livery stable says there's a big one brewing, due by morning."

The old Indian was seldom wrong about the weather. And mention of the stable reminded me that there was no point in my staying hidden, since Ulysses' presence there was advertisement enough that I was in town. The sooner I was seen out and about the less suspicion there'd be, and, in any case, I needed to pick up the provisions I'd come for. As well as a few more.

Doc would be holding office hours in the room next door. "Stay in the bedroom," I ordered Lotus, who pouted a bit and then grimaced at the pain it caused her cheek. Whether she understood the words or not, she clearly understood their meaning when I bound her leg to the bedstead with my belt. She could easily enough get free, but she could also count on my returning for the belt. And for her.

I went off into town, hoping my coat hid the piece of rope holding up my trousers. A stop at the bank with my little sack of gold nuggets and dust came first. Then I returned greetings from acquaintances ranging from gamblers to church ladies as I lugged my sacks of cornmeal and beans and a bit of salt and sugar from the general store along the wood plank sidewalk. Once back at the livery stable, I deposited my supplies next to Ulysses' stall. "A couple more parcels will be delivered from the store," I told Ed Sawyer. "I'll be packing up tomorrow morning at first light to try to get ahead of the worst of the storm." Old Many Bearclaws, tending an injured horse a couple of stalls away, grunted skeptically.

Then, instead of going toward Doc's place, I found myself veering toward Chinatown. I'd been there before, out of curiosity; now I went right for a general merchandise store and picked up a big sack of rice and a few tins of tea. I waited to pay while the old woman at the counter stroked a length of embroidered silk a customer was considering. "*Mei-lai, mei-lai,*" she said, over and over. My skin tingled. "*Mei-lai?*" I asked, as well as I could manage, when the potential customer had left without purchasing. "What does that mean?" She gave me a shrewd, considering look. "Beau-ti-ful," she said at last.

My parcel, when I departed, contained the silk fabric tucked beneath the rice and tea. Beautiful. Never, even in the days when I'd been young and generally acknowledged to be female in spite of my size and gawkiness, had anyone thought to call me beautiful.

It was still three hours until first light when I fetched Ulysses at the stable and loaded him. The snow was just beginning. Doc helped me add on what was still at his place, largely in silence, having done his duty the night before by trying, without conviction, to deter me.

"How much do you really know about this woman?" he'd asked. "How can you be sure she won't knife you in the back and take off with your horse?"

"I know my horse," I'd said shortly. He hadn't bothered to point out that there could still be a knife in my back before she found out that Ulysses wouldn't cooperate.

When we'd about finished loading, though, he played his trump card. "Know anything about birthing babies?" he asked, with studied casualness.

I thought about Lotus' rounded breasts and curving belly, and understood what he meant. I won't deny that a pang of anxiety struck me, along with a pang of something else made up of both joy and sorrow. I tucked those thoughts away for future reflection. "I've helped deliver foals, and been with my sisters for a few of theirs. I can manage," I said. There was no point worrying about it now, at any rate. The choice was clear.

"Well," Doc said, "if this can all be smoothed over in time, with people moving on and enough money in the right hands, maybe you'll be able to come back. Let folks see Jack Elliott with his woman and child. Stir them up a bit." He slapped my flank companionably, and grinned.

When we were mounted on Ulysses, Lotus was wrapped again inside my coat. I was the one who must have looked to be with child, but there was no one about yet to see.

Ulysses shifted a bit, getting the feel of the heavy load of passengers and supplies. If need be, once we were safely away and snow covering our tracks, I'd dismount and walk a good deal of the way to my cabin in the distant hills, but I trusted him to get us that far. He'd been the one to get me into this, after all.

Doc walked beside us for a few paces. "You're sure, Jack?" he said one last time.

"I'm sure," I said. "This is what I want. I keep what I find." Lotus tightened her grip on me under the coat. Her voice still whispered through my mind. "*Mei-lai,*" she'd said, and shown how she'd meant it. *And I keep what's found me*, I thought. With scarcely a signal from reins or heels, Ulysses quickened his pace, and we were on our way home.

BULL RIDER

Sacchi Green

Amsterdam.

Am-ster-god-fucking-*damn*!

Sin City of the '70s, still sizzling in the '80s. Cheap pot you could smoke in the coffeehouses, but that's not what lit my fire. Sex shows and leather-toy shops? Coming a whole lot closer; but what really ignited a slow burn low in my Levi's were stories of the working girls displaying their wares behind lace-curtained windows. Something about the dissonance between elegance and raunch struck a chord. "Fine old buildings," ice-maiden Anneke had told some of the Australian riders, with her slight, *Mona Lisa* smile and a sidelong glance at me. "Many visitors tour the Red Light district just to view the...architecture."

I should have tried harder to figure Anneke out. A damned fine rider, in total control of herself and her mount, she was all blonde and pink and white with cool, butter-wouldn't-melt-in-her-mouth self-possession. But a certain Preppy Princess with a long chestnut ponytail and a cute round ass—and delusions of being a world-class equestrienne—had been using up too much of my energy at the time.

That was all over now. With a vengeance. A fair share of it mine, true; but I still needed to drown my sorrows in whatever fleshpots I could find. I was not going to leave Europe without at least a taste of decadence.

You don't get to taste much, though, without a few guilders clinking in the pockets of your jeans. Which I didn't have. Damn near didn't even have the jeans. First French-tourist jerk-off to point at my ass and say, "'Ow much?" came close to losing his business hand. "Chienne! Pour les Levi's!" he hissed, rubbing his numbed wrist.

"More than you've got!" I stepped away, and he scurried in front of me with a fistful of bills. "No way," I said, lengthening my stride until he dropped back. Before I made it across the Centraal Station plaza I'd had two more offers, Spanish and

Japanese, and damn sure would have taken one if I'd had any alternate covering for my BVD's. But, after that fiasco at the Equestrian Tournament, I'd left behind everything except my hat, buckskin pants, and fringed jacket. And I'd pawned the leathers to raise plane fare home. Too damn cheaply, if even torn jeans reeking of horses and stable muck were in this much demand.

Maybe the stable muck was the selling point. Authenticity. I could've made a fortune if I'd known enough to dirty more jeans! The question now was, could I parlay all that authenticity into getting laid? I had twenty-four hours before my flight to find out. And a conniving little preppy to purge from my system.

Oh hell, there it went again, like a movie in my head. My jaw and fists clenched—and my clit, too—as I sat on a bench at the edge of the square and spread a map across my knees. I lowered my head as though the names of streets, canals, and landmarks were all I saw.

She'd planned it from the start. All those weeks spent coaching her to signal the horse with her knees—to wrap her thighs, naked and moist, around my neck—to lift her tight little butt in rhythm with the horse's gait—to tilt her hips to the thrust of my demanding hand—and all along she'd known that moment would come.

She'd been about to come herself, which only made her moment better. I saw it in her eyes as they went from deep and velvety to glittering and triumphant. She focused on something over my shoulder. My fingers slowed, and she switched all her attention back to me. "Eat me, Toby! Eat me!" she commanded, pushing my head toward her pussy. The musk of sex and the rich aromas of hay and horses blended into a powerful aphrodisiac. I delayed a bit, inclined to make her beg; then she flicked her little pink tongue over her lips like a kitten licking drops of cream, and I forgot everything but getting my own mouth into her cream, and my own tongue deeply into where it would do the most good.

She'd never wriggled with more abandon, never let her gasps and moans and ultimate shrieks rip so free. No faking it, either. Her internal spasms surged right through her pussy into my mouth and hands and rocked me to my toes, but it was no tribute to my skill. When I came up for air I saw her eyes fixed again on someone behind me, and a look on her face like the proverbial cat who's deep-throated the canary.

Some instinct made me roll away just before his fist could connect. It's a wrench to shift from surging lust to fight-or-flight, but I made it fast enough to have ten feet and the business end of a hayfork between us before he could swing again. I recognized him from the picture she'd shown me. Charles, the fiancé. I almost felt sorry for him.

"You goddamn fucking dyke!" he sputtered at me, as much pain as rage in his voice.

"Oh, Chub, do you always have to state the obvious?" Miss Ponytail languorously brushed hay out of her chestnut hair. "Afraid you can't do as well as a stable hand?"

Stable hand. I swung the hayfork toward her, then back toward Chub's more physical threat.

I'd worked my way through the same elite Eastern women's college she was lounging through. Stable hand, stable manager, eventually assistant riding coach; what she called me didn't matter as much as the contempt in her tone.

"So, 'Chub,'" I said. "Let me know if you need any more pointers." I hurled the fork just barely over his head into the bales of hay behind him, and got out of there fast before he could pick himself up off the floor.

Any sympathy evaporated late that night when he caught me alone in the barn and came at me with rage in his eyes and a serious bulge in his pants. Poor dumb bastard. I left him hurting so bad he wasn't going to have the means to please Miss Preppy anytime soon.

If I'd left it at that, I might still have been able to fly back to the States on the chartered plane with the rest of the equestrian team. If I hadn't charged into the Bitch Princess' room, shoved her face into the pillow, immobilized her with my knee between her shoulder blades, and taken my knife to that long chestnut hair until no fancy hairdresser was going to be able to conceal all the ragged gaps without cropping it even shorter than mine, the police and the International Equestrian Organization officials wouldn't have been called into it. But I did, and they were, and I barely got away ahead of arrest with my passport and leather duds and the clothes I'd been wearing to load the horses into the vans for the transport plane.

So here I was in Amsterdam. I'd fed the chestnut hair strand by strand to the wind from the back of some Hungarian biker dude's motorcycle when he'd picked me up hitching on the outskirts of The Hague. The breeze here in the city was pretty light, smelling of canals and the ocean, but as I folded my map and stood and ran my fingers through my hair, I tried to imagine the hot scent of her expensive perfume and greedy pussy being blown away over the North Sea.

Then I headed for the Walletjes Red Light District in search of replacement memories.

Okay, decadence is a subjective concept. Packaged, Health-Department-Inspected sex doesn't do that much for me, and the cruising scene seemed to be, no surprise, mainly the boy-meets-boy variety. There had to at least be a women's bookstore somewhere; I can handle that scene, as long as I can steer the conversation to the better bits of Colette, just as I can coach show riding and could compete myself if I could afford a show-class horse, even though at heart I'm Western all the way. But literary foreplay, especially with language barriers, wasn't what I had in mind.

The ladies of the night weren't disappointing, exactly; the tall, elegant windows glowed with discreetly red-tinted light, and the flesh casually displayed was enticing enough. One blonde, dressed only in a long white men's shirt, saw my interest and treated me to a knowing smile over her shoulder as she straddled a chair and did a slow grind on its plumply upholstered seat. But a paying customer caught the vibes and knocked on her door. After a close look, he invited me to come in, too; I declined. The window shade came down. I moved on.

The neighborhood provided plenty of rosy-fleshed occasions for fantasy, but none of the others quite did it for me. I began to have a sneaking suspicion that one particular pink-and-white-and-blonde vision had been making my subconscious simmer. I sure as hell wasn't going to find her here, but I might know where I could. For all the good it would do me.

Anneke had always been civil, but reserved. Once, when I'd helped her with an emergency repair in the tack room, she'd said, "Toby, you should be riding that fine horse, not her," with a nod of her head toward Miss Preppy.

"Could never afford it." I wrestled with multiple interpretations. Riding the horse instead of riding the girl?

"No, nor could I." Her trace of accent was tantalizing. "The brewing firm that employs me keeps a show stable for...what is it in English? Public relations?"

"That's it," I said. "You work for them? I thought you must be family."

"No, I work summers in their Amsterdam clubs, as bookkeeper and assistant manager. The newest is a country-western bar on Warmoesstraat, all the rage, like that movie *Urban Cowboy*. They would go crazy for you there, Toby!"

Then she was gone, and like an idiot, I didn't follow up. Now it hit me hard just who I wanted to go crazy for me, just what smooth, white skin I wanted to raise a flush on, what cool, half-smiling lips I wanted to suck and bite until they were red and swollen and begging for more. And whose butter I wanted to melt in my mouth.

How hard could it be to find a country-western bar in Amsterdam? I even remembered the name of the street. Had she meant me to? Anneke had always been so collected, so focused on her riding. Maybe I'd been afraid to try anything, afraid it might matter too much.

The neon outline of a rodeo bull rider told me I'd found the right place. I hesitated in the doorway, well aware that I didn't have the means to buy a lady a beer, and even if I did, this might be the kind of place where a move like that could get me thrown out. Then again, the way the people inside were rigged out in wannabe-Western gear, where could I get more mileage out of my battered hat and authentically work-worn (and pungent) denim vest and jeans?

It was early, but crowds were building. Behind the bar a large woman with a generous display of pillowy breasts scanned the room as she wiped the countertop. When her gaze crossed mine it moved on, stopped for a beat, then swung back.

Without looking away, she pulled a phone from under the counter and spoke briefly into it. *Oh shit*, I thought, *are the police here looking for me?* My "victims" couldn't have wanted that much publicity. Then a grin lit her round-cheeked face as she replaced the phone and beckoned to me. I might've resisted the good-humored gleam in her eyes, but the foaming stein of beer she offered was something else again. I hadn't had anything to eat in almost twenty-four hours, and nothing to drink but water from public fountains.

"On the house, honey." Her nametag said "Margaretha," but her accent said New York. "You look like you might liven this place up. Ever ride one of those?"

I followed the jerk of her head. Through a wide archway I saw, rising above the sawdust on the floor like some futuristic mushroom, a mechanical bull just like the one Travolta and Winger rode in *Urban Cowboy*.

I wiped beer foam from my mouth. "You mean, does my ass live up to the advertising of my Levi's? Lady, you have no idea."

"Don't bet on it, darlin'." Her assessing look assured me that one way or another, a good time could definitely be had. Much as I appreciate older women, though—hell, one saved me from fratricide—my hopes for something else grew. If it wasn't the police she'd called, who on this continent but Anneke would have described me to her?

"Yeah," I said, "I've ridden those, and the snorting, stomping, shitting versions too. For another beer and some of those hefty pretzels, I'd be glad to demonstrate."

"Wait a while." She refilled my stein and slid me a bowl of pretzels and cheese-flavored breadsticks, and I did my best not to stuff myself. Some things are better on a less-than-full stomach. Bull-riding is only one of them.

"So, where are you from, Toby?" she asked, chatting me up while keeping a close eye on the door.

"Montana," I said. I definitely hadn't told her my name.

"They let women ride bulls in rodeos there?" she asked.

"Not yet. Not officially. Except at small local shindigs where anything goes." I paid close attention to my beer and pretzels, not wanting to talk much about it. But there was no way I could keep from remembering the surge of wild triumph when I outrode them all, even my brother Ted. The pounding of my blood—the pressure building until I had to explode or die—and the revelation that, to achieve explosion, I needed to wrap myself around Cindy's full, smooth curves.

Back when we were twelve, Cindy hadn't minded a little mutual exploration. She'd been away for a few years, though, and this time, as I tried to pull her close, she twisted loose and ran around the grandstand to throw herself on Ted. Another revelation, that life was a bitch, seared me. No matter how much I could work like a man, even beat the men at their own games, their rewards were officially off-limits to me.

I was young and naïve, and the shock filled me with rage. I leapt for my brother, and only the intervention of Miss Violet Montez, sultry lead singer for the intermission entertainment act, kept me from killing him.

"Hey, Tigrina, come with me." She pressed herself against me as Ted struggled to get up. "I have what you need. And what you don't even know you need." And she surely did, or close enough.

When I rode back to the ranch at daybreak, too drained to sort out the remnants of pleasure and pain and smoldering resentment, Daddy was waiting in the barn. He couldn't quite meet my eyes. "Looks like maybe you'd better go east to school the way your Mama always wanted."

"Looks like," I agreed. And that was that. Someday I'll find the words to tell him that it wasn't his fault. I'd never have survived being raised any other way. And how could he, after letting me know all my life I could do anything a man could do, tell me that the one thing I couldn't have was a woman of my own?

Besides, he'd have been wrong. Going to a women's college didn't make a lady of me, but I sure learned a lot about women.

Not that there isn't always more to learn.

Anneke came through the door and stood for a minute, cool as ever, with just a hint of defiance. "I'll be damned!" Margaretha muttered from behind the bar. "I knew you'd made an impression, but Jeez!" From the dropped jaws and arrested strides of several waiters I got the feeling that they weren't used to seeing Anneke in tight, scant denim cutoffs and a gingham blouse molded to all the delectable curves below those peeking out over her plunging neckline.

Body by Daisy Mae; face by Princess Grace. A divine dissonance, but what the hell was I supposed to do with it in a public place and a culture I didn't wholly understand?

I sure had to do something, though, with the surge of energy pounding through my body. "Maybe it's time for a ride," I growled, and jerked my head toward the room with the bull.

"Good idea." Margaretha shoved some coins at me across

the bar. "Go for it!" As I turned away, she grabbed my shoulder and swung me back. "Take it a little easy. She may not admit it, but she's new to this." She didn't mean the bull.

I set the controls on "extreme" and vaulted aboard the broad wooden back, my hat held high in the traditional free-arm gesture. It was a damn good thing the bull was mechanical; my body could handle all the twists and lurches without involving my brain. Matching wits with a live, wily, determined bull would've taken concentration I couldn't spare, with Anneke on my mind.

I was vaguely aware that a crowd had gathered. The music was "The Devil Came Down to Georgia," and Anneke was leaning against a nearby post watching with her *Mona Lisa* smile. Less vaguely, I realized I was going to be sore tomorrow—though nowhere near as sore as I'd like to be unless some vital moves were made. When my wooden mount slowed to a stop and the room held still, I tossed my hat toward Anneke, who caught it deftly and allowed her smile to widen. Then I shifted my ass backward to make room and held out a hand to her. With no hesitation she let me pull her up to straddle the bull.

Someone, maybe Margaretha, put more money in the machine and set it on "easy"; the music changed to "Looking for Love in All the Wrong Places"; and I was in the kind of trouble worth dreaming about.

Riding without stirrups can be an erotic experience all by itself. Riding with Anneke's ass pressed into me, kneading my crotch with every heave of the bull, was sublime torture. Her slim back against my breasts made them demand a whole lot more of my attention than they usually get, while her own luscious breasts...I nuzzled my face against her neck and gazed over her shoulder at the rounded flesh gently bouncing and threatening to surge out of the low neckline. From my vantage point, glimpses of tender pink nipple came and went. Much as I wanted more, I didn't necessarily want to share.

"Your décolletage is slipping," I whispered into her ear. Instead of adjusting it, she turned her head so her smooth cheek curved against my lips.

"Help me, Toby," she murmured. "Hold me." And I was lost.

I cupped her breasts, gently at first, as the motion of the bull made them rise and fall and thrust against their thin gingham covering. Then I felt her back arch slightly, and her flesh press more demandingly into my hands. There was no way I could help moving my fingers across her firming nipples. I felt her soft gasp all the way down to my toes.

Her ass began to move against me independent of the bull's motion. My clit felt like it was trying to scorch a passage through my Levi's. My grip on her breasts tightened, and her nipples hardened and pulsed against my fingers as she leaned her head against my shoulder. "Toby," she breathed, "You are making me so sore!"

"Want me to stop?" I teased her tender earlobe with my teeth.

"No...don't stop...make me sorer still, please, Toby..."

How could I refuse? I unbuttoned her blouse at the waist and slid my hands across her silky belly before filling them with the even silkier flesh of her breasts. Then I drove her to as much sweet, sore engorgement as hands alone could provide. My hungry mouth made do with the soft hollows and curves of her neck and shoulders, feeling the nearly soundless moans she couldn't suppress vibrate directly from her body into mine. Her pale hair was coming loose from its intricate chignon, so I pulled out the fastenings with my teeth and let the golden curtain fall across the marks my mouth left on her skin. Her hair gave off a faint, clean scent of herbs and roses.

I hadn't forgotten our audience, but I was beyond caring. During my first wild ride there'd been whoops and cheering, but when Anneke joined me the sounds had dwindled to a low hum, an almost communal moan. Somebody put more coins in the machine, and "Looking for Love in All the Wrong Places" played on.

My problem was the accelerating need to get right down to it in ways even permissive Amsterdam couldn't handle. Or, if it could, I couldn't.

"We have to get out of here," I growled against Anneke's cheek. She gave a slight nod.

"Soon," she said, with a shuddering sigh. "Help me turn." I admired her flair for showmanship as she swung one leg over the pommel, poised briefly in sidesaddle position, twisted so that her hands could brace against my shoulders, and pushed herself up and over until she was facing me astride.

Okay. A little more for the paying customers. Just a little. My hat, now upside down on the floor, had become a target for a fair number of coins and bills.

I urged Anneke's legs up over my thighs and got a firm grip on her waist. She leaned her head back as I savagely pressed my mouth into the hollow of her throat and let anger flicker through desire. New to this, was she? New to what? Performing with a woman? What had she done here with men?

My mouth moved down and Anneke leaned farther back, both of us as balanced as if our moves had been choreographed and rehearsed a hundred times. I tore at her shirt with my teeth until the buttons let go and I could get at her arched belly. A collective sigh rose from the audience as the fabric slid aside to leave her round breasts and jutting, rose-pink nipples naked. I knew what they wanted, but there was only just so much I could share.

She lay so far back now that her legs were around my hips and only my grip kept her upper body from sliding off the gently heaving bull. I probed my tongue into the ivory rosebud whorl of her navel as her thighs tightened and jerked.

My clit jerked too. I ran my mouth down to the waistband of her shorts and then over the zipper, biting down gently just where the seam pressed against her clit. The fabric was wet and getting wetter. Our musk rose like a tangible cloud, mixed with the scent of roses and the earthy reek of the stables.

I bit down harder, tugged at the thick seam, pressed it into her, and knew by the spasmodic thrusts of her hips I could make her come right now, right here. And knew I wasn't going to.

My streak of exhibitionism may be as wide as the Montana sky, but some desires are too deep, too intense, too close to the limits of self-control for any but private performance. I pulled Anneke upright and kissed her long and hard, letting her feel the sharpness of my teeth. "There's an old show-biz saying," I said against her mouth, my voice harsher than intended. "Always leave 'em wanting more."

I swung us both to the floor and stood, still holding her in my arms, until the ground stopped heaving under my feet. Her legs tightened around my waist, and so did her arms around my neck, reminding me, for all the enticing tenderness of her flesh, that she was a world-class athlete. The dazed look in her blue eyes retreated slightly. "But Toby, what if *I* want more?"

"You'd damned well better want more. You're going to get it. But not here." I started toward the door, not knowing where I was going. Hands reached out as we passed, some just stroking us, some stuffing money into my jeans.

Margaretha called out; Anneke turned, laughed, and caught the big old-fashioned key spinning toward her through the air. She shouted something in Dutch, and thrust the cold iron down inside the waistband of my BVDs. It slid, of course, much lower, producing new and interesting sensations as we ran hand in hand through the Amsterdam night.

The little houseboat rose and fell gently on the moonlit canal. Anneke went down the steps to the deck, turned, caught me by the hips, and burrowed her face into the crotch of my jeans. My legs nearly failed me.

"Mmm," she said, inhaling deeply. "I never thought to breathe anything as sweet as the smell of a horse. But mixed with the scent of a woman...." All her cool reserve had melted. She looked up at me with eyes darkened by night and arousal, and just a trace of laughter on lips still swollen from my kiss. "I never thought to touch a woman, either, until I had such dreams of you I thought I must go mad!"

I came down the last few steps and pressed her against the low door to the living quarters, trying desperately to feel in control of a dangerously reeling world. When I kissed her as gently as I could, her tongue came tentatively to meet mine and my clit lurched as though it, too, had been touched.

"But Toby," she whispered, turning her mouth away just enough to speak, "I must get the key! I must...is it all right?" She touched my crotch lightly, then drew her hand up along my zipper to my belt.

"Yes...," I managed to gasp. It wouldn't have been all right for anyone else. Even now, I couldn't let her slide her hand down into my pants before I had mine deeply in hers. It was too late for control—I knew I was going to lose it any second, going to come at the touch of her fingers on my throbbing, aching clit—but I'd be damned if I was going to come alone.

Experience counts for something. And Anneke wasn't wearing a belt. I had my whole hand curved around her pussy before she'd gotten farther than the waistband of my briefs. She gasped, and paused, as I worked my fingers between her folds, not penetrating yet—the night was still young—just gently massaging the increasing wetness and circling her clit with my thumb tip. She arched her hips forward, but her hand slid down over my mound, and in desperation to distract her—and myself—I lowered my mouth to one breast and licked at her pink nipple until it was hard and straining. Then I sucked her, hard and harder, biting a little, and she pressed herself deeper into my mouth. Her gasping breaths turned into deep moans, but her hand still moved down and her fingers curved in imitation of mine.

I pressed my fingers deeper, moved my thumb faster, harder, demandingly against her clit, and her fingers moved too, tentatively, but more than enough to push me to the edge. The iron key, shoved back now between my asscheeks, only intensified the sensations.

I had to cheat. I gripped her wrist with my free hand and raised my head. "Wait," I said against her lips. "Just feel, feel it all." Then I covered her mouth with mine and sucked and bit and probed and worked my whole hand back and forth in her slippery depths, spreading her juices up over her straining clit, stroking faster and faster until she spasmed against me and sobbed into my hungry mouth. Finally I let her pull away enough to breathe.

"Toby," she gasped, "please, let me, I have to...let me touch you!" She struggled to move her hand against my grip.

I had to let her. And had to bury my face in her soft neck in a vain attempt to muffle the raw cries tearing through me on waves of explosive release.

She withdrew her hand, and the dripping key, slowly and sensuously. "Oh, yes," she sighed, "much, much better than the dreams. And there is more?"

"More," I assured her, still breathing hard. "All you can handle. This was just a taste."

She smiled wickedly and touched her tongue to the key. "A fine taste!" Then she turned, and the door swung open.

In the snug interior, lit by a hanging lantern, I opened her to pleasures she hadn't yet dreamed of. I took it a little easy, since she was, after all, new to this; then, as her demand grew, she drove me to extremes. And invented new ones. Being with someone whose strength matched mine, who, like me, had as great a hunger to touch as to be touched, was a new and disconcerting experience.

By morning, when Margaretha dropped off some coffee and hot rolls and my hat filled with cash, we were both sore and exhausted. And as high if we'd just won the gold.

"Take all this." I dumped the money on the bed between Anneke's splayed legs. "If my half is enough, could you get my leathers out of hock and send them to me? I'll find the pawn ticket...in a minute...if I ever manage to move..."

"Maybe I shall find a way to deliver them in person." Anneke rolled over to straddle my thigh. "You won't mind, Toby, if I wear those snug trousers a bit, maybe ride in them? And think of you, and get them very, very wet?"

"We could send them back and forth," I said, "until they're seasoned enough to travel on their own. But in person would be a damn sight better." I found the energy to flip her over; maybe the coffee was kicking in. I nuzzled my face into the pale-gold fur adorning her finely seasoned pussy. "Just how wet did you have in mind?"

Exhaustion forgotten, I was ready to ride again.

CONTRIBUTORS

After working in the fashion-design industry in New York for the past eleven years, **Crystal Barela** writes: "I have left the insanity. I am trying on small-town life in Southern California. I've found the perfect setting for spending some quality time with my laptop and thinking dirty. If you liked this story, get out your vibrators, gals, 'cause there is more to be published in 2005. Email me for details or any comments you want to share, at erotikryter@yahoo.com."

Cheyenne Blue combines her two passions in life and writes travel guides and erotica. Her erotica has appeared in *Best Women's Erotica, Playgirl, Mammoth Best New Erotica, Best Lesbian Erotica, Best Lesbian Love Stories,* and on many websites. She divides her time between Colorado, USA, and Ireland, and is currently working on a book about the quiet and quirky areas of Ireland. You can see more of her erotica on her website, www.cheyenneblue.com.

C.B. Calsing grew up on the Central Coast of California and holds a bachelor's in English from Cal Poly, San Luis Obispo. She now resides in New Orleans, where she writes avidly and edits for Liquid Silver Books and *The Deconstruction Quarterly*. Visit her official website at www.deconstructionpapers.com.

M. Christian (www.mchristian.com) is the author of the critically acclaimed and best-selling collections *Dirty Words, Speaking Parts,* and *The Bachelor Machine*. He is the editor of *The Burning Pen, Guilty Pleasures,* the *Best S/M Erotica* series, *The Mammoth Book of Future Cops* and *The Mammoth Book of Tales of the Road* (with Maxim Jakubowski), and over eighteen other anthologies. His short fiction has appeared in over 200 publications including *The Best American Erotica, Best Gay Erotica, Best Lesbian Erotica, Best Transgender Erotica, Best Fetish Erotica, Best Bondage Erotica* and...well, you get the idea.

Amie M. Evans is a white girl, confirmed femme-bottom who lives life like a spontaneously choreographed performance. She is a published literary erotica and creative nonfiction writer, experienced workshop provider, and a burlesque and high-femme drag performer. Her most recent published works have appeared in *Ultimate Lesbian Erotica 2005; I Do/I Don't: Queers on Marriage; On Our Backs: The Best Erotic Fiction, Vol. 2; Back to Basics: A Butch/Femme Erotic Reader*; and *Up All Night*. She also writes gay-male erotica under a pen name.

Chuck Fellows is a transgendered queer who lives in western Massachusetts. She has published a couple of things, but prefers writing for an audience of one. Many of her short stories have been called "Queer Hallmark Love Mush," but not this one. When she is not working at writing or writing at work, she can be found weaving on her loom, riding her motorcycle around western Massachusetts, or reading a book from one of the many piles that inhabit her house.

Shanna Germain divides her time between writing for a living and writing for joy. This falls into the joy category. Her erotic writing has appeared in a variety of publications and anthologies, including *Blowing Kisses, Clean Sheets, Heat Wave,* and *The Many Joys of Sex Toys*. You can read more of her work, erotic and otherwise, on her website: www.shannagermain.com.

Nipper Godwin is a genderqueer, polyamorous, bisexual switch, born in the Bronx, raised by wolves, educated by the Seven Sisters, and currently dedicated to keeping as many plates spinning at one time as is humanly possible. Nipper's work has appeared publicly in *On Our Backs: The Best Erotic Fiction, Vol. 2* and in more private locations from sleazy motels on Admiral Wilson Boulevard to undisclosed locations in the Somerville/Charlestown area.

Co-editor **Sacchi Green** spends her time in western Massachusetts and the mountains of New Hampshire, with occasional forays into the real world. Her work has been published in five volumes of *Best Lesbian Erotica,* four volumes of *Best Women's Erotica, Best Transgender Erotica, The Mammoth Book* *of Best New Erotica 3, Penthouse, On Our Backs,* and a knee-high stack of other anthologies with inspirational covers.

Bryn Haniver, a nature lover, scientist, ocean junkie and sexy B-movie aficionado, writes fiction from both coasts of North America with occasional jaunts to the Caribbean. Previous anthology credits include *Taboo, Down & Dirty 2, A Taste of Midnight,* and *Delicate Friction.*

Jay Lake's stories appear in half a dozen languages in markets around the world, as well as his collections *Greetings from Lake Wu, Dogs in the Moonlight,* and *American Sorrows.* Jay is editor or co-editor of the *Polyphony* anthology series, *All-Star Zeppelin Adventure Stories, 44 Clowns, TEL: Stories,* and other projects. He lives in Portland, Oregon, and can be reached through his website at www.jlake.com.

Caralee Levy's erotica has been published by *Clean Sheets* and is slated to appear in several anthologies, including *Binary: Best of Both Worlds.* She has a master's degree in history and enjoys researching historical settings for her fiction. In her spare time, she enjoys gardening; listening to worldbeat music; and mothering her three dogs, two cats, and tank of fish. Her website is caraleelevy.home.att.net.

C.A. Matthews now shares his house, hopes, and lunch money with Becky, the love of his life. They met online, and it is her inspiration that runs through all his stories. He writes on holidays mostly because, once the juices start flowing, he has to see whatever he is doing through to its climax.

Skian McGuire is a working-class Quaker leatherdyke who lives in the wilds of western Massachusetts with her dog pack, a collection of motorcycles, and her partner of twenty-two years. Her work has appeared in *Best Lesbian Erotica, Best Bisexual Erotica 2, The Big Book of Erotic Ghost Stories, On Our Backs,* and a variety of webzines including *Suspect Thoughts* and *Scarlet Letters.* She's a past champion of the Amazon Slam (a Best of Boston poetry venue), and her slam poems have appeared in *Pinned Down by Pronouns* and *I Do/I Don't: Queers on Marriage.*

Val Murphy is a newcomer to the erotic short-story market but an old (carpal-tunnel-suffering) hand at hot fantasies. She'd like to thank the editors for publishing her first erotic fiction, "Rope 'Em and Brand 'Em." Val is awaiting publication of her erotic poem, "Cowboy," in the upcoming anthology *Velvet Heat*.

Transman **Jake Rich** is thrilled to have his work included here, with so many distinguished writers. He thanks his Muse, S.G., for her unfailing encouragement and support. And he hopes to one day again see his writing in print. Stay tuned!

Toby Rider seldom sits still long enough to write down the stories in her head, but she's published one piece in *Ultimate Lesbian Erotica 2005* and has decided she likes getting those steamy contributors' copies well enough to try it again a time or two.

Stephen D. Rogers' proudest moment (until now) was his acceptance from the now-defunct *Lesbian Short Fiction*. More news can be found at www.stephendrogers.com.

Julia Talbot resides in the Southwest of the United States with her dog and several houseplants, and has not quit her day job. She has a penchant for blank books, gay porn, and big, ugly hats. She can most often be found in coffee shops and restaurants, scribbling in her notebook and entertaining other diners with her mutterings. She has several novels and short stories published with Torquere Press, including *Jumping Into Things* and *Perfect*, and has stories on websites such as Deathlings.com.

Co-editor **Rakelle Valencia** has jumped into the smut-writing business with both booted feet. Besides co-editing this anthology, she has stories published and upcoming in *On Our Backs, Best Lesbian Erotica 2004* and *2005, Best of the Best Lesbian Erotica 2, Naughty Spanking Stories A-Z, Hot Lesbian Erotica, Ultimate Lesbian Erotica, Best Lesbian Love Stories*, and a fine assortment of other publications to stack on the shelf beside her articles on Natural Horsemanship.

Fargo Wellington is a buff of Wild Western History. And, oh, if her parents ever found out she was using her education to write smut! Hence the pseudonym.

Connie Wilkins has published stories mainly in the science fiction and fantasy genre, including her Jintsu Press e-book collection *Wild Flesh*, but fantasy is, after all, a pretty broad concept. Her work has also appeared in *Wet: More Aqua Erotica* and *Embraces: Dark Erotica*.